SURPRISE WITNESS

A STEIN & ASSOCIATES THRILLER

MARIAN K. RIEDY
IN COLLABORATION WITH TANJA STEIGNER

Black Rose Writing | Texas

ISBN: 978-1-68433-966-2
PUBLISHED BY BLACK ROSE WRITING
www.blackrosewriting.com

Printed in the United States of America
Suggested Retail Price (SRP) $19.95

Surprise Witness is printed in Sabon

*As a planet-friendly publisher, Black Rose Writing does its best to eliminate unnecessary waste to reduce paper usage and energy costs, while never compromising the reading experience. As a result, the final word count vs. page count may not meet common expectations.

To my siblings, a refuge in any storm,
and not bad company when the sun shines, either.
– M.K.R.

SURPRISE WITNESS

Vietnam - 1973

He stops at the sound. A footfall. Charlie, or some animal? His buddy, Moose, had sworn he found tiger tracks while on post last week. He shivers in the cold dark of an enveloping fog, looking up for the slight comfort of the weak light of the predawn sky. Silence again.

A second later, the jungle erupts with blasting AK-47s. He drops to the ground, heart hammering. He fumbles for his radio, but the M-16s are already responding. A grenade explodes far to his right, and the clatter of the rifles to his rear subsides. He rises and heads down the well-trodden track between the elephant grass. Shots ring sporadically in the near distance.

About twenty yards ahead, on a slight rise just off the path, he sees three other soldiers, backs against a towering tree.

A single shot from an AK-47 explodes nearby. The second before he dives, he sees one of the men under the tree drop to the ground. He counts to ten before he cautiously rises to one knee. The two soldiers left standing take off at a brisk trot. One of them is carrying a medic's bag. Before they get more than a few yards from the tree and the downed soldier, an illumination shell explodes overhead. He glimpses a flash of silver.

He would never have found it in the grass, but in the increasing light of the approaching dawn, he spots a chain lying on the path. He wonders briefly how the poor guy's dog tags ended up over here. He shrugs, snags the tags off the ground, and walks back to the body. He stands staring at the downed soldier for a moment, then kneels and rummages through the guy's pockets. Empty.

A harebrained idea flashes through his mind. Crazy, yet it seems fated to happen. He reaches up to feel for the carotid. The medic surely checked, but he needs to be sure. Dead. No doubt. He kneels a moment longer, palm on the dead man's chest. He carefully drapes a chain, dog tags dangling, around the neck of the corpse, rises, and runs off the way he had come.

CHAPTER 1
A DISASTROUS POSITION

Trial Day 1
Washington, D.C., 2019

Standing in the well of the courtroom, Will surveyed his domain for the next two weeks. The public gallery opened in front of him. The rows of wooden, pew-like benches, separated from the well by a low, wooden rail, seated one hundred twenty-eight persons, according to a plaque on the wall.

The prospect of all those spectators would daunt the uninitiated. Will, however, had tried dozens of cases here and knew that he would be performing for only a handful of people. These larger courtrooms filled only for trials in which a well-known politico or business titan was on display, accused of some sex offense, corruption, or obstruction of justice.

Mind elsewhere, Will fiddled with the knot of his tie. His nervous tic would disappear once the trial started. Will's strategy, and strength as a trial lawyer, was to avoid becoming a distraction. He purposefully blended into the background. The jury's attention should be on the witness, not the attorney.

Will crafted his appearance to suit his chosen role. He wore an off-the-rack, charcoal-gray suit, white shirt, and maroon tie. He'd had his hair cut a week ago, instructing his barber to trim it neatly above the ears and off the neck. His natural features needed no camouflage. Of medium height and weight, with a round face, narrow chin, regular features, light brown eyes, and sandy brown hair, Will invited no attention.

He turned and looked up at the raised dais from which the judge would preside. To Will's left loomed the jury box, a platform enclosed by a four-foot, polished brass railing. Inside the box sat twelve, wooden, straight-backed chairs arranged in two rows. The furniture had been selected to keep jurors awake, not for comfort. *Voir dire*, or the jury selection process, had taken place the prior Friday. When the case was called, the six jurors would walk right into the box. The witnesses would stand and be sworn in the boxy enclosure between the jury and the judge before taking their seats to give their testimony.

In front of the jury, two rectangular tables, each with two chairs, faced the judge. The one closest to the jury, reserved for defense counsel, was unoccupied. Taylor Baylie, the attorney for the defendants, had not yet arrived. The other table would be Will's station. Between counsel tables stood a podium equipped with a microphone for direct and cross-examination. Will preferred to stand closer to his witnesses and rarely took refuge behind the podium.

The doors at the back of the courtroom swung open. Cassandra Robins, Will's colleague at Stein & Associates and second chair for the trial, marched in. She strode up the aisle, seemingly unburdened by the heavy litigation bags she carried. Her navy-blue skirt suit snugly fit her ample curves. A white silk blouse accentuated her caramel complexion. With her widely spaced brown eyes, prominent cheekbones, and shiny, coal-black hair, professionally coiffed, Cassandra looked every inch the successful D.C. native that she was. Watching her approach, Will, as always, silently admired Cassandra's casual beauty.

Cassandra smiled at Will as she took her place at counsel table. Will grinned as he sat in the chair beside her. "Loaded for bear, I see," he said.

"Always," Cassandra responded, eyes sparkling.

Will turned when Jim Kresge, the firm's administrative assistant, escorting their client, tapped him on the back. José Marquez lowered himself carefully onto the wooden chair, in the style of those in the jury box, directly behind Will. Unlike the jurors, José perched on the stuffed, beige throw-pillow that Jim had carefully placed on the seat.

José was dressed much like his attorney, in a dark suit, white shirt, glossy silk tie, and polished black loafers. To the practiced eye, it was evident that José wore a designer label tailored, at one time, to fit. Now, his suit jacket strained tightly over an uneven lump high in the center of his back. He sat stiffly, elbows tucked against his sides, as though it would hurt him if he moved.

Which it would. José had only last week been released from the hospital after his third back surgery since the accident. José's orthopedic surgeon, Dr. Moraski, had to fuse two more thoracic vertebrae. Unfortunately, contrary to an early, hopeful prognosis, José's spine continued to deteriorate.

José would have to be in attendance during the entire trial. The jury expected as much. The ordeal of being judged for days on end by total strangers was grueling for every plaintiff. José had to bear the additional discomfort of seventy-two fresh surgical sutures under the heavy bandages covering them. He had to discontinue his pain killers, too, at least for today. José would be called to testify, and his mind had to be sharp.

Will had considered filing for a postponement of the trial. But this close to the scheduled trial date, the judge's calendar would be booked for a year, if not more. José could not wait that long.

Will caught José's eye. "Almost time now," Will said, smiling.

José nodded.

"Ah, great, right on time," Will said, looking into the courtroom behind José. "It's your dad and Benjy."

Good, Will thought, as the Marquez family walked hesitantly up the central aisle to take seats in the front row of the otherwise empty public gallery. José's face, sad in repose, brightened when he twisted around and saw his father and son.

Will would not allow José's young son, Benjamin, to spend much time in the courtroom. The experience would not be good for the boy, and the jury would not approve. On this opening day, however, José needed the comfort of his son's presence.

The door to the well behind the judge's dais opened. The judge's clerk walked in, followed by the bailiff. Will swung around and bid them both "good morning." Will knew the clerk's name was Susan. The bailiff was a new guy Will had not previously seen. Baylie and a younger attorney bustled into the well and sat at their table. A few minutes later, a knock sounded on the door behind the judge's dais. The bailiff cried: "All rise."

Showtime, Will thought, as everyone in the courtroom rose. José stood as well, slowly and shakily, with Jim's hand planted under José's elbow. Will glanced back and grimaced. He would get José excused from that ritual before the first break.

"Good morning, Your Honor," came the chorus.

"Good morning, everyone," Judge Nancy Storer replied. She gathered the long skirt of her black robes with a practiced sweep and sat in her high-backed, black leather swivel chair. "Call the case, Susan, then, counsel, identify yourselves for the record."

Three hours later, almost to the minute, Will paused, looked up from the yellow legal pad he was holding, and asked, "Could I have a moment, Your Honor?"

"Of course," came Judge Storer's prompt reply.

Will scanned his notes, reviewing the testimony he had elicited from José after counsel's opening statements. Had Will succeeded in giving the jury a glimpse of the man Will had grown to admire and respect? Would the jurors empathize with José?

José was raised in Gaithersburg, Maryland, an only child. José's father, Mauricio, worked as a temporary, seasonal construction worker. His mother, Berta, cleaned house for a family in Bethesda. Money was tight. When José was in eighth grade, Mauricio landed a full-time, permanent job with one of the largest general contractors in the D.C. Metro area, TRJ Construction. Life improved for the Marquez family.

José did well in high school and was offered a full scholarship to attend the University of Maryland. He turned it down after a lengthy discussion with his parents. Instead, he took a job working alongside his father at TRJ. Seven years later, José met his bride-to-be, Alicia Hoffman, while delivering work orders to corporate headquarters in Reston, Virginia, where Alicia worked as a secretary.

José dreamed of one day owning his own business in the construction industry. Alicia convinced her husband to return to school to obtain his associate degree, to bolster his chances of doing so.

Degree in hand, José, with his father's help, launched his contracting company, just days after José turned thirty. José served as the president and public face of J&A Builders. Mauricio managed the crew. The company began with modest, single-family homes, but J&A thrived and expanded into apartment and office building construction.

And then, finally, after years of trying, Alicia got pregnant. The Marquez family joyously welcomed baby Benjamin into the world.

Two years ago, the Marquezes' good fortune abruptly evaporated. Alicia was diagnosed with pancreatic cancer. She was dead in four months, leaving José with their three-year-old son, Benjy. Shortly after he buried his wife, José stepped on a sheet of plywood covering a heating duct while inspecting the site of a four-story office building under construction. The wood splintered, sending José tumbling helplessly down the open shaft. Three stories below, he crashed flat on his back, shattering his cervical spine.

Will did not dwell on the details of José's injuries and subsequent treatments during José's testimony. Instead, José's surgeon, Dr. Moraski, would walk the jury through the medicine. Will had José focus on how the accident affected his day-to-day life.

José spoke of his pain and disabilities. He spent far more time, however, describing the effects of his accident on his son. Benjy cried when José left home, again, for surgery or rehab. Before José's fall, Benjy shouted with joy as José ran behind Benjy's wobbling bike, hand steady on the boy's shoulder. Now, Benjy's lip trembled as he watched his father walk slowly and stiffly to the table for dinner.

José worried about his family's future and that of his business and his employees. Several construction sites had already shut down, and a dozen workers let go. José was responsible for client development. He had not been able to do that job since his accident, and no one else was qualified to step into his shoes.

Will conferred with Cassandra, then glanced over at the jury. The six women sat attentively, but impassively. Not a hint of emotion showed on any of their faces. A pang of uncertainty swept Will, but he pushed it aside. Too soon to tell what they thought of his client. And too many other things to deal with right now.

He stepped away from the jury box and nodded to Taylor Baylie, first chair of the team representing the defendants. Stein & Associates had sued the manufacturer and distributor of the plywood José purchased to use as a protective cover for the open duct. The complaint alleged negligence and strict product liability as the primary claims.

"Your witness," Will said, taking his seat.

Baylie nodded. Before rising, Baylie conferred with his associate in low tones and wrote a few notes on his legal pad. While Baylie prepared, Will worried.

The cross-examination by opposing counsel was always fraught, particularly when the client was on the stand. Will was sure that he knew the facts of the case inside and out. He and his colleagues had collected and studied every document they could get their hands on that was conceivably relevant to any issue in the case. They had exhausted the witnesses, asking question after question about what had happened and why. But still. Will could have missed something damaging, and Baylie might have found it. If so, it would be coming out momentarily, in cross.

Baylie knew what he was doing, Will could tell right away. He began by asking if José was comfortable or if he needed a break. José confirmed he was ready to continue. Baylie said he was sorry about what had happened to José and wished him a full recovery. Then, having proven to the jury that he was a good person, just doing his job, Baylie started swinging.

The first attack came from a line of questions emphasizing José's lack of experience in construction management. José was only a "carry and pound" guy, in Baylie's words, before he founded J&A. Even after that, José had to "learn while doing," as Baylie would have it. Will thought José was holding up fine, answering politely but pushing back on Baylie's insinuations.

Then, Baylie turned to the day of the accident, trying hard to expose some fault on the part of José or his company. The experts on both sides had agreed that the use of the plywood panel to cover the open duct was appropriate. No stronger material was required. The experts disagreed about why this specific panel failed to hold José's weight.

Will's witnesses, having examined the splintered remains, opined that the panel was defective before J&A Builders got their hands on it, a "lemon" due to a manufacturing error. Baylie's experts thought that the panel's remnants met specifications. Therefore, a defect must have been created during storage or handling by J&A.

Those experts would have their day in court. Right now, Baylie was trying to convince the jury that José should have observed the defect—however it came to be—himself and avoided stepping on the panel. Baylie would then argue that José had been a cause of his own accident. In other words, José had been contributorily negligent. In D.C., that would mean a defense verdict.

Will had anticipated this line of attack and prepared José. Baylie made no headway.

Will glanced at his watch. Noon. This cross had been going on for an hour. José needed a break. Will stood.

"Excuse me, Your Honor, but this may be a good time for the lunch break. It's been a long morning for the jury."

"I was thinking the same thing, counselor," Judge Storer replied. "Mr. Baylie?" she inquired. "Unless you are close to finishing your cross, let's break for an hour."

"Only a few more questions, Your Honor," Baylie responded, "and I would prefer to wrap this up before we break."

"Very well," the judge said. She turned to her jury. "We very much appreciate your time and your attention, and I promise we won't abuse either."

Will noticed that every one of the jurors smiled. He stifled a chuckle. Will had talked to dozens of jurors after his trials. They commented on what a pleasure it was to be included in the proceedings now and again. Even a simple recognition of their existence, particularly by the judge, counted. Otherwise, the judge talked to counsel, counsel talked to the witnesses, and the jury was ignored. The jurors' perception was, however, entirely false. Everyone in the well, particularly the lawyers, was focused intensely on the jurors.

The judge continued, "We'll take an hour's break for lunch in a few minutes. Proceed," she nodded at Baylie.

Baylie picked up a stack of papers from his table. "May I approach, Your Honor?" he asked. The judge nodded. Baylie walked over to José. "I am handing Mr. Marquez Defendants' Exhibit AA, and I have a courtesy copy for the clerk and Mr. McCarty."

Will and Cassandra huddled over the documents, Exhibit AA, that Baylie handed to Will. Nothing surprising. José's income tax returns for the ten years preceding the accident. These documents had been requested by the defendants in discovery. The firm would be asking the jury to award José the amount of his past and future loss of earnings due to his injuries. They would accordingly have to prove José's actual lost income and loss of earnings potential. The income tax returns were, therefore, relevant and had been turned over to defense counsel.

Mr. Baylie got right to the point.

Q:These are copies of your income tax returns for the last ten years, correct?

A:Yes.

Q:Are they accurate?

A:I presume so. That is, Mr. McCarty got them from the IRS, as far as I know.

Q:No reason to question their accuracy, then, is that correct?

A:None that I know.

Q:And this is your signature on the forms, correct?

José shifted in his seat, awkwardly twisting one shoulder, grimacing. He nodded.

Will leaned forward, studying his client. What was going on? Had José's pain worsened? Or was José reluctant to answer? What did José not want the jury to know? Will had no idea, which was a disastrous position to be in during the client's cross-examination. Will's heart raced.

Q:Please answer audibly for the record, Mr. Marquez.

A:Yes, that is my signature.

Q:What is the social security number on the 2007 return?

José's face paled, and his forehead glistened with sudden sweat. He read off the series of numbers in a tight voice.

Q:What's the number on the 2016 return?

In the split second before José answered, Will realized what was coming. He bolted to his feet. "Your Honor, may I approach?" Shouting was forbidden in Judge Storer's courtroom. Will had almost crossed that line.

Then, Baylie did. "Objection!" he boomed. "Answer the ..."

"Counsel," Judge Storer interrupted sternly, "I will not have this kind of conduct. Now ..."

"I instruct my client not to answer," Will spoke loudly, taking the risk of further angering the judge by cutting her off. She could throw him out of her courtroom. He had to take the chance. Will moved out from around his table and started towards the judge's dais.

"This is contemptible ..." Baylie began.

"Enough, both of you," the judge pounded her gavel to underscore her command. "Approach the bench."

Both lawyers scurried forward. Judge Storer turned on the "husher," a white-noise generator in the ceiling which prevented the jury from hearing that which they should not. "The jury needs their break now," the judge said. "When we return, I expect counsel to behave themselves. Right now, I am seriously displeased with you both."

CHAPTER 2
FAKE ID

Cassandra clutched her pen in her right hand, unconsciously clicking it. The phone crushed to her left ear rang for the fourth time. Come on, pick up, Cassandra mumbled under her breath, glancing around at the other attorneys, all on their phones, scattered around the patio outside the side door to the courthouse. She only had an hour.

"A. Stein & Associates," finally, their receptionist answered. "How can I help you?"

"Beebe, it's Cassandra. Put me through to Aaron, please."

Luckily, her call had come during the daily lawyers' meeting. With the team together, Cassandra would get the best advice for Will. He surely needed it, as Cassandra quickly explained to her colleagues over the speakerphone in Aaron's office.

Will realized the trap Baylie had set just as defense counsel was wrapping up his cross-examination of José. Baylie would ask José, point blank, whether he had filed his older tax returns with a fake social security number. Will had no choice but to interrupt because he did not know what José's answer would be.

Will did not, at the time, understand how or why José had used a fake social security number. Will did know, however, that doing so was a federal crime. Presumably, José knew as well. Would José deny having done it? Will could not knowingly allow a client to lie under oath. On the other hand, he would not let his client confess to a crime on the stand, either. It was possible that the statute of limitations—the time limit for initiating the prosecution of a crime— had expired, but Will was not sure. He also had to worry about the jury's reaction if José confessed to the deed. In any event, Will had to stop the questioning. He needed time to find answers.

After the judge called the break, Will and Cassandra questioned José in the privacy of the witness room. José explained that he bought a counterfeit social security card years ago when he was an undocumented immigrant. So, now they had another problem on their hands. José was now legal because of his marriage to an American. But could he still be deported because of that old infraction if he testified to it today?

"Will had no idea about this little problem?" Cassandra heard Marlon's disembodied voice.

"None," Cassandra answered.

"It was clever of him to see what was coming with that line of questioning, then," Marlon noted, uncharacteristically impressed.

Marlon White, the most senior associate in the firm, was extremely bright and a talented lawyer. He had fixed any number of potentially disastrous legal errors committed by his colleagues. Marlon had their backs, come what may, with no hesitation or complaint. He could also drink like a fish and hosted terrific firm parties, but he could be acerbically critical and always corrected everyone else's grammar.

"Yeah," Cassandra replied, "but Will doesn't see it that way. He was angry at himself for not discovering the fake card himself and mad at José for not bringing it to his attention. The five-hundred-dollar sanction Judge Storer imposed because Will interrupted the cross didn't help matters, either. Once we got back to the witness room, Will yelled for five minutes before he calmed down enough to get to work. That's when he told me to call you guys. So, we now have just over fifty minutes of the lunch break to figure out what to do."

"Do about what?" Cassandra heard Betsy ask. Betsy must have arrived late to the meeting, Cassandra thought.

As Aaron recounted Will's dilemma, Cassandra pictured her newest colleague, Betsy Thornhill, listening closely to Aaron. Betsy, the only lawyer in the office from an Ivy League school, was almost as good a lawyer as Marlon. At five-foot-ten, with shoulder-length blonde hair caught back in a headband, hazel-eyes in a tanned, oval face, and the wiry muscled arms and legs of a runner, Betsy looked good in her suits. Cassandra, a clothes horse herself, approved.

Yet, Betsy never joined the rest of the gang at the "Bomb," as they called their regular watering hole in the Bombay Club across Farragut Park from the office. Betsy did not share stories from the nephew's birthday party or the disastrous date as the others did. The only tidbit Cassandra knew about Betsy's personal life was that she had some connection to Jeff Howard, a member of the Virginia State Senate. Cassandra wondered how long Betsy would last at the firm.

"I'm sorry I asked," Betsy riposted when Aaron had finished.

Cassandra smiled as she heard her colleagues chuckling. The tension across her shoulders eased. The familiar scene unfolded in her mind's eye: Aaron's fourth-floor office, spanning the entire floor of the building, floor-to-ceiling windows facing downtown D.C. on three sides; Aaron sitting at his mammoth mahogany desk; and Cassandra's colleagues seated in the deep, padded maroon leather chairs arrayed in a semi-circle in front of Aaron.

On top of the pile of magazines, articles, motions, and briefs on Aaron's desk—the usual legal paraphernalia—lay an obstetrical forceps. To the right of his desk towered a human skeleton attached to a pole embedded in a raised platform. The skeleton, leaning on the baseball bat around which its bony fingers were wrapped, sported a red, white, and blue tie around its neck and a Washington Redskins cap on its skull.

Aaron's firm specialized in medical malpractice law. And his was one of, if not the best in town.

"Will should call Marla Tuckman if he hasn't already," Aaron's voice called Cassandra back to the problem at hand. Marla, she knew, was a top-notch immigration attorney. Will had retained her to help him snatch Norma from the maws of Immigration and Custom Enforcement a few months ago.

"He did," Cassandra replied. "She's incommunicado on a two-week vacation, according to her voice message. Will tried her associate, but he's in trial and unavailable until late this afternoon."

"Okay, then, everybody, go make your calls," Aaron commanded. "Try any other immigration lawyers you know, Assistant United States

Attorneys, or Federal Public Defenders. A State Department lawyer would be good, too. Get to work. Get Will some answers."

* * *

Late that afternoon, Cassandra stepped off the elevator with Will and Jim behind her. Beebe, at the front reception desk, jumped up to open the glass doors to the office suite for them.

"Day one, and you already look exhausted," Beebe exclaimed.

Cassandra stepped back to let Jim with his load in first. Beebe was right, Cassandra thought. Even tall, broad-shouldered, gym-rat Jim stooped a bit, although he did have a legitimate excuse. He lugged a heavy litigation bag in each hand and three, large poster boards under his right arm.

"Well, what happened?" Beebe asked. "Did you already lose your jury because of José's unexpected testimony?"

Will looked at Beebe. He smiled wanly and stepped past into the office.

"I think we cleared that hurdle cleanly," Cassandra answered Beebe, "but we need to revise our strategy going forward. Is Aaron in?"

Beebe confirmed that the boss was in, as were Marlon and Miranda Patel. Cassandra headed toward her office to drop her briefcase and call an expert witness scheduled to testify the next day. Then, she would join the others for a brainstorming session.

CHAPTER 3
THE ARTIST

Far to the south and a time zone west of where the Stein lawyers conferenced, Paco hit "send" on the email to his friend, Marlon. Paco closed his laptop, leaned back in his chair, and stretched. The calendar tacked on the wall caught his eye. Today was the anniversary of the day he met Marlon, a decade ago. For once, on that day, fortune smiled on him.

***

Paco sat outside a café on the town's central plaza, finishing his morning coffee. Earlier, he watched a handful of merchants arranging their wares in the arcades circling the plaza. Echoes from their idle chatter occasionally broke the silence of Paco's isolated village, perched high in the mountains, nestled among towering purple peaks.

This was Wednesday, a day for work. The arcades and the plaza would fill only on the weekend, when local artisans and farmers and their neighbors and friends gathered to gossip and provision for the week to come.

Two men entered the empty plaza from the southwest portal, directly across from Paco. Of similar build and height—slender and a hands-breadth shorter than Paco's six feet—both wore khakis and polo shirts. The brunette sported a bright pink polo and the blonde a robin's egg blue. Dockers and baseball caps completed their ensemble. Tourists, obviously, and Americans most likely, Paco thought.

Outsiders rarely found their way to this remote, if picturesque, hill town. A few intrepid souls came to see its well-preserved colonial architecture. Paco ordinarily avoided those visitors. An instinct, which he immediately quelled, drew him to these two, however. On second thought, he rose, dropped a coin on the café table, and stepped onto the rough cobbles of the plaza floor.

Paco advanced no more than a few meters when the tourists stopped and turned back towards the portal. Heads tilted back, they inspected the portal's carved wooden lintel. Paco hesitated, then continued across the plaza.

"Excuse me," Paco said, and the tourists turned to face him. Paco stuck out his hand, smiling. "Welcome to my hometown. I'm Paco."

The brunette's lips crooked, a slight frown on his narrow, high-browed face. Paco understood the man's disquiet. Paco did not look like the locals who accosted visitors in every tourist destination in Mexico, offering their services as guides. Still, the stranger's ingrained politeness trumped his hesitation. He returned Paco's gesture, reaching out to shake.

"Hi, I'm Marlon. Marlon White. And this is my husband, Allen James."

As he and Allen exchanged greetings, Paco stifled a smile. Marlon meant to drive Paco away, leaving the couple in peace, by his proclamation of the men's relationship. Gay marriage was unheard of in solidly Catholic Mexico. Clever, Paco thought, and preferable to the supercilious rebuff given by most tourists to the locals. His interest in this couple deepened.

"I would be delighted to show you around," Paco said. "I've lived here for a very long time. Although you have a guidebook," he motioned to the Fodor's clutched in Allen's left hand, "I can take you off the beaten path."

Marlon raised a hand in protest, but Paco persevered. "It would be my great pleasure," Paco said. "This is a small town, and the families are close-knit. We don't see many tourists. I am on my own. The break from my ordinary solitude would be most welcome."

Marlon and Allen exchanged glances. Allen shrugged.

"Okay, then," Marlon said. "Lead on."

Paco motioned the couple towards the portal through which they had come, and the three started walking, abreast.

"Why is someone like you living in the mountains in Mexico, and alone?" Allen asked.

Paco flapped a hand. "Later. I'm not at all interesting. What brings you two here?"

Marlon explained. Allen persuaded him to embark on a two-week road trip through Mexico. "Not exactly my idea of a nice vacation. I only agreed under duress."

Allen laughed. "Oh, come on. It was high time to do something other than stay in a five-star hotel and eat in Michelin-rated restaurants. I promised to drive, planned the trip, and insisted on buying an emergency break-down kit …

"… the need for which filled me with horror," Marlon finished Allen's sentence. "We'd be leaving AAA and the rest of civilization far behind."

Paco laughed out loud, for the first time in months.

By mid-afternoon, the three were companionable. Paco knew Allen was a corporate lawyer specializing in mergers and acquisitions. Marlon, also an attorney, specialized in medical malpractice. Marlon told the story of his and Allen's first date and described their "perfect" wedding. They discussed the North American Free Trade Agreement and found common interests in classical music and American civil war history.

Paco suited the American couple as a guide, as well. He satisfied Marlon's fetish for detailed information by filling in the blanks in the Fodor's description of "must-see" sites. After Allen revealed his desire— to find a local treasure no ordinary tourist would discover—Paco fulfilled his wish. He led the couple down a roughly carved, stone staircase into a hidden, underground chapel in the cathedral. Inside the tiny, dim room, lit only by the candle Paco held, a marble altar, streaked with lime green veins, glowed from within. On the altar lay a golden pyx embedded with magnificent emeralds. Not in the guidebook, Allen trumpeted triumphantly.

Lunch did not arise as a topic until, at 3:00 p.m., Marlon announced that he was starved. And exhausted. Allen was a runner and unfazed by the hours of wandering around on the cobbled streets. Marlon did not believe in exercise, as a rule. On the rare exception when he exerted himself, it took its toll, as it had today. Paco suggested that Marlon and Allen return to their hotel and have a siesta. He would retrieve them at 6:00, and they would go to Paco's humble home, as he put it, for cocktails and dinner.

After leaving his new friends, Paco imagined Marlon and Allen speculating about him.

With his auburn hair pulled back into a short tail, freckles, grey eyes, and flat English vowels, Paco was certainly an American by birth. Paco had admitted to being born in Texas but avoided specifics, as he did when telling Marlon and Allen that his occupation was as a teacher and historian.

A mystery: An intelligent, widely read, late-middle-aged, American man living alone in a Mexican hill town for decades, friendly, but with a watchful reserve. Paco did not intend to enlighten them.

Two hours later, Paco led his guests up a narrow, stone staircase to the second floor of a worn, stucco house next to the cathedral. The first floor of the building served as the rectory, where the resident priest lived, Paco explained. He opened the narrow wooden door at the top of the stairs and bade his guests enter.

Paco watched his guests take in his one-room apartment. A bar with three stools divided the room into a living space on the left and kitchen on the right. The appliances in his kitchen had aged gracefully, Paco thought. The narrow, one-doored refrigerator had a weathered ivory hue, as did the four-burner gas stove. Gleaming, steel-colored pots, pans, griddles, and sieves of professional quality hung on hooks above the bar. The molé sauce bubbling in a pot on the stove wafted a rich smell through the room.

Paco had furnished his living area with a low couch covered with an unadorned red cloth and two wooden, upright chairs. He chose the simple, unobtrusive furniture to highlight the room's centerpiece: A magnificent, twenty-square-foot area rug, a tapestry embroidered with an enormous, green and scarlet quetzal in full flight on a background of variegated jungle greens.

Past the living area, on the left, an area curtained off from the main room signaled Paco's sleeping quarters. On the right, against the far wall, stood his nondescript desk on which sat a PC and three monitors.

When Paco gave them a brief tour, nodding towards the door catty-corner to the desk with a "WC" stenciled on it, Allen's gaze turned toward the Dell tower on the floor beside the desk. He had noticed Paco's high-end computing capacity.

Paco sat his guests in the living area and offered them martinis. He knew from the day's meandering conversations that Marlon and Allen both preferred very dry gin martinis for cocktail hour. The three chatted while Paco completed dinner preparations in the kitchen.

"Are you the artist?" Allen asked, pointing to the wall across from the kitchen, on which hung a dozen eight-by-ten, black-and-white photographs in clear, lucite frames.

Paco laughed. "I took the pictures, if that's what you mean," he answered.

"You're far too modest," Allen responded. "Those are the work of an artist."

"You seem to have a thing for birds," Marlon said, sipping his drink. "Are all of them local?"

"Yes," Paco answered. "This area supports a rich diversity of flora and fauna because of the varying altitude, rainfall, and vegetation in the surrounding district. I am particularly drawn to the beauty and grace of the birds. Watching them disappear, high in the skies, lifts my spirits."

Paco served empanadas with the molé, black beans, rice, and corn tortillas, accompanied by several glasses of Malbec. After the meal, Paco excused himself and disappeared into his curtained sleeping nook.

A couple of minutes later, Marlon exclaimed, "The Pearl Fishers!" as the opening notes of "Au fond du temple saint" from Bizet's opera filled the room. "Amazing sound," Marlon continued. "What kind of equipment do you have?" he asked as Paco lifted the curtain and reentered the living area.

"An old vacuum tube amplifier," Paco answered, smiling. "It's been a beast to keep working, but you can't beat the quality. And a turntable and vinyls."

Marlon nodded his head appreciatively. "Why am I sure you've got quite a collection of those vinyls, Paco?" he asked wryly.

Paco grinned. "We'll work our way up, in terms of emotional intensity, starting with this aria. We'll end the evening with Don Giovanni. Drink up, for the night is young."

Three hours later, Allen began abstaining from Paco's offer of refills. Marlon, however, stumbled on his return trip from the loo.

Paco leaned his head on the back of the sofa and closed his eyes. The alcohol and opera in such good company had disarmed him. He felt a tear run down his face. He leaned forward, put his face in his hands, and wept. When he had calmed himself, Paco told his story.

It was 1968. People's Park in Berkeley was far away, but Paco, a senior in high school, was doing his best to get in on the revolution. He would not have gotten very far except his girlfriend had an older cousin who lived in Austin. The cousin, Linda, had gotten a scholarship and was attending the University of Texas. Linda was a flower child, as she put it. Every so often, Paco and his girlfriend saved up enough from their occasional jobs to take the bus into Austin to stay with Linda. Paco learned a lot from Linda and her friends. Linda even let him try a toke of marijuana, though she would not let a "little kid" try her hash brownies.

Once, while in Austin, Paco joined Linda and her friends in a march protesting the Vietnam War. The university students told Paco about draft dodgers fleeing to Canada to avoid fighting in an unjust war. Paco thought the draftees had another reason to escape. The images he saw on the evening television news of the fighting in the jungle frightened Paco. Still, it was all far from Paco's remote, rural community deep in Texas.

Paco registered for the draft when he was eighteen, as required by law.

One week after his high school graduation, Paco walked out to the street in front of his house to get the mail. He recognized the return address on the one envelope lying in the box. Heart pounding, he extracted the single sheet bearing his draft notice.

"As many times as I run it through my head, the next few days remain a blur," Paco told his guests. "I do know I skipped the date I was supposed to report for duty. I sold my bike and took the bus to the airport in Houston. Canada seemed too far from home, so I bought a one-way ticket to Mexico City at the TWA counter."

"Did you have your passport?" Marlon asked. He looked like he was sobering up quickly.

"No, of course not," Paco answered. "I didn't have one. I didn't know I needed one. I didn't know where or how I would live in Mexico, or anything about the consequences of dodging the draft. I was only eighteen. Young and stupid." Paco smiled wanly.

"The ticket agent, a pretty blonde lady in a red uniform, pointed me towards the gate for my flight. I joined the handful of other passengers in the departure lounge. Everybody but I wore a business suit and had their faces buried in a newspaper. I sat on one of the hard, plastic seats and stuffed my mom's battered blue Samsonite between my feet."

"I reached into my duffle for the peanut butter and jelly sandwich I had brought. I stopped and sat upright when a man in a Texas State police uniform walked into the lounge. The officer scanned the area, then started towards me. Maybe the nice ticket agent sent him, I thought in a last burst of hope, because she had directed me to the wrong gate. The police officer grabbed my arm."

"He took me into a room marked 'official personnel only' and sat me down on a straight wooden chair. A minute later, two other men in suits, not uniforms, came in. One pulled an ID card from the breast pocket of his jacket and held it out. I have no recollection of the name on the card, but he was FBI. He told me I was under arrest for the federal crime of violating the Selective Service Act. I must have looked confused because he said, 'dodging the draft, coward.'"

"How did they find you?" Marlon asked. "And so quickly! What would have been the penalty if you'd been convicted? Do ..."

"I don't know any of that," Paco interrupted. "All I know is what happened. I was scared shirtless on top of being tired and confused. I remember thinking I deserved what was coming. I'd screwed everything up. My dad would ..." his voice trailed off.

Abruptly, Paco hauled himself to his feet. "I need one more shot," he said. "Anybody else?" Allen and Marlon demurred.

Paco silently strode to the bar and poured Tequila into his glass. He took a swig and, still standing, wrapped up his story.

"The FBI agent said I had one alternative to jail. If I renounced my U.S. citizenship, I could go free. Not back home, but on to Mexico. I had my boarding pass, and that's all I would need. So, that's what I did. Took an oath and relinquished the U.S. of A. For good. Forever."

Paco lifted his empty glass in a mock toast. His knees buckled. He slid down the side of the bar onto his backside, landing heavily, eyes closed.

He felt a touch on his forearm, then Marlon's voice. "We'll be back tomorrow with a pot of coffee from the café. Around noon."

***

A chime from Outlook woke him. Paco sat up abruptly and looked at his watch. He had fallen asleep over his reminisces.

Paco opened his laptop and read the email from Marlon, excitement growing. His friendship with Marlon had become, over the years, the focal point of his otherwise dismal existence. Paco had not thought that this relationship could grow in importance. Yet, it had. Marlon had just handed him his ticket out. Perhaps.

CHAPTER 4
UNDOCUMENTED

Will rose from his chair and walked to the wall of windows on the east side of Aaron's office. The spring dusk softened the top of the Capitol Dome, barely visible at the other end of Pennsylvania Avenue. He began to pace.

"Okay, I dealt with José during the afternoon session," Will began. He stopped and glanced at his colleagues. "But I've got another problem."

"Go on," Aaron commanded. The other attorneys sat quietly, prepared to conference all night if Will needed them.

"I'm not sure what to do about Mauricio," Will said. He resumed his pacing.

Mauricio was Will's star fact witness on liability. Mauricio managed J&A's building materials on-site. He would tell the jury how the company purchased, transported, stored, and handled those materials. Based on Mauricio's testimony, or the factual foundation he would establish, Will's two expert witnesses would opine that J&A's processes met industry safety requirements. In other words, J&A did not cause the defect in the plywood. The culprit had to be the defendants.

"I planned on calling Mauricio to testify tomorrow, in fact," Will concluded, "but I need to know what's coming in terms of his status before I do. José is a citizen, but what do I know about Mauricio? Nothing. I'd like you guys to be here for Mauricio's story and then help me decide what to do."

"Is Mauricio here?" Marlon asked.

"No," Will answered. "José is, though. It took some real convincing to get José to tell us what he knows about his father, by the way, which confirms that I do have a problem."

"I understand why José would be reluctant to spill the beans," Cassandra said. "If Mauricio is exposed as undocumented, he could be arrested and deported. His life, and his family's, destroyed in a heartbeat."

"I know," Will said impatiently. "That's why we're here, after all. I can't do anything to risk Mauricio's secrets coming to light. José wouldn't want me to, either. I'm certain. But I need Mauricio's evidence in this trial." Will massaged his forehead heavily.

Will signaled Jim, who stood post at the closed door to Aaron's office. A few minutes later, Jim returned with José.

"Have a seat, José," Will motioned, "and tell us about your dad. Start with when and how he came to the United States, please."

"Dad crossed the border from the state of Tamaulipas in Mexico without papers when he was sixteen, fleeing his family's extreme poverty. He made his way to Houston, found a room in the home of another Mexican migrant, and got day jobs in construction. Dad settled into the local immigrant community."

José looked at Will, who flashed an approving smile. José continued.

"Dad could fill his stomach in his adopted country, for which he was grateful, he told me. He was also hard-working and ambitious, despite his lack of any formal education. Dad wanted more than hauling lumber and pounding nails for the rest of his life. His undocumented status stood in his way. Dad knew he had to become a U.S. citizen to succeed."

"Dad's status bothered him for another reason, as well. Dad was raised a Catholic, and he sat in the village church with his family every Sunday morning. He heard the village padre warn, time and again, that lying was a sin. Sinners went to hell unless the sinner confessed and was given absolution in the sacrament of penance. Nobody at the construction sites where Dad worked ever asked him if he were legal. Technically, then, he had not lied, but he still felt guilty. Dad feared confessing to a priest in America, however. He knew a Mexican priest could not disclose what was said in the confessional, but he was not sure about American priests."

"Wait a minute," Miranda interrupted José's story. "I thought employers were required by law to check the immigration status of prospective employees. But nobody asked your father?"

José shrugged. "The rules change over time, and so do enforcement efforts. Back then, at least in Texas and in construction, nobody asked. Nobody cared, I guess, because the undocumented Mexicans were cheap labor."

"Still are," Marlon observed. "I mean, way underpaid for the backbreaking work they do, like shingling roofs and harvesting grapes."

"Soon after my dad got back from the war, things changed," José continued. "Companies weren't hiring without social security cards, and that's when Dad bought his counterfeit card."

"He what?" Miranda asked.

"What war?" Will asked simultaneously.

"Vietnam," José answered. "Back to your question in a minute, Miranda. Just after Dad turned eighteen, one of the older immigrants he had befriended told him about the service-to-citizenship opportunity. Dad jumped at the chance. He asked around, found out where to go, took a bus, and presented himself at the closest Army Recruitment Center to enlist. He was shipped off to Vietnam."

"Interesting," Marlon observed, rhythmically tapping the fingers of his right hand on his knee as though caressing the keys of a piano.

"Dad served his tour, returned to Texas, and sent in his application for citizenship, along with a copy of his separation papers. To his dismay and disbelief, his application was denied. He had no idea to whom to complain because he did not know who was responsible for the decision or why it had been made. So, he sent letter after letter to various offices at the State Department and Department of Defense. He received a few canned responses—'this office has no jurisdiction over the events at issue'—but nothing at all helpful."

"Dad took a bus to Annapolis and found the office of his district's representative in the Maryland State House. Lacking an appointment, he waited for hours. Finally, an aide to the representative met with Dad and listened to his story. When Dad finished, the aide shrugged and said the Feds had made their decision, presumably the right one. There was nothing his boss could do."

"Dad gave up. He bought his counterfeit social security card, as his old friends in Houston had advised. He went back into construction jobs, fell in love with my mom, Berta, another undocumented Mexican, and married."

"Mom was pregnant with me when she traveled to see her parents' family physician in Mexico. Mom needed medical care, a pregnancy-related complication, I was told. My folks couldn't afford the treatment in the States. I was born prematurely in my grandmother's house in Mexico. Because I was not born in the States, I was undocumented, like my parents. I bought my own counterfeit social security card to get jobs. When I married Alicia, an American citizen, I became a citizen."

"After which you sponsored your father for his green card, I suppose?" Cassandra asked. Cassandra would never take on the representation of a client in an immigration matter, as she was far from an expert in that field. She worked *pro bono* at an immigration law clinic earlier in her career, however, and had some basic knowledge of the rules.

José shook his head, no. "You can't adjust someone's status unless the preexisting status is legal, which Dad's wasn't," he answered. "Except, in some circumstances, through marriage. I got lucky."

The room fell silent.

Will stood.

"Sit down, Will," Aaron said testily. "It's getting late, and your pacing is getting on my nerves."

Will sat.

"We have to assume Baylie will ask Mauricio about his status if you put him on the stand," Aaron said. "If Mauricio were legal, his son would have been, too. But Baylie knows José was undocumented before he married his American wife."

"I agree," Will said, "but do you think Mauricio's service record trumps the fact that he's undocumented? That is, would the jury overlook the immigration problem because Mauricio served his country?"

Aaron shrugged. "You can't be sure." He shifted his gaze to his senior associate. "Marlon, what do you think?"

"Forget the jury for a moment," Marlon responded. "Remember what you said earlier when we were talking about José, Will. If Mauricio admits his status in open court, that fact is on public record. What if the immigration authorities find out about him? We don't know the answer to that."

Will's shoulders slumped. "I can't call him. Damn it!" He pounded his fist on his knee.

"You'll be fine," Marlon said. "There has to be another employee who can testify to the materials handling issue. He might not be your best witness, but you can make it work."

"Yeah, come on, Will," Cassandra said as she stood. "Let's get back to work. I'll reread Mauricio's deposition and identify candidates for replacing Mauricio. I'll draft the revised witness list to file tomorrow, too. You can decide who you'll call tomorrow instead of Mauricio and get him or her lined up to be in court on time."

Will looked around at his colleagues. He felt a surge of renewed energy.

"Sounds like a plan. Oh, and José." Will turned to his client. "I'm sorry I kept you so long. You must be exhausted. Jim will take you home now."

A few minutes later, Aaron's big corner office was empty and dark.

CHAPTER 5
TAKE THE FIFTH

Will maneuvered his Prius through the tight fit into the garage as the motion sensor light came on. He glanced into the rearview mirror to make sure the garage door closed completely. He would have to get to that rusty mechanism and grease it one day.

As he reached for the door handle, his reflection in the mirror caught his eye. He was reminded of Marlon's comment, one evening over drinks, on Will's appearance. Will would have made a perfect spy, Marlon had said. Will understood. With his unremarkable appearance, Will blended into a crowd. Marlon had hastened to add that Will had a great smile, however. The face in the mirror grinned. Gathering up his old leather briefcase, Will got out of the car and unlocked the lower-level door to his house.

"Norma, I'm home," he called as he crossed their finished basement and started up the stairs. He glanced at his watch and grimaced. Ten o'clock. He had to get to bed soon to get an early start tomorrow.

Norma met him as he reached the top of the stairs. They murmured greetings as she leaned in for his embrace and kiss. She took his hand and led him toward the kitchen. For the first time since he had left for court that morning, Will relaxed.

"Wine?" Will asked. Norma nodded her approval. Will took a chilled bottle out of the refrigerator, opened it, and poured her a glass. He chose a Corona for himself and popped off the cap. Just one, he thought as he leaned back onto the granite counter. It would help him sleep.

"How was your flight?" Will asked. Norma had returned earlier that day from Spain. An engineer, Norma worked for a multinational wind energy production company. Part of her job included travel to assist in wind farm inspections.

Norma yawned in reply. Both laughed.

"Fine," she replied. "Uneventful." She took a sip of her wine. "How's the trial going?"

Will filled her in, skimming over all of it except the revelation about José's fake social security card.

"What did you decide to do about it?" Norma asked.

"Punt," Will answered. Norma, whose exposure to American football was decidedly limited, looked confused. "We did the best we could with limited options," Will explained. "We couldn't get advice from anyone during the break. It was lunch hour, after all. So, Aaron instructed me to have José 'take the Fifth.' Aaron told me exactly how to do it. When we all looked surprised, he said it had happened to him, once, years ago. It worked for him, and maybe it would for me and José."

"And?" Norma inquired.

"Worked like a charm," Will answered. "I requested that the clerk read back the last question from the transcript, which she did. I rose and said in the most solemn tone I could muster: 'Mr. Marquez, do you choose to utilize the rights guaranteed to you and other citizens by the Fifth Amendment to the United States Constitution and refuse to answer that question?' José said, 'I do.' And that was that. Went right over the jurors' heads. None of them batted an eyelash."

Norma laughed. "You've told me Aaron is good," she said.

Will nodded. "Really good."

Will was on the verge of telling Norma about his other immigration problem but bit his tongue. The District of Columbia had abolished the marital privilege. He could and did tell Norma almost, but not quite everything.

Norma yawned again and said she was ready for bed. She invited Will to join her, but he declined.

"Tired but wired," Will explained with an attempt at a grin.

Norma nodded. They had been married long enough that she knew what Will was like during a trial. She kissed him and retired to their bedroom.

Will, restless, idly fingered the stack of mail on the kitchen counter. Might as well do something constructive, he told himself, extracting a letter from the top of the stack.

He opened the envelope addressed to him from the District of Columbia Bar Association. The enclosed letter announced the two candidates for the upcoming election for the president of the organization. Will would vote this year, as he always did. Not recognizing either from their pictures, he scanned the candidates' bios. Will noticed that one of the candidates originally hailed from Baltimore. He had attended high school at Gilman, an exclusive private school outside Baltimore.

Will's father had tried so hard to get Will into Gilman, but Will's application was rejected. The lump rose in his throat. After all these years, Will chided himself. Still, he let the wave of embarrassment and disappointment run through him, anyway.

After Gilman rejected him, Will's father comforted him. He assured Will that he would do as well in life as those kids who grabbed the Gilman golden ring. Will would have to work harder than they.

After attending a local community college, Will finished his degree in biology at Catholic University. He taught high school biology in Baltimore public schools, studying for his law degree at night.

With his law degree in hand, Will hit the job market hard. He mailed dozens of applications to law firms across the D.C. metropolitan area. He took the only job offer he received, with a sole practitioner in Gaithersburg, Maryland.

Will tried routine slip-and-falls and car accidents for ten years before his luck turned. He landed a job with Aaron Stein. To Will, a position at Aaron's was good fortune, indeed. He knew, however, how the corporate bar looked down on med mal practitioners. No graduate of Gilman would have considered working for Aaron.

Will shook himself back to the present. He had to try to get some sleep. He had already made a bad mistake in this trial. He would not allow himself another.

CHAPTER 6
AN UNPLEASANT SURPRISE

Trial Day 2

The clock on the wall behind the Judge's dais read 4:10 p.m. They had been at this since 1:00 p.m. Will needed a break.

"Give me a minute, Your Honor?" Will asked. Judge Storer nodded.

Will smiled at Dr. Moraski, perched jauntily at the edge of his chair in the witness box. Of course, Will thought, José's treating doctor was unfazed. What had been a grueling three hours for Will and far too much for most witnesses to handle was nothing to this doctor. He performed ten-hour, life-and-death surgeries daily.

Will turned and strode back to counsel's table to check his notes. Ready to wrap it, he decided. He returned to his usual examination post in front of, but not crowding, his witness.

Q: What, in your opinion, is José's prognosis, Dr. Moraski?

Glancing at the jury box, recognizing looks of uncertainty, Will rephrased.

Q: What does the future hold for José in terms of his physical condition, given what has happened to him?

A: José will, unfortunately, suffer from recurrent back pain all his life. His movements, particularly his walk, will be stiff and ungainly because of the fusions to the vertebrae I had to perform to save his life. The severe trauma to his spine from the fall will cause continued deterioration of the vertebra. Therefore, he is likely to need additional surgeries as he ages.

Q: Would you please tell the jury what you mean by "continued deterioration"?

Dr. Moraski rose, the pointer he had used earlier in the afternoon still in his hand. He walked to the easel sitting directly in front of the jury box. He indicated the cervical spine on the life-size illustration of the human spine drawn on the poster board propped on the easel. In his clear, tenor voice, Dr. Moraski began his explanation.

A:This is C-6, directly below the site of the first fusion ...

As the jury listened attentively to Dr. Moraski, Will's thoughts momentarily drifted. He knew he was decidedly old-school in using poster boards and paper documents. The younger lawyers used a laptop and flashed digitized images on the white board hanging on the wall to the left of the jury box. After decades of doing it his way, however, Will stuck to the tools with which he was most adept.

Trying a case was already like being the ringmaster in a four-ring circus, without adding new technologies to the mix. In the center ring, Will struggled to get the witness from meandering off into damaging territory. Opposing counsel interrupted with objections which Will fought to overcome. He had to argue with the judge over unfavorable rulings without showing disrespect. Last but most importantly, Will clued the jurors with every word he spoke and every move he made. He must convey honesty and integrity and win the jurors to his side. To be further distracted by crotchety electronic gadgetry was more than Will could handle.

Dr. Moraski concluded his testimony and returned to the witness box.

Q:Do you hold the opinions you have testified to today to a reasonable degree of medical certainty?

Clumsy, Will knew. He had to ask the question, though, to establish the final element of admissible opinion evidence.

A:I do.

Will hesitated, giving the jurors time to absorb Dr. Moraski's grim predictions and him a moment to consider asking one more question. He had another witness with the answer he wanted. His vocational rehabilitation expert would testify about José's diminished work capacity and loss of future earnings. Still, he could see that Dr. Moraski had established a good rapport with the jury. Two of the jurors nodded appreciatively when Will walked the doctor through his impressive credentials. All of them remained attentive to Dr. Moraski's testimony even through the driest stretches of technical medical details. Go for it, Will decided. The worst that could happen was an objection from Baylie.

Q:Will José be able to work again, in your opinion?

No objection from Baylie, to Will's surprise. He glanced over. Baylie was not looking at the witness but down at his notepad. Hah, Will thought. It had worked. Baylie was too busy thinking about his cross.

A:How much he is going to be able to do for his company is a big unknown. But he certainly will not, physically, be able to play the dominant role that he has in the past.

A:Thank you, Dr. Moraski.

Will turned back and nodded at Baylie. "Your witness."

Two hours later, Will and Cassandra sat motionless in their cab. They had been lucky to nab it just outside the courthouse, on the corner of Third and E. But now, they were stuck in rush-hour traffic. Will leaned back against the headrest and closed his eyes.

"What is it about this trial?" he asked petulantly. "I'm a good lawyer. I prepare. Thoroughly. I don't get unpleasant surprises. In this one, I've already had two," he groaned.

Towards the end of his cross-examination of Dr. Moraski, Baylie handed the court clerk, the witness, and Will copies of a document. Will realized, with a jolt, that this document was not in his file. He had barely a second to absorb its contents.

Baylie asked that the document be admitted in evidence. Will stood and objected. Summoned to the judge's dais, the attorneys argued furiously but, as far as everyone else in the courtroom was concerned, silently. Judge Storer had activated the husher.

"Your Honor," Will began, "we asked for all relevant documents in discovery. The defense did not produce this one. They cannot use a document they failed to disclose before trial."

Judge Storer switched her attention to Baylie.

"We only received this document from the insurance company yesterday, Your Honor," Baylie responded. "Besides, Mr. McCarty could and should have had all of Mr. Marquez's medical records whether or not we provided them. That's his job."

"Overruled," Judge Storer said without hesitation. She admitted the document, the record of an emergency room visit José made to Sibley Memorial Hospital three months ago.

José had been a passenger in a company vehicle driven by one of his newer employees. A Mercedes SUV rear-ended their truck on Western Avenue. The cops came. The driver of the SUV admitted fault and was given a ticket, and insurance information was exchanged. Neither vehicle appeared to be damaged, and José claimed he was fine. However, because José was only a month post-op, his employee insisted on driving his boss to Sibley.

José's recent car accident was as much a surprise to Dr. Moraski as it was for Will. And Baylie pushed the witness, hard, to admit that the impact of the collision worsened José's condition.

If Dr. Moraski had caved to the pressure, his testimony would have thrown a very big wrench into Will's case. Will claimed that all of José's damages, totaling in the millions for medical expenses alone, were caused by his fall at the construction site. Baylie was trying to shift the blame, and a sizeable percentage of the damages, to the car accident.

To Will's immense relief, Dr. Moraski, calmly but firmly, rejected Baylie's theory. When Baylie tried to cut him off, Dr. Moraski insisted on explaining to the jury why the recent accident caused José no harm.

After Dr. Moraski left the stand, Judge Storer excused the jury. She also reminded them, as she did every day, not to discuss anything about the evidence or the trial with another juror, family member, or anyone else. She then adjourned court for the day.

José apologized profusely to Will as he and Cassandra packed their bags. "I didn't purposefully withhold the information," he explained. "I simply forgot all about the accident. It was such a minor fender-bender.

I was in the ER only a half hour or so, and a thousand more serious matters captured my attention between then and now. I am so sorry."

Will struggled to conceal his irritation with his client. Will had been blindsided. Again. Will's surprise had been evident to Baylie and the judge. That stung. He remembered that feeling too well. Will stumbled badly in his early trials. He began to doubt his ability to play in the big leagues in Washington. He worked harder. He had succeeded, but all could too easily be lost.

Will pulled his attention back to his client. José's cheeks were drawn, and a sickly, grayish pallor darkened his light caramel complexion. It was not José's fault, Will scolded himself.

"It's okay," Will said, putting his hand on José's shoulder. "I understand, and Dr. Moraski stopped Baylie in his tracks, anyway. Jim will take you home now. Relax and get some rest."

Their cab lurched forward just as Cassandra reached over and patted Will's hand. "You're a med mal lawyer, Will," she said soothingly, "and a very good one." Will's thoroughness was renowned throughout the med mal bar, among both plaintiffs' and defendants' lawyers. "But you haven't handled a personal injury case in ages. Personal injury is a different world, you know."

Will sighed. He thought back to those slip-and-fall cases he had tried for so many years. The big battles focused on the client's credibility. Was that back pain, of which the client complained, real or a ploy to run up the bill for damages? Aaron's cases centered on medicine and science. "Yeah, you're right," he agreed. "The roadmaps for success in the two are very different."

"And I don't think Baylie scored any points with the jury, do you?" Cassandra asked.

Will sighed, again, but opened his eyes and sat up. He had expressed confidence for his client's sake, but he had his doubts. "Maybe not," he said. "Won't know until it's over. Anyway, let's think, what all do we have to do between now and 9:00 tomorrow morning?"

CHAPTER 7
PRO BONO

Betsy set down her ladle and straightened herself. Cradling her back with both hands, she leaned back and stretched.

She caught the eye of the woman in front of her station: Diminutive, of uncertain age—she could have been thirty or sixty—swathed in layers of Goodwill-quality sweaters despite the balmy April evening. She stood, head down, face hidden under the brim of a Washington Redskins baseball cap.

Betsy snatched up her ladle. "Sorry about that," she murmured.

The woman lifted her tray towards Betsy. The cap, perched loosely on her head, slipped back. "No worries," she said, smiling, and "thank you," after Betsy filled her bowl with soup. The line moved on.

Betsy volunteered at Rachel's Kitchen. Known as the neighborhood soup kitchen, Rachel's rarely served its namesake dish. The nonprofit boasted, instead, of its "good food for good people." Every meal included fresh fruits and vegetables, along with heartier fare. This evening, however, the chef had made vegetable soup.

Betsy glanced down the line of tables to her left. She would need to refill the bread baskets soon. Enough carrot and celery sticks remained on their trays to do for the evening, she decided. Another volunteer would check the urns of coffee on the last table in the line.

Betsy mechanically dipped and poured the soup, smiling and nodding a hello now and again. Her thoughts drifted to her morning's phone conversation with Jeff Howard.

Jeff had called as Betsy was gathering her things to leave her apartment for work. He had decided to throw his hat into the ring for a run at the U.S. Senate. Initially, he had hesitated, because of his age, but the Republican National Committee assured him that his popularity among voters from both parties in the Commonwealth outweighed his years.

"After all, seventy-year-old candidates are in vogue, these days," he had said, a smile in his voice. "Anyway, I'd like you to be a part of my team. A small part, because I know you've got a lot on your own plate right now. And I should have asked you properly, over lunch, but I'm tied up in Richmond right now."

"What role do you have in mind for me?" Betsy had asked.

Jeff explained. He had served in public office for decades, as a member of the House of Delegates for six terms and in the Virginia Senate for two. He was an open book to the citizens of Virginia. This race for the U.S. Senate, though, was on a different level. Every detail of his life would be closely scrutinized. Many of those peering into his past would be looking for dirt.

"Is there any?" Betsy joked.

"Nothing worse than the occasional keg party in college," Jeff responded lightly. Betsy caught the serious tone in his voice, however. "But we need to be prepared for anything. Remember when the 'swiftboat' rumors crushed John Kerry's presidential campaign? We need to anticipate problems like that before they arise. You know me so well, you're smart and creative, and you know how to solve problems. Dig anywhere. Pull up anything somebody might consider a weed, so to speak. Tell me about it. Then we'll deal with it."

"I'd love to help," Betsy responded. "And, of course, I believe you are the best man for the job and am behind you one hundred percent. But, as you said, I've got a lot going on right now. I still feel on shaky ground at the firm. I'm on probation, I think. And you already have such a talented staff."

"I understand," Jeff's supportive voice came through the line, "but think about it. We'll have to come up with another approach quickly if you don't come on board. So, please let us know as soon as possible."

Jeff had asked Betsy to let Vincent know of her decision. Vincent Bainbridge, Jeff's chief of staff and best friend, managed the complex inner workings of Jeff's senatorial campaign.

A tap on her shoulder interrupted Betsy's thoughts. She turned, cupping her left hand under the dripping ladle.

"Your hour is up," the eponymous Rachel, standing behind Betsy, said with a smile. Rachel reached out to take the ladle and Betsy's place on the line.

Back in the pantry, Betsy untied her apron and hung it on its peg. Now was the time to decide, she thought, before she was buried in a brief again.

She wanted to say no. She needed to stay focused on the firm. In the end, loyalty won out. She owed Jeff her new life, after all.

Betsy's old life ended the day after she turned eight. She remembered the blue-frosted layer cake, Betsy's favorite color. Her grandmother had baked it to celebrate Betsy's birthday. The next morning, as Betsy and her grandparents ate breakfast, a knock sounded at the door. The police.

Her grandfather shooed Betsy from the kitchen before he beckoned the policeman to come in. Half an hour later, her grandmother appeared in Betsy's bedroom to tell her why the police had come to their house.

Betsy realized, later in life, that few eight-year-olds would have been told the whole story. Her paternal grandparents, both retired teachers, believed it best to be open and honest, however. Betsy would come to know what happened to her parents eventually. Why not get it over with now? Her grandparents also recognized Betsy's precocity. They did not hold back.

Betsy's parents, Thomas and Natalie Thornhill, both graduated from Antioch College. Shortly after graduation, they joined an "antifa" group crusading against fascism. Organizing protests and distributing anti-fascist pamphlets became the Thornhills' full-time job.

At the time, Betsy knew only that her parents worked in "politics" and had to travel for work. Accordingly, from time to time, when her parents were away, Betsy stayed with her grandparents, who lived in rural Ohio.

The night Betsy turned eight, Thomas and Natalie, toting carbines, crashed a dive on the outskirts of Charlottesville, Virginia. The place was known to be a hangout for local neo-Nazis. One of the customers in the bar ended up dead.

The dead man had no criminal record. His buddies at the bar swore no one in the place had exhibited any aggression, except the Thornhills. The Thornhills were charged with felony murder. They would be tried in the "rocket docket" in the Federal District Court for Eastern Virginia. Justice would be delivered swiftly.

After the policeman gave his report and left, Betsy's grandparents called the local sheriff's office. They did not have spare cash on hand, but the bank might loan them money to hire a lawyer to represent Thomas and Natalie. But how would they find an attorney in Virginia?

The sheriff assured them that an attorney, paid for by the government, would be appointed. Don't get your hopes up, though, the sheriff warned. The evidence against Thomas and Natalie was damning.

Later that morning, Betsy lay in her bed, staring at the ceiling, when she heard the phone ring. Her grandmother entered Betsy's bedroom and sat on the side of her bed. She reached up and softly stroked Betsy's wet cheek.

"Good news, sweetie," her grandmother said. "A fancy lawyer in Richmond volunteered to represent your parents. A real lawyer, not one of those the government provides. Name's Jeff Howard."

"But," Betsy sat up, "how will you pay him?"

"He's doing it for free," her grandmother answered. "Donating his time. Something called *pro bono.*"

"For the public good," Jeff translated for Betsy later. Most attorneys paid lip service to their obligation to provide free legal services, but Jeff took his duty seriously.

Jeff lost the case. The jury found the Thornhills guilty as charged. Thomas and Natalie went to prison for life, with no possibility of parole.

Natalie's parents, moneyed Chicago folks, publicly disowned Natalie. After the trial and conviction, they would have nothing to do with Natalie's daughter. Betsy had no other family, so her paternal grandparents took on the job of raising their granddaughter.

Six months after the trial, her grandparents sat Betsy down in the living room. They explained to her that Jeff had called soon after the trial. He felt terrible about the case. Perhaps taking on a felony murder charge had been over his head. Natalie had told him all about her smart, beautiful daughter. Jeff and his wife wanted children but had not been given that blessing after years of marriage. Jeff asked them to consider whether Betsy might come to live with him and his wife, with adoption being the ultimate plan, if it all worked out.

After repeated phone conversations, and much soul searching by her grandparents, the adults decided it would be best. Jeff could give Betsy a much better life. If Betsy wanted it.

Betsy agreed to meet Jeff. He flew to Ohio. Betsy remembered him as a tall, blonde man, about her father's age. He seemed kind, and he smiled easily.

Betsy, still numb, looked at her grandparents closely for the first time since her world crumbled. The wrinkles in her grandmother's face had deepened noticeably. Her grandfather's eyelid had acquired a tic, and his hand shook when he raised his coffee cup to his lips.

Betsy nodded. She would go with Jeff.

The pantry door swung open, interrupting her thoughts. Betsy smiled at the other volunteer who entered, serving trays piled on her outstretched arms. Betsy wondered how long she had been standing there staring at the apron she had just hung. An apron just like the one her grandmother had worn.

So, Betsy would dig into Jeff's past, as he had asked. She thought she knew her mentor and role model inside and out. She admired all of him. Still, nobody was perfect. Betsy wondered what she might find.

CHAPTER 8
A RED FLAG

Marlon set a bowl of olives on the counter in front of Allen. With a block of parmesan cheese, a loaf of crusty Italian bread, and a glass of wine or two, this would be their dinner.

Comfortably dressed in jeans and t-shirts, the two of them ate at the kitchen island tonight. Marlon and Allen took their meals in the formal dining room of their townhouse in Cleveland Park only when joined by enough guests to exceed the kitchen's seating capacity.

"Welcome home," Marlon said, raising his glass in a toast. Allen had returned from a three-day trip business trip to New York City earlier that afternoon. "How were your meetings?" Marlon continued.

The couple caught up on the events of the last few days. Allen had much to say about the three new partners in his firm. Marlon's news centered on Will's trial.

"It sounds as though that trial is the only thing going on in the office," Allen observed as he broke off a chunk of the bread.

"That's about right," Marlon responded. "It's odd. Usually, when two lawyers are in trial, the rest of us are doing double duty covering their other cases as well as our own. This week, except for Luke, who is in Los Angeles covering three back-to-back depositions, we all have light calendars."

"Too bad I'm swamped, or we could have taken a day off and done something fun," Allen sighed. "But back to the trial. Don't you have some concerns about Will's strategy?"

Marlon had not disclosed any confidential information about Mauricio to his partner, but Allen could read between the lines. Allen questioned Will's decision to remove Mauricio from his witness list.

"As I understand it," Allen said, "Baylie knows the Marquezes were illegally in the States because of José's employment records. He knows José is now legal, having married an American. Baylie does not know Mauricio's status because the question was not asked during the discovery phase. Wouldn't pulling Mauricio off the witness list now be a red flag to Baylie? Might he even contact the immigration authorities?"

"That would be an extreme measure, even for a defense attorney," Marlon responded drily.

Allen laughed.

Marlon had a dim view of select members of the defense bar who hit below the belt. The greater number, however, he respected. The feeling, Marlon knew, was mutual.

"Speaking of Mauricio," Marlon continued, "I mentioned his name to Paco in my last email to him. I told him Mauricio served in Vietnam. Nothing about what happened after, of course. That's confidential. Paco wanted all the details. I'll have to get that information from Will."

"Another addition to Paco's Vietnam project?" Allen asked.

"Yep," Marlon answered.

When they dined in Paco's apartment that first and only time, years ago, Marlon and Allen had wondered why Paco owned such sophisticated computing equipment. Later, Marlon found out that Paco used it for what he called his Vietnam project. Paco had collected and stored thousands of pages of documents over the years, and he continuously added to his library. Anything remotely connected to the Vietnam War was fair game.

When he first learned of Paco's project, Marlon thought it odd that the man obsessed about the thing he had sacrificed his life to avoid. But, on reflection, Marlon decided it made perfect sense.

Marlon rose to clear their dishes. "Shall we have a glass of wine on the patio?" he asked.

"Sorry, but I've some work to finish before tomorrow," Allen answered. "You go ahead. It's such a beautiful evening. I'll be upstairs in the office."

Twenty minutes later, Marlon settled onto the orange canvas seat cushion of a white wicker love seat. One of a pair, the chairs crowded their brick-paved, handkerchief-sized patio, surrounded by a ten-foot wooden privacy fence. Marlon placed his phone, laptop, and wine onto the glass-topped wicker coffee table between the love seats.

The traffic noise from the nearby city streets ebbed as the twilight deepened. Marlon opened his laptop and clicked on Paco's email. Paco had sent his latest story.

Marlon had been intrigued enough by Paco's unmoored life to exchange a few emails with him after returning from Mexico. Marlon expected nothing more from their encounter than this occasional correspondence. Even those would taper off over time. Friendship did not seem in the cards.

For one thing, Paco's story did not add up. Marlon had done the legal research when he returned home. Only a voluntary renunciation of citizenship was valid. A renunciation made to avoid a threatened punishment would be considered involuntary and invalid. Paco's renunciation to avoid going to jail was invalid.

An eighteen-year-old man alone in a foreign country could not have known this, of course. The mature man would have questioned the validity of his status, however. The no-man's-land of statelessness was too dreadful a condition to go unchallenged. Paco would surely have contacted an American lawyer. If the events Paco described to Marlon and Allen had, in fact, happened, Paco would have had his American citizenship returned to him.

The truth, Marlon presumed, was that Paco flew to Mexico City and voluntarily relinquished his U.S. citizenship before an American consul to avoid being drafted. According to the law, a renunciation under these circumstances was "voluntary" and binding even if done in order to avoid the Selective Service laws.

Why Paco had lied to them Marlon did not know. Perhaps Paco wanted to secure a friendship with the Americans who unexpectedly crossed his threshold. He may have thought his revised version of events put him in a more sympathetic light. Understandable, Marlon told himself. Plus, the story Paco told them was mainly true. Paco was stateless, alone, and adrift, regardless of how he had gotten to that point. Still, the lie bothered Marlon.

Marlon also, initially, found little to say in his occasional emails to Paco. Other than a love of opera, they had little in common. Paco's return messages were perfunctory, as well.

A year passed, and almost two months since their last correspondence, when Marlon received a brief note from Paco, bearing an unexplained attachment. Paco had sent him a short story, a simple vignette.

In spare but powerful prose, the story developed the harsh, internal conflict of a soldier in Vietnam. His father was proud of his warrior son. The young man wanted out of the war, whatever it took to get there.

Intrigued by the striking imagery in Paco's story, Marlon responded promptly.

Paco:
Is this why you've collected your Vietnam library? As the source for your fiction? Anyway, I thought the story well done. It was as though you'd been there!
Marlon

Paco's answers came immediately.

Marlon:
No, the fiction is ancillary to my study of the history of that war. I'm obviously a novice writer, but thank you for the compliment. Herman Melville had been to sea, but much fiction is written by authors unlike their characters and lacking the fictional experiences given them.
Paco

Paco's stories kept coming. Marlon eventually convinced Paco to allow him to submit one of the stories, under a pseudonym, for publication. The magazine accepted it, and the critics of military fiction reviewed it favorably. Paco never achieved wide readership, but he published regularly and made decent money from his work.

Through their regular correspondence, the relationship between Marlon and Paco deepened. They discovered their mutual interest in music theory, philosophy, and political science, in addition to history.

Marlon marveled at Paco's erudition, given that Paco was entirely self-taught.

On a lighter note, Marlon kept Paco abreast of the activities of his day-to-day life, and that of the firm. Paco requested as much. An escape from his isolated exile, Marlon supposed.

Of Paco's daily life, Marlon learned little. "Nothing ever happens," Paco responded, when Marlon asked.

Paco also objected to using video conferencing, which Marlon suggested. They used the technology a time or two, but Paco complained that the distorted images distracted from the conversation.

Marlon accepted their friendship for what it was. The lie on which it had been founded faded into the past.

Marlon opened the attachment to Paco's most recent email and began to read.

When he had finished, Marlon saved the story to Paco's file, then opened Outlook. He hoped Paco was still up and on his computer.

Paco:
This is unlike your usual war stories. A deserter?
Marlon

Marlon did not have to wait long for a response.

Marlon:
If you haven't read Tim O'Brien's incredible book, "Going After Cacciato," you should. Anyway, it got me wondering what might have happened to a real Cacciato who did get away.
Paco

Well, okay, Marlon thought. He would put the O'Brien book on his "to do" list.

Marlon's phone rang. Leaning over the coffee table, he peered at the screen. His dad, according to the caller ID. Marlon sighed. He had nothing to report that would impress his dad enough to catch his attention. Therefore, if Marlon answered, he would be subjected to a litany of last month's accomplishments by his dad's three stepchildren and seven step-grandchildren. Marlon let the call go to voice mail.

He gathered his things and headed into the house. He had time to review his notes for tomorrow's interview with Vincent Bainbridge, Senator Jeff Howard's chief-of-staff, before turning in. The transcript of his meeting with Bainbridge would add to Marlon's growing collection of interviews with Vietnam War veterans and their loved ones.

Paco's passion for the archives of Vietnam had sparked Marlon's interest, to his colleagues' amazement. The previous achievements Marlon had set for himself focused on the fine arts. Two years ago, Marlon memorized the score of Wagner's magnum opus, *The Ring Cycle*. Nothing remotely martial had appeared on Marlon's lists, before now. He and Paco, chronicling the war experiences of Vietnam veterans, aimed to write and publish a book.

Marlon had worked hard to get a meeting with the Senator himself who, Marlon knew, was a veteran. Senator Howard had volunteered and served a tour of duty as a private first class in the Army in Vietnam before attending the University of Virginia. His staff remained adamant, however. The Senator was far too busy to make himself available for Marlon's history project. Marlon wondered if his tight schedule confirmed the rumor that Howard was considering a run for the U.S. Senate. At any rate, as a conciliatory gesture, his staff had offered up Vincent.

Marlon had consulted Paco about the interview tomorrow, as he always did. Paco knew far more about Vietnam than Marlon did. With his wealth of knowledge, Paco proposed questions for the interviewees that never would have occurred to Marlon.

The question Paco suggested for Bainbridge surprised Marlon. Surely, Howard had nothing to hide. If he did, Bainbridge would never disclose it. Well, Marlon would know soon enough.

CHAPTER 9
A DNA MATCH

Trial Day 3

Miranda stopped by the small conference room on the way to her office. She knew Will and Cassandra would be in early this morning, finishing their preparation for the third day of trial.

Will looked up from the legal pad on which he was taking notes. Cassandra sat across the table from Will, shrugging into the jacket of her navy-blue suit.

"Good morning," Miranda said. "Ready for the day?"

"I hope so," Will answered, "but Peyton is on the stand this morning, and that makes me nervous."

Miranda knew that Peyton Richards, their materials science expert, was an inexperienced witness. He had testified as an expert witness in only one other trial. The alternative, however, was Frank Nugent, a grizzled, seventy-year-old who had not had a job in industry for years. Instead, he made a good living testifying, primarily for plaintiffs' lawyers. The jury might question Nugent's credibility after the defense, in cross-examination, established that ninety percent of Nugent's sizeable annual income came from testifying on behalf of plaintiffs. To avoid that risk, Will opted to take a chance on an amateur.

"I met Peyton at his hotel for breakfast this morning to review his testimony," Cassandra said, addressing Miranda. "He seemed solid."

Will nodded, reached down, and hauled his big litigation briefcase onto the table as he stood. He grabbed a stack of yellow legal pads and deposition transcripts and packed them into the bag.

"Let's hit it, Cassandra," Will said.

"Good luck, you guys," Miranda called as the lawyers trouped out of the conference room.

"Thanks," Cassandra said. "I'm feeling optimistic. I think Peyton will do well." She grinned. "It's sure our turn to have a good day."

Miranda laughed. The elevator chimed as its doors opened. Will and Cassandra headed to court.

A half an hour later, Miranda glanced at her watch. Almost 9:00 a.m. She picked up her pace. Chad would not care, but Miranda hated to be late.

She smiled as an early childhood image crossed her mind: Her mother, Paula, hurrying Miranda out of the door to their house as Miranda struggled into her coat. Paula insisted that they arrive at Aunt Judy's for their regular Sunday night get-together at least ten minutes early. Maybe not strictly an inherited trait, Miranda thought, but close enough.

Miranda entered the park at the northwest corner. She took the diagonal path toward the park's eponymous statue of the Marquis de Lafayette. Chad would be waiting for her with breakfast from Chesapeake Bakery.

Last evening, Chad offered to swing up to Bethesda to get a bag of Miranda's favorite bagels. Miranda accepted, although Chad would have to fight the worst of rush-hour traffic both ways. She had mostly forgiven Chad for planting a bug in her phone last fall. She understood why he had to do it, once he explained. Still, there was no reason to give him a short shrift. She would let him go out of his way to be extra solicitous a few more times.

As she neared Pennsylvania Avenue, Miranda spotted Chad leaning back against the Marquis's pedestal. Eyes closed, his face tilted up to the warm, April sun. She was tempted to surprise him with a kiss on the cheek but resisted. She was not sure how he would react if startled like that.

Chad had spent a good part of his life dodging and feigning, uncovering the secrets of others while carefully protecting his own. Miranda had the overall picture by now, five months after they started dating. He would not or could not tell her the details, however. Miranda was not sure of the reason for his reticence. Chad was one of the good guys. After all, he had handed the identity of a data hacker wanted by every national intelligence agency in the world to the National Security Agency. Case closed, and the Agency eternally grateful.

Or not, Miranda corrected herself. Marlon had his suspicions about Chad. Marlon thought Chad and his partner, Ed Dante, pulled a fast one on the NSA. The agency failed to retaliate for reasons unknown to the lawyers. Either way, Miranda did not care.

"Heh, Chad, wake up," Miranda said teasingly. Chad opened his dark, brown eyes framed with those long, thick lashes which Miranda envied, and smiled broadly. It was the smile that first attracted Miranda. It still did, complemented by his slender, wiry frame, four inches taller than her own, and the silky blonde hair that he wore neatly trimmed. Plus, he was super smart and made Miranda laugh.

Initially, Miranda supposed Chad's interest in her would quickly wane. She had enough bad experiences with men to keep her expectations low. Plus, Chad was way out of her league, she feared.

At forty-seven, Chad was ten years her senior. Miranda had been to Europe, but Chad had circled the globe, more than once. Miranda had a good job and owned a two-bedroom house on a quiet, tree-lined street in American University Park, a block from the Metro station. Chad lived in the mansion in McLean, Virginia, overlooking the Potomac River, that he had purchased from Ed Dante when Ed left the country. Chad was movie-star handsome. Miranda disliked her nose and thought her brown eyes too small for her wide, heart-shaped face. Yet, to Miranda's surprised delight, the relationship seemed to be working just fine.

Chad straightened, reached for Miranda, and pulled her in for a hug. The couple joined hands and strolled west on the wide pedestrian walkway into which Pennsylvania had been transformed after 9/11, towards their destination.

Parker Evans' tattered, orange pup tent squatted on the park lawn directly across the promenade from the White House.

"A prime spot," Miranda remarked to Chad as they approached. "Parker must have camped in Lafayette Park all night to get it."

To the right of the tent stood a wooden easel that once may have been painted white. Its muddy brown frame, mottled with grey streaks, held a poster board. Six-inch lettering hand-painted in a garish shade of

red admonished: "Don't be a Fossil Fool." Pictures of
bears, flooded bayous, and raging forest fires were ta
around the slogan. The poster board on the easel to th
its counterpart, proclaimed "Vietnam Veterans Against
images of weapons, explosions, and exhausted, bloody faces from Syria
and South Sudan and Gaza.

Parker was nowhere to be seen.

Chad bent down and peered into the dark interior of the tent.
"Parker, you in there?" Chad called.

A head, pate close-shaven, emerged. An extra-large pair of dark
glasses hid most of the face. It peered left, then right.

"Well, if it isn't my favorite couple," Parker said, clumsily
extricating his torso from the tent through its small, oval opening.

Chad, grinning, looked over at Miranda, who blushed, then
blanched. She involuntarily placed her palm on her chest as Parker stood
to his full, six-foot height. He looked worse than his poor polar bears,
she thought.

"You're sick again," Miranda said, stumbling her words, kicking
herself mentally for her rudeness. And for stupidly stating the obvious.

Miranda first met Parker when she joined Stein & Associates right
out of law school, twelve years ago. Parker, a long-time friend of the
firm, always made friends with Aaron's new associates. He took
Miranda out to lunch during her second week on the job. The next
weekend, Parker and Miranda walked for hours on the trails in Glover
Archibald Park. Miranda, smitten, adopted Parker as the father figure
she never had.

Miranda's father, Peter Patel, abandoned her and her mother, Paula,
shortly after Miranda was born. Miranda inherited her glossy brunette
hair, brown eyes, and olive skin from her father, a first-generation
Italian whose immigrant parents had shortened Pescatelli to an
Americanized version of their surname. Miranda was also left with an
abiding distrust of the sincerity of a man's commitment.

Parker broke Miranda's emotional dam around men. Parker told
Miranda she was brilliant and beautiful enough times that she believed
him. Believed Parker saw her that way, at least. Because of Parker,
Miranda was receptive when Chad came into her life.

And now here Parker was, on this beautiful spring day, at death's door, according to his appearance.

"It's my kidneys," Parker confirmed. "Giving out on me."

"The amyloidosis?" Miranda asked.

"Yes," Parker answered with a grimace. "The disease isn't flaring up again. But, because I've had it so long, the amyloid buildup over time is destroying my kidneys."

"You need to be on dialysis," Chad asserted, eyeing the yellow skin stretched tightly across Parker's skeletal cheekbones.

"Yes," Parker agreed, "and I tried it. The treatment about killed me. Long story, for another day. I've got a better option, anyway. The best. A kidney transplant."

Lordy, Miranda thought. The poor guy was delusional, presumably from his renal failure. No surgical team would agree to transplant a kidney into a sixty-five-year-old with the disease Parker had. If he could find a surgeon who would do it, Parker had no money to pay for the procedure. Besides, a donor would need to be a tissue match with Parker. What were the chances of finding one? Slim to none, Miranda figured.

"Oh, Parker," Miranda said softly, reaching out for Parker's hand.

Parker grabbed Miranda's hand excitedly.

"I know, almost too good to be true, isn't it?" Parker's grey eyes sparkled. "But I found a person whose DNA matches mine. Closely. She'll be a perfect kidney donor."

Miranda stepped back, nonplussed. She traded glances with Chad, whose normally unreadable face showed a trace of alarm. Parker's mental condition was worse than she had feared, Miranda thought. Parker could not have found a DNA match. He had no living relatives.

Parker had been part of the Stein & Associates family since the early 1980s. Parker stumbled on Aaron's name on a list of attorneys representing veterans in a class action filed against the U.S. government. The plaintiffs, all veterans, claimed damages arising from their exposure to Agent Orange in Vietnam.

Parker asked Aaron to take on his case. Previously, Parker had gone to the VA hospital in Baltimore complaining of severe fatigue, weight loss, and swelling under his left armpit. The doctors diagnosed amyloidosis, a rare disease in the general population but not so rare in Vietnam vets exposed to Agent Orange.

Although Aaron had volunteered to be on the list, he, as yet, had no client and was not a member of the trial team on the Agent Orange case. Aaron knew enough about it, though, to advise Parker that he would probably not qualify for the class. Settlement negotiations were well underway. The plaintiffs' lawyers accepted 1972 as the cut-off year for the eligible in-country service period. The Department of Defense claimed it used no Agent Orange in Vietnam after 1972.

Parker, who was deployed as an Army private in Vietnam in 1974, laughed harshly. "You could smell it," he sneered.

Aaron nodded. "I believe you," he said, "but for purposes of this lawsuit, what I think doesn't matter. I'm sorry."

Many years later, the government recanted. All Vietnam veterans having symptoms of diseases associated with Agent Orange exposure became eligible for disability benefits. Luckily for Parker, in the interim, his disease fell largely quiescent. The VA doctors warned him, though, that he was not cured. Parker's symptoms abated. He regained strength and weight.

Parker struggled to make a living, as he had since the war. He had returned to his hometown when he got back to the States, but there was little for him there. His dad, Parker's only surviving parent, died unexpectedly while Parker was in Vietnam. Parker inherited thirty-eight dollars and a one-story, two-bedroom house. The building badly needed structural repairs, and its aging appliances functioned fitfully.

The local economy, like that of the nation, floundered. The oil embargo, soaring inflation, and tight credit made jobs hard to find for a high school graduate with no skills save those necessary to survive in a jungle. Parker's small, rural community was still solidly in support of America's war effort. Local business owners would have bent over backwards to hire a vet. If they had a job to offer. And if Parker had looked willing and able to work.

Instead, Parker spent his time feeding the marijuana addiction he had acquired in Vietnam. He quickly fell in with the sketchy high school seniors who supplied him drugs.

Parker angered quickly and for no apparent reason. He would slam his fist full force onto the bar, toppling nearby beer glasses, startling the other patrons of the darkened pool hall. He awakened in the pitch dark of the bedroom he once shared with his brother, sweaty, heart pounding, woken by his nightmares. His dreams of gunfire and explosions and panicked shouts and screams seemed more real than the tangled sheet clutched in his hand. Parker knew, much later, that he was suffering from post-traumatic stress disorder. At the time, however, only a handful of medical specialists knew of the disease. The townsfolk considered Parker a disaster of his own making.

For a year, Parker spiraled downward. Unkempt and ill-fed, he survived on charity and the occasional odd job he was able to pull off during his increasingly rare, lucid days. He spent hours lying in his bed, staring at nothing. His brother's high school girlfriend pulled him back from his abyss.

Parker had occasionally come across Lydia in town when he returned from the war. Early on, he had tried to engage her in conversation, without success. He could not blame her, though, when she snubbed him cold. Could have been worse, he had thought. A slap across the face would have been more than warranted. Parker was standing at the sink in the kitchen, all these months later, wondering vaguely why the tap water was rusty, when Lydia walked into the house. The jelly jar Parker had been filling shattered on the floor when he dropped it.

It took weeks. She failed in her first attempts to rouse his anger, pride, and hope. Shame is what got him, in the end. And remorse. For what he had done to his brother.

Parker cleaned himself up and made a little money shoveling manure for a local farmer. As soon as he was able, Parker got on a bus to D.C., putting miles between him and his memories.

At the time he first met with Aaron, Parker was unemployed, again. He had been working as a garbage collector for the city until, as his symptoms got worse, he had to quit.

After he turned down Parker's case, Aaron hired him as the firm's messenger. On his bicycle, Parker delivered briefs to opposing counsel across town and pleadings to the courthouse.

Marlon had thought it an odd hire, he told Miranda later. The tall, skinny, thirty-year-old with prematurely greying hair hanging loose to his shoulders did not fit the ranks of the hale teenagers with bulging calves speeding east down K Street to meet filing deadlines.

Parker eventually graduated to a better job. Still, his name continued to appear on the firm's holiday party guest list. Aaron regularly took Parker out for lunch. Aaron had, unaccountably perhaps, developed an affection for the man. As did they all. Chad, too, the moment Miranda introduced them.

"You got her contact information from the DNA matching service, right?" Miranda asked.

Parker nodded.

"Of course, I'll contact her as you ask," Miranda said, a note of hesitancy in her voice, "and see if she will meet with me. But there must be some mistake."

Chad shot Miranda a look. Not disapproving, exactly, but Miranda pivoted.

"I'll call her as soon as I get back to the office," Miranda assured Parker.

A fool's errand, she thought, to be undertaken only for Parker.

CHAPTER 10
A COMPLEX MAN

Marlon stood, as did Vincent Bainbridge. The two men reached across the conference room table separating them and shook hands. Marlon glanced at the clock high on the wall behind Vincent. A little after three in the afternoon. He would be driving from Howard's campaign headquarters in Richmond into D.C. during the worst of rush hour. Oh, well, it was worth it, he thought.

"You'll email the transcript to me." Vincent did not ask. He commanded.

In appearance, Vincent matched the chief-of-staff model from popular culture. A short man, Marlon estimated him at five-foot-six inches tall when Marlon entered the room in which Vincent stood against the far wall. Vincent's white shirt strained against a belly bulging above his belt. A square, thrusting jaw dominated a mottled face. His short, salt-and-pepper hair needed a trim and his rumpled, nondescript brown suit a press. Vincent did not look up from his mobile until Marlon cleared his throat.

Vincent started the interview with a demeanor matching his appearance: brusque, pushy, prickly. He warmed up considerably once Marlon performed his magic.

His colleagues marveled at Marlon's ability to adapt his persona to suit his witness. Marlon had a sense for the demeanor to which any one witness would best respond: paternal, professorial, counselor, confessor, devil's advocate. He could then play that role to the hilt.

For Vincent, Marlon played an earnest, humble-verging-on-obsequious James Boswell, duly recording every heroic detail of the great man's life. Vincent succumbed. He stopped barking answers. The formal interview became a conversation.

Q:Tell me about Jeff's parents.

A:Jeff's father, Jared, landed with the first wave of Marines on Guadalcanal. That should tell you a lot about him.

Q:Yes, it does. What did Jared do after the war?

A:He went to college on the G.I. Bill. After he graduated from the University of Richmond, he got a job as a loan officer in a local bank. He had worked his way up to chief financial officer by the time Jeff was in grade school.

Q:And Jeff's mother?

A:A stay-at-home mom.

So far, Marlon already knew the answers to his questions. All this was public information. He would stay on safe ground for a few more questions and then start digging.

Q:As chief financial officer of a bank, Jared had the means to send Jeff and his younger sister to private school. Why didn't he?

A:Jared harbored political ambitions. With his eye on an eventual run for public office, Jared decided public schools were the sounder political choice. As it turned out, it didn't matter. Jared ran once for city commissioner. He was defeated in a landslide and never tried again.

Q:So, Jeff fulfilled Jared's dreams of public service. The old man must be very proud of his son.

Vincent grunted. Marlon saw an opening.

Q:How would you describe Jeff's relationship with his father?

A:Jared was a Marine, through and through. He was strict and demanding. But he loved Jeff, provided well for the family, and always had Jeff's best interests at heart.

A nonresponsive answer if ever he had heard one, Marlon thought. He would move on, however to Jeff's service in Vietnam and early professional career.

After high school, Jeff had volunteered, following in his father's footsteps, although as an Army private, not a Marine. After his tour of duty, Jeff attended the University of Virginia. Jeff and Vincent, fortuitously paired as roommates, became fast friends. Jeff stayed at the University of Virginia for his law degree. He married his wife, Helen, and took a job at a prestigious law firm in Richmond.

Marlon turned the subject to Jeff's relationship with Betsy. Betsy rarely spoke of Jeff with her colleagues at the firm. However, the basic facts regarding their relationship were in the public record. Marlon would try for more.

Marlon learned from Vincent that Jeff and Helen intended to adopt Betsy, but Helen's baby arrived before that happened. Betsy had been settling well into the Howard household. Yet, after the baby came, Betsy withdrew. Jeff and Helen did their best to make Betsy feel a part of the family again, but Betsy kept her distance.

Fearing Betsy would not regain her happiness if she stayed in the Howards' home, Jeff changed course. He called on close friends to form a foster consortium, in effect. This cohort of responsible, respectable, caring adults shepherded Betsy to adulthood, although Jeff remained the constant presence in her life.

After about a year, when Betsy had outgrown her jealousy of Helen's baby, Betsy returned to the Howard home for extended periods. Betsy spent her holidays and summer breaks with Jeff. When Betsy was away living with one of her foster parents, Jeff spent hours on the phone with her, keeping up with Betsy's day-to-day affairs. He took Betsy on a month-long tour through Europe after her sophomore year in high school.

In short, Jeff remained the dominant influence in Betsy's life. He also remained the primary source of her financial support. Jeff paid the tuition for the bachelor's and master's degrees in physics Betsy earned from the Massachusetts Institute of Technology and for her law degree from Harvard, Vincent explained.

Marlon threw a few softball questions, then turned to what puzzled him most. Why had Jeff risked his marriage and reputation in a traditionalist city in a conservative state by taking in a stranger? A young girl whose radical, left-wing parents were in jail for felony murder, at that.

Vincent paused and scowled for the first time since the interview began. "Are you suggesting Jeff acted improperly?" Vincent asked.

"Not at all," Marlon said, injecting a hero-worshipping note of surprised reassurance into his tone. "I'm wondering whether Jeff's Vietnam tour had anything to do with it, or how his time in Vietnam affected his character. That's what I'm really looking for in these interviews. The influence of W.W.II on the lives of the 'Greatest Generation' who experienced that war has been well-chronicled. I don't see that long-term retrospective among the dozens of extraordinary books written about Vietnam. That's what I'm working on."

Vincent cocked an eyebrow. "Big job," he said curtly.

Marlon started to answer that he was well up to the task. He stopped himself, remaining in character. "Wildly ambitious, I know," he said, raising his hands, palms out in protest. "And my efforts at 'armchair psychology' aren't likely to be of interest to anybody but me. Still, humor me. Was there a connection between whatever Jeff experienced in Vietnam and what he did for Betsy?"

Vincent said nothing. He had probably thought Jeff was a crazy fool for bringing Betsy into his home, Marlon concluded. Most likely, Vincent had tried to talk him out of it. But Vincent would not criticize his boss in front of Marlon and was at a loss for another explanation for Jeff's behavior. Marlon decided to bypass the subject of Betsy, specifically, and ask the larger question.

Q:Do you think the war changed Jeff?
A:Nah. He went in, did his duty, and came home.

Well, that got him nowhere, Marlon thought. He would have to find his answers elsewhere.

Marlon returned to his list of anodyne questions about Jeff's political career and his views on a wide range of issues facing the Commonwealth and the nation. Vincent, back on familiar and comfortable grounds, answered readily.

"One last thing," Marlon said. The two-hour block of time he had been granted was coming to an end. "The veterans I have met told me everybody screwed up somehow in 'Nam. Went with the territory. Naïve, eighteen-year-old boys a world away from home, figuratively if not literally lost in the jungle." Marlon smiled broadly. "Come on, Vincent, tell me about the 'blotch' on Jeff's war record," Marlon said, index fingers vigorously air-quoting to remove any sting.

Vincent chuckled. Marlon, inwardly, sighed with relief. This question had been Paco's idea. Marlon had feared an explosion from the staffer, or at least a very cold shoulder.

A few minutes later, Marlon took his leave. He assured Vincent, as had been agreed, that Marlon would send the transcript of the interview to Vincent's office for vetting. Anything to which Vincent objected would never see the light of day.

"I'll email you the transcript later this afternoon," Marlon said as the two men walked out of the conference room into the adjacent corridor. "I've got a transcription app on my phone. The document should be ready by the time I get back to my office." With a last "thank you" from Marlon, he and Vincent parted ways.

Out in the parking lot, unlocking his Volvo sedan, Marlon thought about Jeff's wartime peccadillo, disappointed. As Vincent had said, nothing of note.

An hour later, less than half the way back to Washington, Marlon decided he would head straight home. With traffic this bad, it would be too late to go to the office by the time he reached the city.

Marlon pulled into the driveway of his townhouse at 6:30 p.m. He climbed out of the car stiffly. One day, he should take a yoga class. He shuddered at the image.

He let himself into the patio and from there entered the kitchen. "Allen?" he called. No answer. Working late again, Marlon decided.

Marlon set his laptop on the kitchen island. He uncorked a bottle of red wine and poured himself a glass. As he sat on one of the island's stools, Marlon opened the computer. After he unwound from the hellish I-95 traffic, he would review the transcript and reflect on what Vincent had told him about Jeff Howard.

These interviews came easily to him, he thought. After all, he had taken thousands of depositions over the years. Soon, it would be time to get to the hard work of writing the book.

Marlon had been the one to suggest that he and Paco write a book. Marlon had recently mastered Schubert's Fantasy in F minor, to his and his teacher's satisfaction, at any rate. He was looking for another challenge that required fewer hours alone and on a piano bench. Paco agreed they should give the book a try. Marlon started researching in a way impossible for Paco: Face-to-face interviews with veterans and their families.

Marlon found himself drawn into the work in ways he had not expected. His life experiences had led him to believe, fairly or unfairly, that he would have little in common with Vietnam veterans. He predicted that he would have difficulty connecting with them as individuals. This had not proven true. Marlon discovered something of value—a point to ponder, an astute observation, humor and courage and compassion—in all their tales. Jeff Howard was a case in point, Marlon thought.

Before today, Marlon would have avoided Jeff if they were thrown together at a cocktail party. The arc of Jeff's life—born with the proverbial silver spoon in his mouth, military service, long-time denizen of the clubby Virginia statehouse, lifelong Republican—had no point in common with Marlon's. Nor did it bear any resemblance to those of the people Marlon admired.

Now, Marlon knew better. The interview with Vincent revealed Jeff to be a more complex man than Marlon had supposed. Jeff, too, had to overcome losses. Hidden behind Jeff's shrill political rhetoric denouncing "welfare queens" and "illegal aliens" lay compassion.

Jeff and his wife, Helen, had a difficult time conceiving. Then, tragically, Helen and their two-year-old son died in a car crash. According to the accident report, Helen skidded on ice and crossed the center line. An oncoming car in the opposite lane plowed into her. Six years after Helen died, Jeff remarried, but he and his second wife, Susan, were never able to have children.

Several months after the accident, the parents of the driver whose car had hit Helen's approached Jeff. The young man, Ted Albrighten, was consumed by grief. He dropped out of school and spent his days locked in his bedroom. He emerged only as demanded by his parents to join them for meals, of which he ate sparingly. Ted lost an alarming amount of weight. The Albrightens asked if Jeff would speak to the boy. Only Jeff could absolve Ted from his crippling guilt. Jeff agreed.

Shortly thereafter, Jeff found time outside of his demanding work at the law firm to launch a juvenile justice foundation. Jeff also lobbied hard, every time the bill was introduced in the General Assembly, against the "three strikes you're out" legislation penalizing repeat criminal offenders.

Jeff seemed to have a soft spot, Marlon thought, for young people, and particularly young men, who made mistakes, with tragic consequences. As different as Jeff's politics were from his, had Jeff sympathized with Thomas Thornhill, Betsy's father? Is that why Jeff had taken Betsy in? It seemed a stretch, but people were complicated. Maybe even the picture-perfect Jeff Howard had made some mistakes in his life.

"Table for two?" the hostess asked, menus in hand, poised to lead Miranda and Chad to a table. Guapo's, a popular Tex-Mex restaurant in Tenleytown, bustled. The mild, spring evening had attracted even more than the usual crowd for outdoor dining on Guapo's expansive, wooden deck overlooking Wisconsin Avenue.

"Yes, and outside, please," Miranda responded, "if there's a table."

The hostess nodded toward an empty spot in the far corner of the deck. She wended her way through the narrow aisle between two rows of tables. With ease, she dodged the tightly packed customers clinking sweating steins of beer and holding out empty baskets calling into the din for more chips and salsa. Chad and Miranda hustled close behind. Their hostess handed Miranda and Chad their menus. A waitress took their orders and left them to a moment of privacy.

"Well, what did she say?" Chad asked. "Tell me everything."

"She agreed to meet," Miranda answered. "I'll take the train to Philly on Friday."

"Yes!" Chad exclaimed, beaming his approval.

Parker had convinced Miranda to make the initial overture to his DNA match and potential donor, Roberta Kurtz. The circumstances were fraught for Parker on so many levels. He feared the emanations of his primal fear, stunned confusion, and desperate hope would drive the woman away.

Parker had succeeded in removing the other obstacles to his transplant, should Roberta agree. To Miranda's surprise, Parker had come up with the money for the surgery. For decades, Parker made weekly deposits into a savings account. He vowed not to touch the account, no matter how desperate his need, unless and until he faced a life-or-death emergency. One of the few lessons from his dad that he had heeded, Parker explained. Some weeks, Parker had only an extra dollar or two for his stash. Over the years, however, the deposits, with interest, reached a sizeable sum. Enough, Parker assured Chad and Miranda.

He found a willing surgical team through his network of fellow veterans. A surgeon, recently retired from The George Washington Memorial Hospital, had served in the same battalion as had Parker. Parker got in touch, and, long story short, Parker had his medical team in line.

Miranda's job was to connect with Roberta and explore her willingness to consider donating a kidney to Parker. The other item on Miranda's list was to figure out how Roberta could be closely related to Parker.

The percentage DNA match between Parker and Roberta indicated that, based on the averages, she was his grandmother, aunt, half-sibling, or niece. Both of Parker's grandmothers were long dead, and he had no aunt or half-sibling, as far as he knew. He supposed it was possible his father had strayed, but the ages didn't work. His father had been dead before forty-two-year-old Roberta was born. That left a niece, also impossible. Parker's only sibling, his brother, John, had died before their father, killed in Vietnam.

Parker made his instructions clear. Miranda was to drop the subject immediately if Roberta reacted negatively to the idea of being an organ donor. What Parker wanted even more than a life-saving kidney was to connect with the relative he never knew he had.

CHAPTER 11
MISSING IN ACTION

Paco switched on the lamp. Sipping from his shot glass of tequila, Paco stared down at the jungle creature embroidered on the rug beneath his feet. The image of the quetzal in full flight—its beauty, power, and freedom—soothed his jangled nerves.

He had just finished reading the transcript of Vincent's interview. Marlon forwarded it to him an hour ago, confirming in the email that Jeff's office cleared the document's release.

Paco's image of Jeff Howard, drawn from public reports of Jeff's career, had not inspired any positive emotions. The personal details Vincent had disclosed did stir Paco's admiration for Jeff's evident sense of justice and works of mercy.

Plus, these characteristics would work to his advantage.

Paco set those thoughts aside. The passage that had sent his heart racing needed immediate attention.

As Paco had suggested, Marlon asked Vincent to confess Jeff's wartime "sin." The one infraction even a spit-shined Marine committed, given the confusing cross currents of military law, testosterone, and the instinct for self-preservation. Marlon had, apparently, not been impressed by Vincent's answer. He had not noted it in his transmittal email. Paco, on the other hand, suspected he had hit the mother lode when he read Vincent's answer in the transcript.

A:Not anything, really. And I'm sure it's in his military service record somewhere, anyway. I was at the Pentagon, civil side, you may know, and on temporary duty assignment in Saigon. Jeff was on his way out. We planned on having some drinks the night before his flight home, and I picked him up at his barracks in Long Binh. He was shirtless when

I arrived, and *sans* dog tags. I asked him what the hell happened. He'd been at a brothel the night before, drunk as a skunk. He lost his tags. He got a reprimand, but nobody gave a crap. Everybody knew the girls lifted gear, when they could, to sell on the black market.

Paco put his glass down on the side table, minimized the transcript document, and opened another file. Pictures. Hundreds of them. The earliest images, grainy and distorted, almost unrecognizable. Paco had studied them all, magnifying glass in hand.

He opened one of the pictures and enlarged it to full screen. Jeff, grinning, arms around the shoulders of the two soldiers flanking him. Paco stared fixedly at the final piece of the puzzle.

Jeff had not lost his tags in a brothel the night before he shipped out. A prostitute had not stolen his tags. Nor had anyone else, for that matter.

Paco rose and walked into the shadowy corner of the room, towards his desk. He opened the top drawer and removed a rectangular box the size of a package of cigarettes. He opened the container and removed a silver chain. Rubbing the shiny surface of the dog tag hanging from it between thumb and index finger, Paco remembered his shock when he discovered its owner was still alive.

During his early years in Mexico, Paco rented a post office box in a town across the border. He had enrolled in a correspondence course that accepted any student who could pay the fee. He slipped across the border to deposit the envelopes containing his homework. At the same time, he retrieved marked-up work returned by the instructor.

One day, Paco found a discarded circular from the American Legion Magazine on the post office floor. The advertisement offered the recipient a free, introductory annual subscription. The ad encouraged veterans and their family members to subscribe and "keep up with fellow men-at-arms." The magazine promised news on American Legion activities and those of other veterans' associations.

Paco accepted the offer and renewed his subscription year after year. He spent long hours sitting at the rickety, wooden table in the one-room, thatched shack that was home then. There, he studied the magazines, searching for a needle in the haystack.

He found it, providentially, in the August 1976 edition of the magazine. A story reported on the first reunion of 138 AVN Co. 19. The article included the list of reunion attendees and the names of those killed and missing in action. The one MIA was Glen Hadley.

Paco, shaken and confused, puzzled over the problem for days. Only one MIA. The man whose dog tags Paco kept in the box on his desk. At least, Paco had thought the tags were Hadley's. The name embossed on the tags, though, was Jeff Howard. How could that be?

When Paco came to the most plausible solution, his blood boiled. After he calmed down, Paco realized his discovery could be used to his advantage. It would take time and effort. He could easily fail. But he had a goal. He kept searching, amassing a veritable library. Anything related to the soldiers who had served in Vietnam, he collected.

The American Legion magazine remained a rich source of information. In it, Company 19's alumni organization published news of its members. These reports included colleges attended, jobs secured, marriages, the births of children, and, as the years went by, deaths. By 1978, all living members were accounted for, except Mauricio Marquez.

Mauricio remained "unknown" in all categories, until 1983. Mauricio emerged from obscurity as "living and working in the D.C. area." After that, silence.

Paco assumed a fellow veteran must have spotted Mauricio and reported the sighting to the magazine. Otherwise, if Mauricio had checked in himself, why disappear again?

Paco got his hands on a photo of Company 19 taken shortly before its last engagement. One of the men, by his appearance, was likely Mauricio Marquez. Eventually, Paco identified most of the other soldiers, including Jeff Howard.

Paco also had a photograph of Mauricio and one other soldier, taken from the rear. He could identify one of the soldiers as Mauricio due to his unusually short stature. The other, his profile facing the photographer, was Jeff.

For decades, Paco could not find another scrap of information about Mauricio anywhere. Then, yesterday, Marlon wrote that the firm represented the son of a veteran named Mauricio Marquez. This morning, Marlon confirmed that Mauricio served in 138 AVN Co. 19.

The news could not have been better. Not only had Paco found Mauricio. He also had access to Mauricio through his friend, Marlon.

Paco's stomach growled. He closed the talisman back in its box. He walked across the room to his galley kitchen and took a ceramic bowl from the refrigerator. Setting the bowl on the counter, Paco pinched off a handful of the mound of dough within and began rolling tortillas.

Paco dropped the first of his tortillas into a bubbling pot of hot oil. He idly watched the browning shell stiffen.

He would make his move. The timing was off, and the outcome far from certain. The cards would all have to fall his way. Paco generally took a dim view of Lady Luck, but he would surely be calling on her now.

His opponent's first play would determine how the other cards fell. Paco had a strong hunch that Mauricio played a role in all this, but he was not at all sure.

CHAPTER 12
A FAMILIAR NAME

Trial Day 4

Will walked into the courthouse cafeteria and headed for the industrial-sized aluminum urns to his left. He set his briefcase on the floor and torqued a Styrofoam cup out of its holder. He filled the cup with what he knew from prior experience would be hot but tasteless black coffee.

Dozens of customers lined the food service tables on the opposite side of the cafeteria from Will. The men, women, and occasional child pushed grey metallic trays down the three-barred rack in front of the clear, nose-high sneeze guards. Mounds of scrambled eggs, bacon, sausages, and biscuits in enormous rectangular serving pans waited to be chosen.

As early as it was, the pans were still piled high, Will noted. The serving spoons perched handily at the near corner of each dish. The tiled floor was clean. Give it an hour, he thought. By then, it would look as though a food fight had broken out. The plastic guards would be smeared with greasy handprints. Smudges of scrambled egg and splotches of gravy on the floor would make for a treacherous passage.

Will took his coffee to a free cashier's station. "Is that all for you this morning, Mr. McCarty?" she asked.

Will smiled, nodding. "Yes, thank you, Thais," he answered. She rang him up, and he inserted his card. Transaction completed, Will looked around the cavernous dining room. He searched for an empty table away from traffic but where Baylie could easily spot him. They had arranged to meet at 8:30 a.m. and would have ample time to talk before the case was called.

Will arrived at 8:00 a.m. He had already made notes of what he wanted to go over with Baylie, but he would review them. He could also go over his direct examination of Bruce Tryon, the expert witness scheduled to testify today, if he had time.

As the noise level in the cafeteria increased, Will paused. He leaned back in his chair and took a sip of his coffee. This place, he thought, was the true heart of the courtroom.

Upstairs, hushed courtrooms lined the corridors. Inside each, the steady pace of the attorney's emotionless voice questioned the well-prepared witness, answering by rote. The judge loomed over the proceeding, her humanity evident only from the stern face emerging from her enveloping black robes. A uniformed bailiff, standing to the ready with arms folded, service pistol in the holster on his hip, squelched any eddy in the smooth flow of the delivery of justice.

Down here, Will heard angry shouts. "Get back here," came from a mother. Early that morning, she carefully groomed and dressed her daughters. An ill-kept child would be taken by the social services folks during the custody hearing they had been called to attend later in the day. Now, mock-angrily playing at the end of the table, her daughters' tight corn rows frayed.

Down here, a man leaped from his chair. He reached across the table and flipped a full breakfast tray onto the lap of the man across from him. "You're dead, you f***ing rat!" the man screamed at his brother and alleged co-conspirator in drug trafficking.

Down here, clients argued with their lawyers. In raised voices, attorneys made deals and broke them. Everyone in the room yammered on their phone to someone apparently quite hard-of-hearing.

Will spied Baylie across the cafeteria and waved. Perhaps, Will thought, Justice should occasionally take off her blindfold and come down here.

* * *

The afternoon before, back at the office, Will and Cassandra had talked over their third day of trial and discussed what would come next.

"Preston went soft towards the middle of Baylie's cross, don't you think?" Will asked.

"Maybe a little," Cassandra answered. "He did concede that 'others could differ' in their opinions about what went wrong with that plywood plank. You firmed up his testimony nicely in redirect, though. And our rehab expert was flawless."

Will nodded. He thought the same thing, but it was comforting to hear confirmation from Cassandra.

"I don't know what to think about what Marlon said," Will wondered aloud. Marlon had relayed Allen's concern about what Baylie might do, given that Will had abruptly scratched Mauricio from the witness list. "Your thoughts?"

"I can't see Baylie doing anything drastic," Cassandra answered. "He's a lawyer, not a border patrol agent. What litigator has the time to contact Homeland Security to report Mauricio as possibly undocumented? And why would he want to? What's it to him?"

"I suppose you're right," Will responded, although he could imagine many reasons why Cassandra could be wrong.

Apparently sensing Will's doubts, Cassandra pressed on. "Baylie doesn't know what we know. In fact, the only thing Baylie knows for sure is that José became a citizen through marriage. Wouldn't Baylie assume that Mauricio got his documents through his son?"

Will, who had been listening intently, shook his head. "Maybe so, until I took Mauricio off the witness list at the last minute. I made the mistake of not being prepared enough for this trial. I compounded that error by rushing to change the witness list. My stupidity might have put Mauricio in grave danger."

"But ..." Cassandra began.

"Look, I don't know Baylie at all," Will interrupted her. "Never met him, never even heard of him before he submitted his answer to our complaint. Baylie might be strongly anti-immigrant as far as we know. If so, he may well act on it, particularly if the jury hands us a big verdict. Against his clients."

"But what can we do now?" Cassandra asked.

"I don't know," Will answered. "But something is nagging me. Something I've seen in the files but can't quite remember. Come on, Cassandra, let's get to work."

He found it in the middle of a deposition transcript. Will sent Cassandra home, as it was late, but not too late to call José. Will knew his client slept fitfully.

José did not have an answer to Will's question. Mauricio had told José it passed muster. The "how" was somebody else's secret and not his to disclose, his dad had said.

Will thought long and hard. He considered consulting Aaron or Marlon. In the end, he decided it was his decision, and he had no other choice. He would have to step carefully. The consequences of a misstep were ghastly.

***

The men greeted each other politely but did not shake hands. Traditionally, when the judge sent the jury out to deliberate, opposing counsel would shake. But not yet. They sat at the otherwise-empty cafeteria table.

"I want to discuss Mauricio Marquez," Will began without preamble. "I pulled him from the witness list because I didn't want two of my witnesses to have to plead the Fifth."

Baylie chuckled. Will forced himself to smile.

"I've reconsidered, though," Will continued. "I'd still like to call Mauricio. But I'm asking you not to raise the counterfeit social security number again. Or anything about citizenship."

"Why would I agree to that?" Baylie asked.

"The jury didn't even notice it," Will responded. "Nobody batted an eyelash. So, what's the point?"

Baylie sat silently, expression neutral.

"It'll speed things up," Will concluded his case. "Mauricio is the only one on the crew who can speak to all the issues I'm going to need to cover. Procurement, inspections, storage, and handling of materials for the company. If he doesn't go on, I'll need to call at least two other witnesses in his stead."

Baylie's brow furrowed. Considering the angles, Will thought. Maybe he would get away with this ploy more easily than he had feared.

"Are you telling me that Mauricio is legal?" Baylie asked, dashing Will's hopes.

"Mauricio is not my client," Will responded, as planned. "I couldn't ask him directly because his answer would not be privileged."

Will paused for a moment as if dredging his memory.

"I remind you," he continued, "that you deposed Bud Prettyman, J&A's director of human resources. Bud testified in his deposition that every full-time employee of the company was cleared by E-Verify. That's the federal government's electronic verification of social security numbers. Mauricio is a full-time employee."

Baylie nodded. "Yeah, now that you remind me," he said. Placing both hands on the table, Baylie preparing to rise. "I'll have to run this by the client, but I'm inclined to accept your proposal. Especially if you can sweeten the deal. Got anything you can give me in return?"

Will did.

He would withdraw his objection to the admission of the videotaped deposition of Baylie's expert in lieu of his live testimony. Will knew it was a valid objection because the expert was within the subpoena power of the court. Judge Storer would require the expert's live testimony unless Will agreed to his absence. The witness wanted to be on the Amalfi Coast, instead of in the courtroom. Will knew he had a deal.

He would call Mauricio to testify first thing this morning, before Baylie had a chance to reconsider. Will had already prepared Mauricio. This was going to work. Will sighed with relief.

Will packed his notes and pens in his litigation bag and headed upstairs to the courtroom. He tossed the remnants of the Styrofoam coffee cup he had methodically torn to pieces during his negotiation with Baylie into the trash can on his way out.

* * *

Betsy pulled down the tray table. She put the latte she had grabbed at the Starbucks in Union Station on the tray, then reached into her bag to retrieve her laptop.

She had had no problem finding an available seat on the Amtrak train to Baltimore even though 9:00 a.m. was prime time for travel. The heavier traffic was southbound, to D.C., at this time of day. Betsy was headed north to consult a radiologist on a pending case. She had forty minutes of free time.

Betsy opened her email. Below the spam report was a secure email from Vincent's office, clocking in at 6:06 a.m. When Betsy called Vincent to confirm that she would work on the campaign, he promised her complete access to all their files. It had arrived.

Betsy clicked on the link in Vincent's email and entered her credentials as directed. The page opened to an index. Scrolling down the entries, she clicked on "University of Virginia, 1975–1979" and choked on her mouthful of coffee. Sixteen sub-headings and, another click, yes, each sub-heading contained sub-sub-headings.

Good luck to any reporter looking for dirt, Betsy thought. Then again, she reminded herself, if that was someone's career, and she was good at it, she would find a way to get through all Jeff's files.

"Not my job, thankfully," Betsy said aloud, prompting a glance from the suited young man across the aisle. Following a quick, mutual appraisal—"too young," "too old"—both returned to their laptops.

Betsy again accessed the main index to the files. She paged through, unsure where to begin. The entry entitled "War Years" caught her eye. Jeff had rarely mentioned his service in Vietnam to Betsy. Maybe she would learn something.

"War Years" included a dozen sub-files, including "Official Service Record," "138 AVN Co. 19," and "Veterans of Foreign Wars." Betsy remembered, now. When she was young, Jeff regularly attended meetings at the local VFW post.

In the company sub-file, Betsy found the names of the soldiers and officers who served with Jeff during his one-year tour beginning in August 1972. Betsy had an eidetic memory, a photographic memory in common parlance. As she read through the list, she automatically memorized the names.

One name she expected to see on the list was missing. The officer on Jeff's Christmas card list.

Betsy, twelve years old at the time, was spending the holidays at the Howards' home. After dinner, Betsy helped Jeff and his wife, Susan, prepare the holiday cards for mailing. Jeff and Susan addressed the envelopes, and Betsy inserted the cards. She noticed an envelope addressed to a lieutenant colonel in Guam and asked Jeff about him.

"He commanded my unit during the last few weeks of the war," Jeff had explained. "It was a tough time. He got me through it."

Probably an error in the document, Betsy thought. But then again, the file in front of her looked like a copy of an official government record. She shrugged, then continued her search.

Betsy scrolled through the next several entries in the company file without opening a page. Then, she came to "First Annual 138 AVN Co. 19 Reunion," which was a photocopy of an article published in the American Legion magazine, dated August 1976.

The article contained selected quotes from the keynote speaker, a Captain (retired) Gregory Hawkins. Captain Hawkins promised that, by the next year's reunion, he would have an updated accounting of the status of the unit's members, including casualty lists, up to the date the unit was deactivated in 1974.

A sidebar in the article chronicled the history of the unit's last major engagement, which occurred in mid-July 1973. According to the story, Company 19 had been decimated. The casualty loss, from unofficial reports, of killed or wounded was in the dozens. The command post was destroyed, bombed to ashes. The company captain, who had rotated into Hawkins's position only a month earlier, lost his life in the blast.

That explained the missing lieutenant, Betsy thought. In the dark, smoky, unfamiliar terrain, survivors scattered. Jeff must have latched onto an intact unit for the last weeks of his tour, commanded by the officer on Jeff's Christmas list. She would confirm this with Jeff.

She scrolled down and found Hawkins' promised accounting. In that last enemy engagement, twenty-one soldiers were killed, and one, the company medic, was missing in action. Betsy made a note of the MIA's name. She would follow up on this, as well.

Betsy spent the next twenty minutes on Jeff's four years attending the University of Virginia. A different plan might occur to her as she got deeper into the material. For now, she thought she would be most useful to Jeff starting near the beginning. Anything about his life needing a facelift would likely have occurred in his youth.

Betsy glanced at the time displayed on her laptop. Outside the window, the familiar outskirts of Baltimore glided by the slowing train. Betsy powered down her laptop.

The door at the end of the car rolled open. The conductor in his Amtrak uniform—white shirt with blue epaulettes, red tie, and black pill box hat—strode in. "Ba-awl-timore, Ba-awl-timore," the conductor called, adding syllabic depth to the name of the city's founder as he walked down the aisle.

Betsy smiled as she slipped her laptop into its protective cover. She rode Amtrak's Northeast Corridor route to Baltimore, Philly, New York, or even Boston whenever she had the time to indulge her preference for the train over flying. She recognized this conductor, although she could not recall his name. Despite the hundreds of times he had made the same announcement, he always sounded delighted to be able to announce that, *mirabile dictu*, they had arrived at their intended destination.

As she was disembarking, Betsy reviewed the list of Company 19 soldiers embedded in her mind. One foot on the platform, she stopped abruptly. She had missed it on the first read. A familiar name. Probably a coincidence, she thought, but she would follow up on it.

CHAPTER 13
THE ALTERNATE JUROR

"All rise," intoned the bailiff.

The lawyers rose from their places at counsel tables. Judge Storer bustled into the courtroom from the door behind her dais. She stepped onto the platform and said, "Please, take your seats," as she took hers. She motioned to the bailiff, who opened the door behind the jury box, disappeared for a moment, then returned with the jurors lined up behind him.

The jurors filed into their box. Not one caught Cassandra's eye. Will told her earlier in the week that the same thing was happening to him. The jurors watched his witnesses and appeared to be listening intently. They remained expressionless, however, and never looked directly at Will.

Juries were hard to read, Cassandra thought, and that is the way it should be. The jurors were to consider the evidence, "without fear or favor," as the judge instructed them on day one. It was unnerving for the lawyers and their clients, though, and this jury seemed particularly stony.

Cassandra glanced around at José. He managed a smile. As they were entering the courthouse after the lunch break, José asked Cassandra to keep an eye on him. He had taken another pain pill to get through the afternoon. "Please make sure I don't doze off," José had said.

When all were in their places, Judge Storer smiled broadly at her jury and said, "I hope you all had a good lunch. Counsel," she turned her gaze to Will, "you may proceed."

Will stood. "I call Bruce Tryon to the stand," he said, looking back into the gallery as Bruce made his way forward. Will motioned Tryon towards the witness box. An unnecessary measure, Cassandra thought as she concealed a smile. Tryon, their expert economist, had testified in hundreds of trials.

When a plaintiff claimed that his damages included future costs, the rules required an economist to calculate the present value of those costs. What amount of money, if invested at the time the jury returned a verdict, accruing interest, would cover the future expenses adjusted upward for inflation?

Dr. Moraski and the rehabilitation expert had testified as to José's needs resulting from his broken back. They outlined what treatments, medications, and therapies José would likely have to undergo over his lifetime. Tryon would tell the jury the amount of money José would need, today, to pay for all that.

Although Tryon's testimony was a critical component of the case, it was dry stuff. If a jury succumbed during any part of a trial, it would be during the economist's testimony. The chances of a juror falling asleep increased after the lunch break, in any event. Will had planned, therefore, to put Tryon on that morning, after Mauricio testified. Two thorny evidentiary issues had arisen as Mauricio gave his evidence, however. By the time counsel argued their positions and the judge ruled, time had run out on the morning session. So, here they were, and Will was doing his best to get the numbers in quickly.

Cassandra had heard Tryon's spiel so many times she could have testified to it herself. She was listening with half her mind elsewhere, pondering the strange conversation she had with the defendants' insurance adjuster over the lunch break.

Baylie had approached their table as Will and Cassandra were packing briefcases to take with them to the courthouse cafeteria.

"Counselors," Baylie began politely. Will and Cassandra nodded their return greetings. "Our insurance adjuster would like to broach the possibility of settling this case," Baylie continued. "Gary Franklin is his name. Will, he'll call you during the lunch break if you have the time."

Will motioned to Cassandra. She understood and gave her cell number to Baylie.

Will did not discuss settlement during a trial. It would, however, verge on malpractice to decline the invitation. It could well be in the client's best interests to settle rather than proceed to a verdict. Whether to settle or not depended on how the evidence was going in, what unexpected glitches had arisen and, most importantly, what terms were proposed. Will enlisted his co-counsel or, if trying the case alone, Marlon or another of the more senior attorneys to talk settlement. Will would not allow himself the distraction.

Cassandra headed outside the courthouse to the courtyard. It would be quieter there than in the cafeteria. She could make do with the power bar she had in her briefcase for lunch.

Cassandra stepped through the doors into the sunny courtyard. She clasped her hands, raised her arms above her head, and stretched. The stiffness from three hours sitting quietly at counsel table in the harsh, fluorescent light of the courtroom that morning melted away.

She wondered what kind of a bird Franklin would be. This would be her first time negotiating with a stranger.

Ordinarily, Aaron and his associates had previous dealings with the defendant's insurance adjuster when he came calling. The medical community in the metropolitan area—individual doctors, physicians' groups, and the smaller hospitals that did not self-insure—regularly relied on the same three insurance companies for malpractice coverage. Having been in the business a long time, Aaron knew those companies' adjusters. But not Franklin, or his employer.

Cassandra's phone rang.

"Cassandra Robins here."

"Gary Franklin. The offer is ten thousand."

Cassandra's face flushed. An insulting, low-ball offer. Only her duty to the client stopped her from immediately hitting the "end call" button on her cell.

"A cheap shot, Franklin," Cassandra huffed. "Call back when you have something realistic to put on the table."

"You'd better think again," Franklin returned. "Your case is paper-thin. Our experts are going to rip even that to shreds. And your client is layering it on heavily. I'll bet the jury thinks he's faking all that pain."

Such an amateur, Cassandra thought. An adjuster who knew what he was doing would be diplomatic. He would acknowledge the strengths of the opponent's evidence, although also pointing out weaknesses. He would negotiate, not shoot down her case with both barrels blazing.

"How would you know anything about José?" Cassandra jumped on that one. "I haven't seen you in the courtroom. Not once." She had never talked settlement with an adjuster whom she had not already seen planted in the gallery for hours, listening intently to the witnesses.

"I've been there," Franklin protested. "You just haven't seen me. Listen," he added, voice deepening, "there's something you should know."

Cassandra did not want to listen to one more word from him. She forced herself to stay on the line.

"Yesterday afternoon, after the jury was released, I saw one of them, the woman with the big, auburn hair, in the lower lobby. She serves as the alternate juror. She was making a call on one of the payphones."

"So?" Cassandra asked.

"A payphone?" was his reply. "In this day and age? When have you last seen anyone use those antiquated things?"

He had a point, she thought. Years ago, lawyers would line up, ten-deep, behind every one of the dozen phones hanging on the lobby wall. Everyone was hoping desperately to have time to make that critical call before court reconvened. Cassandra always entered the courthouse through the lower lobby. She had not seen anyone making a call down there for ages.

"I hung around, curious," Franklin continued. "A few minutes after she made her call, the juror left the courthouse. She walked directly to a shiny, black stretch limo pulling up to the curb. The back passenger side door was opened from within. The juror got into the car, and off they went."

"Why are you telling me this?" Cassandra asked.

"She said during *voir dire* that she was a nurse's aide," Franklin reminded Cassandra. "Yeah, right. Since when do nurse's aides ride in limos? Either she lied to the judge, or someone is going to an awful lot of trouble to be nice to her for some reason. Either way, you've got a problem. A problem with your jury."

CHAPTER 14
A LONG SHOT

Marlon lifted the latch on the gate, pushed the heavy, wooden door open, and stepped into the garden behind Miranda's house. He sniffed, sneezed, and balefully eyed the emerald- green grass glowing in the afternoon sun. Newly cut, Marlon thought.

Neatly trimmed forsythia bushes lined the picket fence to his right, a scattering of lemon-yellow blossoms clinging to the branches even this late in the season. The riotous fuchsia azaleas on his left, on the other hand, were in full bloom. A giant hosta plant, at least six feet in diameter, grew in the far corner of the garden, next to the sliding glass doors leading into the house. Around the base of the hosta a row of orange zinnias nodded cheerfully. The sunken, brick patio between the garden and the house had been neatly swept.

Miranda must have hired a gardener, Marlon decided. This well-tended plot was not her work. Miranda had many talents. A green thumb was not among them.

Marlon took a seat on one of the stools at Miranda's high-top patio table. Idly tapping his fingers on the tabletop, he pondered yesterday's conversation with Miranda.

Miranda had encouraged Marlon to interview Parker. Today.

"He's in bad enough shape from his disease," Miranda said. "The anxiety of waiting to see what Roberta says is likely to do him in. You could help Parker pass the time by keeping him occupied."

"I don't know why I didn't interview Parker long ago, when I first embarked on this project," Marlon responded. "I guess I hadn't thought about him in connection with Vietnam for a long time. Parker was just ... Parker."

"Agreed, then," Miranda confirmed. "My backyard would be a good place for it. Parker knows the place well. He'll be relaxed. Plus, it'll be quiet, and outside, in the sunshine. Parker hates to be indoors. He'll be in infinite blackness soon enough, he said."

"Is he doing anything to prevent slipping into eternity other than waiting for a miracle donor?" Marlon asked. "And isn't someone at the VA looking after him?"

"Parker tried homeopathic remedies when he first realized he was failing," Miranda answered.

"Bah," Marlon retorted. "Foolishness. Herbs won't fix Parker's diseased kidneys."

"Steve Jobs tried it for his liver cancer," Miranda objected.

"And when that didn't work, he turned to westernized medicine and a transplant," Marlon noted with satisfaction.

"Anyway," Miranda had continued, "Parker's symptoms got worse, so he went to the VA for a round of dialysis. Unfortunately, the procedure roused his post-traumatic stress disorder, which had been dormant for so many years."

"I've never heard of dialysis provoking PTSD," Marlon observed, "but I know that PTSD is not a 'cookie cutter' disease. It affects people in different ways."

"Exactly," Miranda confirmed. "Anyway, something about those helpless people tethered to life-saving machines echoed his memories of the war. The image of a medic on the battlefield, kneeling by a downed soldier, holding high the bag of blood dripping through the transfusion tube, is what Parker sees."

"But what PTSD symptoms would interfere with dialysis?" Marlon asked.

"Parker's blood pressure shot up dangerously high while he was on the machine," Miranda had explained, "risking a massive stroke. But, without the dialysis, Parker will die."

"Oh, dear, the proverbial rock and hard place," Marlon said. "Poor guy. I'm so sorry, and for you, too, Miranda. Which did Parker choose?"

"He's discontinued treatment," Miranda answered. "He's terribly worried about what will happen to Lydia when he dies. It'll be even worse, though, if he's incapacitated by a stroke, Parker thinks. If that happened, they would both need help."

They had agreed Miranda would pick Parker up in Lafayette Park and bring him to Miranda's house. Marlon, knowing Miranda did not lock her garden gate, would let himself in and meet them there.

He remembered Lydia, Marlon thought, although he had not seen her in years. He recalled a sunny, open-minded person, not well-educated but a good conversationalist. Marlon shuddered. Dementia was a terrifying prospect.

Lydia had begun exhibiting symptoms of early dementia when only in her early 60s. Parker became Lydia's caretaker.

The two had stayed in touch after Parker fled to D.C. from his hometown, Lydia having shamed Parker out of the dark hole he had created for himself. In the early 80s, Lydia took a clerical job at the Department of the Interior and followed Parker to Washington. The two became good friends. "Only friends," Parker explained to the lawyers. Lydia, like Parker, never married.

Marlon's phone beeped. "Fifteen minutes," Miranda had texted. Marlon opened the laptop he had brought with him. He would have time to read the second installment of Paco's story about the deserter.

"We're here," Marlon heard Miranda call from inside the house. He looked up from his computer as the glass door onto the patio slid open. "Sorry to be late," Miranda said as she crossed the threshold, followed by Parker.

Marlon stood, smiling. "Not a problem," he said, and stepping forward, he reached for Parker's hand.

"Did I cover the plywood panel performance specs with Claudia this afternoon?" Will asked Cassandra. Cassandra sat across the conference table from Will. A stack of legal pads lay neatly organized on the table in front of her.

"Just a sec," Cassandra answered, reaching for the topmost pad. Their materials expert, Claudia Sanderson, had been the last witness to testify that afternoon. Cassandra began flipping through pages. "Check," she said a few moments later, "that evidence is in."

Will was almost set to rest his case tomorrow, on the fifth day of the trial. Before doing so, though, he had one last task to complete.

An examination in the courtroom frequently went astray. All too often, a witness would jump ahead, digress, or get lost. The series of questions and answers carefully prepared in advance had to be rearranged, rephrased, or jettisoned on the spot. The judge's grant of opposing counsel's objection—"Move on, counselor"—compounded the problem. An entire line of questioning had been ordered off limits.

Will had to ensure that everything he had planned to get in evidence had in fact been elicited from his witnesses. To do that, he compared his prepared examination questions with Cassandra's notes of the testimony.

"Okay, that's it," Will said as he closed his trial notebook.

"Did you get a chance to talk to Aaron?" Cassandra asked as she stood and stretched.

"Not yet," Will answered. "I'll get to it."

An hour earlier, during their cab ride back to the office from the courthouse, Cassandra told Will about her conversation with Franklin. Will's response was lukewarm.

He could think of dozens of innocent explanations for the limo pick-up of the juror. Maybe she cleaned house for one of the local, millionaire televangelists as a second job, and he was picking her up after a visit to the Hill. Whatever. She was an alternate, anyway. She would not deliberate on the verdict unless another juror was excused for some reason.

Still, they had agreed that they could not simply sit on it. Cassandra would ask Jim to do some online research to see if he could find anything about this juror that had not come out in *voir dire*. Will would call Aaron to see if he had any advice.

"Okay," Cassandra responded. "Anything else we need to do before tomorrow?"

"I've got a couple of things to wrap up, but you should go on home," Will said, motioning Cassandra out of the conference room. "I'll see you at court in the morning."

After Cassandra left, Will took a few minutes to compose his thoughts. Then he rose and walked down the corridor to the large conference room.

As he stepped into the room, Will felt a swell of pride. Looking like a movie set of a well-heeled Wall Street law firm, this space always reminded him that he had made it. He had left the shabby classrooms of his undistinguished night law school far behind.

A twelve-foot-long walnut conference table, seating eighteen, dominated the room. Floor-to-ceiling bookshelves, lining three walls of the room, housed hundreds of volumes of reported decisions from the state and federal courts of the District of Columbia, Maryland, and Virginia; law reviews from the top schools; and dozens of medical textbooks and journals. The night lights of downtown glowed behind the sheer, beige curtains pulled across the windowed south wall of the room.

All was serene and quiet, save for in the far corner where Benjy and Jim sprawled on the carpeted floor. An open Monopoly board scattered with green plastic houses and red hotels lay between them.

"I passed 'go,' and you didn't pay me my two hundred dollars," Benjy's shrill, five-year-old voice complained.

"I did, too!" Jim protested.

"You didn't," Benjy insisted, "and I think I'd be the better banker."

"He's right," Will interjected from his post at the door. Jim, Benjy, and Mauricio, who was sitting on an ottoman pushed against the far wall, overseeing the boys' game, looked up. Mauricio laughed.

Mauricio had returned to Aaron's office early in the afternoon, after he had testified and lunched with José and Will. Will asked Mauricio if he could stay at Aaron's until Will returned from trial. Will wanted to discuss something with him in the privacy of their offices.

"That is so unfair," Jim protested jokingly, then joined Mauricio's laughter.

Will smiled and, giving a little wave, told them he would pack his briefcase for the evening and return in a second. Will hurried to his office.

Jim was the last in the series of Aaron's attorneys and staff who had gladly volunteered to keep an eye on Benjy while Mauricio was down at the courthouse. Ordinarily, Benjy would have been in his preschool. Mauricio had been dropping Benjy off because José was in trial. This morning, Mauricio had to be in D.C. for court before Benjy's school opened. So, Benjy spent the day inspecting anatomical models, getting his first lesson in Bridge, or playing games, depending on the respective caregiver's interests or pedagogical philosophy.

As he packed his briefcase, Will thought again what a fine witness Mauricio had been. Mauricio, a noticeably short man, a tad less than five feet tall, and stocky, had come to court neatly if modestly dressed. He wore a blue button-down chambray shirt and khakis, both neatly pressed. With his thick head of grey hair, bronzed complexion, deeply lined face, and gnarled hands, Mauricio's appearance announced to the jury that this was a man used to hard work and long hours on a construction site.

On the stand, Mauricio spoke softly, but with conviction. Will was sure, or as sure as he could be at this point, that the jury believed every word. Mauricio had convinced the jury, as he had Will, that his company's handling and storage of the plywood had been to industry standards. Nothing J&A Builders had done or failed to do caused the defect in the plank that had shattered under José.

In his direct examination, Will largely stayed away from Mauricio's past. Will did ask a few questions about José's education. He established that José's mother died of complications of a stroke two weeks after José's wedding day. Will also asked about Mauricio's lengthy experience in construction before they founded J&A.

Otherwise, Will kept Mauricio focused on José's accident. Will had decided that this was implicitly part of his deal with Baylie. Both lawyers would stick to the facts relevant to the case. Accordingly, Will did not ask, and the jury did not know about Mauricio's service in Vietnam.

Will knew, though, and he was troubled by what had happened. Or not happened, as it were. Through some bureaucratic error, Mauricio lost the right to U.S. citizenship that he had earned for his military service.

Will worried, too, that Mauricio's status put him and his family at risk. Mauricio somehow passed the E-Verify test, but as a matter of fact he was undocumented. Somebody on a mission to root out undocumented persons would not be fooled so easily.

Will deposited his briefcase at the door to the office suite. Returning to the large conference room, he glanced into the far corner and smiled. Neat piles of the Monopoly currency lay in front of Benjy.

"Can you stay a few more minutes?" Will directed his question at Jim.

"Sure," Jim called as he picked up the dice for another roll.

Will motioned Mauricio out into the hallway. Mauricio joined Will, and the two leaned companionably against the reception desk, shoulder to shoulder.

Will started to speak, then hesitated. José had made it clear that the topic was not one to be broached lightly. Will glanced at Mauricio, who was looking at Will expectantly.

"I think the firm should see if there is anything we can do about your status," Will began quietly.

Mauricio shook his head, no, vigorously. "No, Will," he said firmly.

"Wait, hear me out," Will continued. "We would only approach trusted sources. The inquiry would be anonymous. We wouldn't tell anybody your name, or anything else personally identifiable. We would only explain, in general terms, what happened, and see if anybody has any ideas about fixing the situation."

"Do you know anybody powerful enough?" Mauricio asked. "You know ..." Mauricio paused. "You know I've been here illegally for a very long time."

"It's a long shot, I have to admit," Will responded, "but it seems well worth a try."

Mauricio stared at Will fixedly. "I trust you to be careful," Mauricio said. "But I can't trust anybody else. Not completely. And you can't promise me there is no risk in this, can you, Will."

"No, I can't," Will admitted.

"Let's let sleeping dogs lie, then," Mauricio said, crossing his arms across his chest.

Maybe Mauricio was right, Will thought. Could it be a mistake to disclose Mauricio's status to anyone outside the firm, even if no name was disclosed? And was Will really doing this for Mauricio? Or was this another attempt to expiate his guilt for repeatedly bungling the Marquezes' status issues during this trial?

From inside the open door of the conference room, Will heard a peal of laughter. Benjy. Will was reminded that there were other interests at stake here.

"Do it for Benjy," Will said, putting his hand on Mauricio's shoulder. "He needs you, as does José. Your family can't be worrying that, someday, you will suddenly disappear, running from the immigration authorities or taken into detention."

Mauricio eventually agreed, although reluctantly.

On the drive home, Will put together a mental list of the people to be called. Aaron's list of politicians to whose campaigns Aaron had donated. That friend of Cassandra's mother, also a Vietnam vet, who had worked as an attorney for the Veterans' Administration for decades. Senator Howard.

Will had forgotten to ask Mauricio if he remembered Jeff Howard. Betsy had made the connection: Mauricio and Jeff served in the same unit in Vietnam. Surely, Jeff would be sympathetic to the plight of his comrade-in-arms, but only if Will could reveal Mauricio's name. Will would have to check with Mauricio.

If Mauricio agreed, Will would have to ask for Betsy's assistance in reaching out to Howard. Howard had recently announced that he was running for the United States Senate. It would be tough for Will to get Howard's ear, but he was sure Betsy could do it.

Will wondered whether Betsy would be willing. Betsy did not mix her personal affairs with office life, as the other attorneys did. Come to think of it, Will had no idea what Betsy thought about undocumented persons. She might have no interest in making any effort on Mauricio's behalf.

Well, one way to find out, Will decided. He would see if Betsy was free to meet on Sunday. Somewhere outside of the office.

CHAPTER 15
THE REPLACEMENT

Trial Day 5

Cassandra, Will, Baylie, and his second chair, whose name Cassandra kept forgetting, sat at their respective counsel tables. Will, fidgeting with his pen, whispered to Cassandra, "What do you suppose is going on?"

Cassandra shrugged. "No idea," she said.

Trial was to have started at 9:00 a.m. It was now 9:20. Judge Storer was a stickler on time. She always gaveled her proceedings to begin at the scheduled hour. If the judge had to take an emergency phone call, her clerk would have informed the lawyers, but the door to the judges' chambers remained closed.

The bailiff was also absent, which was unusual once the courtroom was open to the public. Maybe one of the jurors had not checked in this morning, and Judge Storer sent the bailiff out with a warrant for the errant juror's arrest, Cassandra thought. She had known the judge to do that. But no, again, the Judge would have let counsel know.

The minutes ticked away. Cassandra saw a bead of sweat drip from Will's forehead down the side of his face.

A tap on Cassandra's shoulder startled her. She swung around.

"Why aren't we starting?" José asked, palpably uneasy.

"I don't know," Cassandra answered. "We'll find out soon enough, I imagine," she said soothingly. "Nothing to worry about, I'm sure."

She was not at all sure, however. She glanced at the other counsel table. The two defense attorneys huddled together, whispering furiously. Did they know something she and Will did not?

The door to chambers swung open. Court personnel spilled into the well of the courtroom. "All rise," called the bailiff as Judge Storer climbed onto her dais. The clerk took her seat at the table to the judge's right.

"Good morning, everyone," Judge Storer said as she swept her robes under her and sank into her chair. "Please be seated."

"What do you think?" Will asked Cassandra, *sotto voce*. "Does she look concerned? Angry?" As Cassandra responded with a shrug of her shoulders, Judge Storer answered Will's question.

"We have a situation," Judge Storer said, looking directly at counsel, "but not one we aren't fully prepared to handle."

Cassandra and Will shared glances as the judge looked down at her notes, then continued.

"Juror Number 6 was taken by ambulance to the hospital early this morning. According to her husband, who called the Court Clerk, it appears she may have had a stroke. Let us all offer our hopes and prayers that it was minor, and she will recover quickly."

Nodding her agreement, Cassandra looked over at Baylie's table. Both defense lawyers scribbled on the yellow legal pads in front of them. What was so complicated about this that it required taking notes, she wondered?

"Accordingly, our alternate juror will take her place in the box this morning," Judge Storer advised, "and we will proceed as scheduled. Will, you've called the last witness and are resting your case this morning, correct?"

Will stood. "Yes, Your Honor," he answered, "but could we please have five before the jury is seated?"

"You have exactly five minutes," the judge answered crisply. "Bailiff?" She motioned the bailiff off to the jury room, from which the reconstituted jury would emerge in moments. Will took his seat beside Cassandra and leaned in for a whispered conference.

"Go call the office," Will said. "Have someone contact Sue Geller and get her into the office right away."

The firm rarely engaged Geller & Associates, Private Investigative Services, as Sue styled her one-person shop. When they did so, it was to locate assets a defendant was trying to hide, dodging a judicial writ of attachment on the property to satisfy an unpaid judgment.

Only once, that Cassandra could recall, had Aaron hired Sue to investigate a juror's background. The time had come to do it again.

"You'd better go back to the office and brief Sue in person," Will continued. "Tell Sue what Franklin supposedly saw, and that we need anything she can find on our new juror. I'll be fine alone here this morning. Let's plan on meeting in the cafeteria for lunch unless you hear otherwise from me."

Cassandra nodded. She rose and reached down to grab her bag. With a nod and encouraging smile for José, Cassandra walked hurriedly out of the courtroom.

Two hours later, the meeting with Sue concluded, Cassandra stood outside Aaron's office building, phone in hand, watching the avatar of her Uber driver approaching. The phone rang. Will.

"I'm on my way back to court," Cassandra answered.

"No need," Will's voice replied. "I'm returning to the office. An emergency motion landed on Judge Storer's desk. She dismissed the jury to free her afternoon to hear argument on the motion. We'll reconvene on Monday."

"How did it go this morning?" Cassandra asked.

"Fine," Will answered. "I'll tell you all about it when I get back."

"Sounds good," Cassandra said. "See you in a few."

Cassandra canceled her Uber, feeling only slightly guilty. D.C., at this time of day, swarmed with would-be passengers. Her driver would easily get another fare.

Just as she wheeled around to return to the office, Cassandra's phone rang again. She did not recognize the number, but she answered the call.

"Hi, this is Cassandra Robins."

"Franklin," the adjuster answered without preamble. "We're raising our offer to $75,000, but it won't stay on the table past the weekend."

Cassandra frowned, thinking quickly. This offer was only slightly less ridiculous than Franklin's first, given that José's past medical bills alone totaled over a million dollars. Were they missing something, some fatal weakness in their case?

Baylie had dredged up that fender-bender and trotted it in front of the jury. He had been trying to convince the jury that the accident was a cause of José's injuries and medical expenses. She and Will thought that ploy had failed. Instead, the evidence supported their claim. All those medical bills and projected costs for future care were the direct results of José's fall through the plywood covering the duct. Will had also built a solid case that the defendants were at fault for the defective board.

On the merits, it made no sense for Franklin to up his offer now. Plus, the alternate juror, the nurse's aide who rode around in limos, had just been promoted. She was now a full-fledged member of the jury. What was going on? Whatever. Cassandra would certainly not disclose her confusion to Franklin.

"I'll pass it along to my client," Cassandra said, "but the offer will be rejected." She ended the call.

CHAPTER 16
DON'T MENTION HIS NAME

Betsy stopped by the receptionist's desk to tell Beebe that she was leaving for her 11:00 a.m. meeting. "By the way, with whom is Cassandra meeting?" Betsy asked.

Betsy had spied Cassandra through the glass-paneled door of the small conference room. Across from Cassandra sat a short, plump woman, whose flaming red hair, cropped short, contrasted sharply with her yellow-and-orange floral print blouse.

"It must be important for Cassandra to have come back from court," Betsy added.

"That's our PI," Beebe answered.

"We have a private investigator?" Betsy asked wonderingly. "I wouldn't have thought a med mal firm had much use for those kinds of services."

Beebe shrugged. She had been with Aaron even longer than Marlon. "Stick around long enough, Betsy," Beebe said, "and you'll see it all. I swear I have." She laughed.

Betsy smiled. "I might do that," she said. "So, any idea what this is all about?"

Beebe shook her head. "Not yet," she answered, "but we'll find out soon enough. There aren't any secrets around here."

Betsy wondered about that but kept her counsel. "Okay, well, I should be back by 12:30 or so if anybody needs me," she said. "See you later, Beebe."

Betsy turned left outside the office building, took another left on I Street, and headed toward Dr. Singh's office on George Washington Circle. She looked forward to discussing a surgery Dr. Singh had performed on a client. The immersion in technical details would dispel her disquieting conversation with Jeff that morning.

She had managed to get on Jeff's schedule for a ten-minute phone call at 6:00 a.m. On the agenda would be several items Betsy had found in Jeff's file.

"Good morning, Jeff," she began the call. "I'll get right to the point as we don't have much time. How well do you know Carter Blythe?"

"I'm not sure I've even met the man," Jeff answered. "The name doesn't ring a bell."

"He was a law school classmate," Betsy explained. "Blythe was disbarred after it was discovered that he cheated on his bar exam. If you had been friends, someone might question your judgment. A stretch, I know, but I'm doing the job you asked me to do."

"Fine," Jeff responded curtly. "We were definitely not friends."

Betsy paused, taken aback. What was up with Jeff? He should have chuckled, thanked her, and told her to keep digging. Unless Jeff was lying about Blythe, which Betsy did not believe, Jeff was simply having a bad day.

Betsy turned the conversation to the real reasons for her call.

Jeff confirmed that, after 138 AVN Co. 19 was effectively destroyed, he had bivouacked with another unit for the last three weeks of his tour.

"The whole thing was coming apart at the seams by then," Jeff said, "and the command structure everywhere in Vietnam was crumbling. Those of us on the ground were doing our best to keep our heads down and get the hell out."

Betsy was not sure why, but she had a hunch she should ask Jeff about Glen Hadley, the MIA from Company 19's last battle. She followed her instincts, which proved the right call.

"Glen Hadley was not MIA," Jeff said.

"What do you mean?" she asked, startled. "You're saying the Army was wrong?"

Jeff laughed harshly. "The Army was wrong about a lot of things. In this case, there's no question about it. I was beside Glen when he was shot dead."

Jeff had first written to the Department of Defense to try to fix the mistake. Receiving no satisfactory answer from the government, Jeff wrote directly to Glen's family.

"I debated whether it would be more hurtful to tell them their son was dead or leave them to the unknown," Jeff said. "In the end, I convinced myself that not knowing would be worse."

"How did the family respond?" Betsy asked.

Jeff sighed heavily. "They didn't want to have anything to do with me, some unknown grunt. They would rely on the *bona fides* of the U.S. Government. I realized they would rather hope than mourn. Which I understood. But it bugged me for a long time."

"One last thing," Betsy said, glancing at her watch. "It's an incredible coincidence, but I've recently met a comrade of yours from Company 19. Mauricio Marquez. His son is the firm's client. I could arrange it if you'd like to see him again."

"Don't you dare mention my name to Marquez," Jeff snarled. He hung up on her.

Betsy, stunned, felt as though she had been slapped. Jeff had never spoken to her like that. Not even close.

Jeff had texted minutes after he disconnected the call with a curt apology. The message had done little to soothe her hurt feelings or calm Betsy's anxiety.

Betsy stopped at the red light on Pennsylvania Avenue. As the seconds on the clock for the pedestrian crosswalk ticked by, she took a deep breath, steadying herself.

Betsy lived with the constant dread of abandonment, the legacy of her parents.

Bright and introspective, Betsy, by her early teens, recognized her fears and understood their source. She fought to overcome those emotions. She tried to put her syndrome under a microscope, study it, and rationalize it away, without success.

Betsy did not develop close friendships with her schoolmates. She avoided social interaction when she could, other than that necessary for politeness' sake. She clung tightly only to Jeff, her one rock.

Jeff, worried about Betsy's isolation, encouraged her to break out of her shell. He taught Betsy to play field hockey and insisted she try out for the team. Jeff was so proud when Betsy made the varsity team in junior high. He convinced Betsy to audition for a role in a local production of *A Christmas Carol* over Betsy's objection that she could not act. She got the part of Martha, one of the Cratchit daughters.

Betsy knew she could succeed at more than her studies. Yet, she did not get satisfaction from those other accomplishments, except for pleasing Jeff.

Susan, Jeff's second wife, tried a different tack. Susan believed Betsy would blossom if she reconnected with her parents.

A quiet, reserved woman, although unfailingly kind, Susan did not otherwise play a prominent part in Betsy's upbringing. Susan did, however, succeed in getting Betsy to explore her complex feelings about her parents.

Betsy could never, afterward, remember a time when Susan said anything definite about the matter. Nevertheless, Betsy was led to conclude that her mother deserved to see her daughter, and vice versa.

Betsy was fourteen years old when she started visiting the federal correctional facility where her mother, Natalie, was imprisoned. She had been terrified that first time, Betsy remembered, but it became routine.

Betsy had not fallen instantly into her mother's arms, literally or figuratively. Over time, however, Betsy renewed her love for her mother if not, completely, her trust.

Her father, Thomas, was another matter. Thomas was bright, probably brilliant, Betsy came to realize. Thomas worked in the penitentiary library. Betsy never saw Thomas, on her rare visits to him, without a book at hand. They could discuss physics, but not much else. Betsy recoiled from Thomas's rigid self-righteousness, his immense sense of self-regard, and unfailing certainty that the end he believed in was worth any means.

Nearing Dr. Singh's office building, Betsy tightened her grip on her briefcase. Why had Jeff reacted as he had to the name Mauricio Marquez? Could they have had an altercation in Vietnam? That made no sense. Jeff was not the type of man who would hold a grudge so long, whatever had happened. None of it made any sense.

She would do as Jeff asked and not pursue the matter with Mauricio. She would also make more of an effort at the office, Betsy decided, as she stepped into the revolving glass door. She would seize the opportunity to do more than get the job done, for once.

* * *

The noonday sun cast a glare on Paco's laptop screen. He shifted the computer into the shadow cast by the kelly-green awning over the table, nestled against the warm stucco of the café's front wall. The proprietor had told Paco that he had been pleased to find a sunshade with a color from the national flag.

Paco took a deep breath. He opened the attachment to Marlon's email: The transcript of Marlon's interview with Parker.

Q: Where do you want to start, Parker? What would be easiest on you?

A: Might as well get the worst over first. I was at school when they delivered the news about John's death. I knew what had happened the minute I set eyes on Dad. He looked as dead as he'd just found out John was.

The next few days are a blur. All I remember clearly is the casket in the parlor of the funeral home. The director told us it had arrived closed and sealed. That was the first time I cried. I'd never see my brother again. Not even his corpse.

We didn't have much of a crowd at the funeral. Dad didn't socialize. John had alienated his friends from earlier days. I hadn't had much interest in anything for a while. Dad and I, Lydia, and John's high school history teacher sat through the pastor's service. Everybody followed the hearse to the municipal cemetery in the funeral director's black station wagon. We watched the casket lowered into the grave. John was buried with military honors.

Q: How had John alienated his high school friends?

A: Oh, he had gotten into that anti-war stuff. He was vocal about it, which didn't go down well in that place and at that time. John got into a fist fight with some guy on the football team, I remember. The kids didn't have much to do with John after that. Probably fine with John, too.

Q: Do you know anything about how John died, Parker?

A: Not much, other than that he got disengaged, somehow, from his own unit. He ended up killed in a firefight between some other unit and Charlie. Shit bad luck, that's for sure.

Q: Were you sent any of John's effects?

A: Only his dog tags. Dad gave them to me. I didn't want anything to do with them. I must have stashed them in the house somewhere, but I don't remember where. Anyway, I never saw them again.

Q: Your brother was killed in the war. Your family had sacrificed enough. Why did you enlist? Why did your father allow you to?

A: Well, I was of age. I finished my senior year of high school, turned eighteen in June, and enlisted. Not sure Dad could have done anything to stop me.

Dad wasn't paying much attention, anyway. He and John didn't agree about much, and they fought a lot. Nothing physical, but nasty. John always said Dad considered me his only real son. But that wasn't true. Not true at all. Dad wasn't around for us an awful lot before, but after John died, Dad checked out.

Q: Okay, your dad wouldn't stop you, but why do it? Why did you enlist?

A: John died because of me. I killed him.

Q: Let's take a break, Parker.

Paco propped his chin on his folded hands, imagining the scene. He should have taken the chance, he thought. He should have sent those letters. Almost too late, now. He turned back to the transcript.

A: I'm okay, now. Let's keep going.

Q: John was killed in battle. What did you mean, you killed him?

A: A week or so after John got his draft notice, I overheard him talking to somebody in our bedroom. I never was sure who it was because the door was closed, and I couldn't hear the other voice. Anyway, John was going to run away to avoid the draft.

I didn't know anything about that stuff, but I got it into my head that it would be a crime. John would go to jail. I thought he'd be better off in Vietnam than jail. Little did I know.

Q: So, what happened?

A: I told Dad. I don't know if Dad physically dragged John to the recruitment center, or what, but John went to the war. I thought I'd saved John. Instead, I'd killed him. I didn't know the word back then, but I needed to atone.

Paco rose and entered the café. He returned to his table a few minutes later with a shot glass of tequila. He took a sip and returned to the transcript.

Paco read about Parker's collapse after returning from the war and his escape to D.C. This pattern of descent and resurrection continued in the city, Paco noted, beginning with Parker's illness and landing at Aaron's.

Parker worked as a messenger for Aaron for three years. Then, using a connection Aaron had with a wholesaler in the garment district in New York City, Parker opened a small women's boutique in a mall in a Virginia suburb close to the D.C. line.

Parker drove to New York City on Sundays, bought inventory, and worked the other six days of the week in his store selling ladies' apparel. He marketed his wares as clothing with a Big Apple cache but at a price affordable to the secretaries and administrative assistants who worked in the office buildings surrounding the mall. He acquired a small but loyal clientele, and Parker was holding his own financially.

Parker bought clothes for a lot of women during those years, but never for a wife. He dated off-and-on but never married.

Then, based on a rumor that the Federal Government was looking at property in the area to build a new Patent and Trademark Office, the landlord raised Parker's rent. Parker looked at his books and decided he could not do it. After ten years of hard work, Parker closed his shop.

Forty years old, with modest savings and a keen eye for a hat suitable for a Northern Virginian fashionista "wannabe," Parker had to start over.

After liquidating his apparel business, Parker found a job as a short-order cook in a diner in Tyson's Corner. The business occupied enough space in a one-story, commercial building to fit six booths, a row of stools at a counter, and a kitchen with a walk-in refrigerator.

Parker schlepped to McLean on a bus from Herndon at 4:00 a.m. for two years. By then, he had scraped enough together to buy a share of the business from the aging owner.

Seven years later, the County exercised eminent domain and condemned the building to construct the new, Tyson's Corner subway line. In a few years, a gleaming, thirty-story steel skyscraper stood where Parker had once happily grilled hamburgers. Those in the know profited hugely from the Tyson's Corner boom, but not Parker. He had been pushed out long before the money rolled in.

Parker was done being an entrepreneur after the diner closed. He found part-time employment at a nonprofit, veterans' service organization located in Southeast D.C.

Until then, Parker studiously avoided making any connections with veterans or veterans' affairs, other than to use the services of the VA medical facilities. As he aged, his feelings changed. He found himself more at home now, spending time with his fellow veterans, than he ever had in his life.

Soon after Parker started at the nonprofit, an anonymous donor kicked in a sizeable sum, and the organization blossomed. Parker's job converted to full time. A year later, he was promoted to director of outreach. Then, somebody "cooked the books." The organization ran out of money and closed its doors.

Parker limped by on public assistance, including public housing, for a couple of years, until he could draw, first, on his military pension, and then on social security. He kept himself busy caring for Lydia, after she moved in with him. He played chess in the park, volunteered for Big Brother, and joined in protests for what he considered worthy causes. It was not for what he had planned and hoped, but it was a decent life, he told himself, until he got so sick again.

Once again, he was going to lose it all. Until Parker found his miracle donor.

Paco, reaching blindly for his shot glass, knocked it off the table. Glass shattered.

CHAPTER 17
A MISSING FATHER

Miranda settled into her seat, warmed by the afternoon sun streaming in the window on her right. The carriage creaked and groaned as the train lumbered along the maze of tracks under Penn Station, on the way south to D.C. She opened the flap of her shoulder bag and reached in for her book. The test kit, containing a snippet of Roberta's hair and a vial of her saliva, nestled in a plastic bag at the bottom of the bag.

Miranda had met Roberta that morning in her rowhouse in the Old City neighborhood in Philadelphia. Roberta was tall for a woman, close to six feet, and slender. Otherwise, Miranda detected no evident resemblance to Parker. Of course, Parker was old, grey, and ill. Roberta looked in her early forties. Apples and oranges, Miranda decided, dismissing any notion that appearances mattered.

Roberta, with whom Miranda had communicated several times via phone and email, welcomed Miranda warmly. She led Miranda through the foyer into the living room, open to the kitchen to the right, and beckoned her to take a seat. From the matching set of ivory-colored, over-stuffed leather sofa and two chairs grouped in the room, Miranda chose the love seat.

"Coffee?" Roberta, still standing, asked.

Miranda smiled and nodded her thanks.

"Cream or sugar?"

"No, thanks, just black," Miranda answered.

Roberta returned from the kitchen a few minutes later with two mugs and, handing Miranda one, sat on the sofa. "I may as well cut right to the chase," Roberta said. "I would have considered it, even though I have no idea how we are related. After all, people donate a kidney to complete strangers. But I can't help you. Can't help Parker, that is. I was born with only one kidney."

Miranda's heart sank. She barely controlled a shudder as the image of Parker's animated excitement on Wednesday passed through her thoughts.

Beneath Miranda's disappointment, she felt anger. Why had Roberta not told her outright? Why drag her here on a fruitless and now painful journey? Miranda's frustration, if not her sadness, disappeared with Roberta's next words, however.

"I could have told you all this in an email or on the phone and saved you a trip, I realize," Roberta said. "But I wanted to hear, face-to-face, from someone who knows him. I'm curious about this person who could be a close relative, yet I've never met him. What's he like?"

Miranda talked for over an hour.

"Your turn," Miranda concluded, "to tell me about you, starting with the big question. How are you related to Parker?"

"Can't help you there, I'm afraid," Roberta answered. "I'm adopted."

Her adoptive parents, Roberta explained, who raised Roberta in a comfortable, middle-class neighborhood just off the Main Line north of Philadelphia, never knew anything about Roberta's birth mother. Nowadays, Roberta knew, it was not uncommon for the parents-to-be, even in an arms-length adoption, to become acquainted with the mother before the child was born. Back when she was adopted, the identity of the mother was clothed in secrecy.

"I could have tried to find her on my own," Roberta continued, "but I never had the desire. I had the means to try. I've worked for the Philadelphia Gazette my entire career. I'm a graphic designer, but I'm friends with a lot of top-notch reporters who would gladly have helped me in my search. I suppose I was happy enough with the parents I had. I never married and never wanted to have children of my own, so I had no need to find my mother to see if I needed to worry about genetic abnormalities I might pass on to a child."

Roberta had risen and walked over to the two, six-foot-tall windows fronting the street below. Her back to Miranda, she said, quietly, Miranda straining to hear: "I'm not sure I want to meet Parker, either.

I've gotten used to being on my own. And why …?" Roberta glanced over her shoulder at Miranda, a troubled expression on her face.

Miranda understood. Why now? Why take on the burden of comforting a dying stranger? Miranda had to convince Roberta to do so, for Parker's sake. But how? The way every journey begins, Miranda thought. With the first step. Get the samples.

"Look," Miranda began, "maybe it will help you decide if we run another test on the DNA match. Earlier, you said this person, Parker, that is, could be a relative. You need to be sure. All I need right now is a snip of your hair and a saliva sample. I'll send these to a commercial DNA testing lab. We'll have the definitive results in no time."

Roberta agreed. Her curiosity got the better of her.

Miranda roused herself from her thoughts. By habit, she had chosen a quiet car and would have to move to another spot to call the office. She decided to stay put. If it had been good news, Miranda would have been on the phone immediately. The real story could wait. She would go straight to Aaron's offices when she arrived in D.C. at 4:25 p.m., if the train was on time.

Miranda cringed at the thought of Parker's reaction to the news of Roberta's medical condition. Parker must have known, all along, that the odds were long that Roberta would be both able and willing to donate a kidney. Yet, Parker's face had glowed whenever he mentioned the match or a donor or his fantastic surgical team. Whether it was reasonable or not, Parker was cautiously optimistic.

He would be devastated, and desperate to find a new home for Lydia.

Parker never admitted as much, but Miranda knew Parker's love for Lydia was not platonic. Miranda also knew that Parker's desires had never been requited.

"She's been the only woman in my life," Parker told Miranda. "We were both loners, but so comfortable with each other around. Before she got sick and moved in with me, we were constantly in and out of each other's apartments. Whenever one of us wanted to get out and do anything, we would call the other."

Lydia needed her own space, Parker had said, more than he did. There were times and places in her life she would not discuss with

Parker. She held other people's secrets that were not hers to reveal, she had explained.

When Miranda started to praise Parker for taking on the burden of caring for Lydia when she got sick, Parker brushed Miranda off. She had lucid days, Parker said, when things were much as normal. In any event, she was always still Lydia.

Miranda would figure out what do with Lydia. Later. Miranda opened the book she had absent-mindedly set on the drink tray in front of her seat twenty minutes ago. She found the page where she left off that morning and began to read.

Two hours later, Miranda walked into Aaron's office. The lawyers, gathered for a meeting, all looked over at her. Faces fell.

"What do we do now?" Miranda asked, after she had related to her colleagues what she had learned about Roberta.

"I think we should exhume John," Marlon said.

"You want to do what?" cried Miranda. "Haul Parker's brother up from his grave? Why?"

"Sorry, Miranda," Marlon said. "I should have said exhume the body that was buried as John."

"That doesn't help me a whole lot," Miranda complained, but she sank back into her chair.

"Follow my logic here," Marlon replied. "The simplest answer to Roberta's mysterious consanguinity with Parker is that John was her father. There is no other candidate. Remember your Sherlock Holmes. 'If you eliminate the impossible, what remains, no matter how improbable, must be the truth.'"

"I get it," Will chimed in. "If John was Roberta's father, John could not have died in the war. To have sired Roberta, John had to have been alive at least four years after he was supposedly buried. The body is someone else's."

"Exactly," Marlon said. "So, we exhume that body and have a pathologist retrieve DNA samples. We compare the corpse's DNA with Parker's. If the DNA in the two samples is wildly different, we'll have solid evidence the buried man was not John Evans."

"The 'why' makes sense to me," Betsy said, "but how would we arrange an exhumation?"

"That's easy," Marlon answered. "Ten years or so ago, we had a client who died, presumably of a heart attack. But no autopsy was done. His widow came to us. Her husband went to his cardiologist regularly. She wondered why, if there was a problem, it hadn't been detected before he died of it. Our expert said we'd need to have an autopsy to tell if there'd been malpractice."

"I remember," Miranda observed. "We called on Laurie Hanus, that sole practitioner we call on for odd jobs. She did whatever it took to get him dug up, sent from a mortuary outside Baltimore to Pittsburgh for an autopsy, and back in his grave in twenty-four hours." Miranda shook her head. "Amazes me still!"

"Odd jobs, indeed," Betsy said wryly.

"We'd have to get the family's permission," Marlon noted, "but that means Parker's. That should be simple."

"I don't see it as simple at all," Miranda objected. "It will upset Parker terribly. For one thing, he'd start thinking he may have mourned a stranger, instead of his brother, for all those years."

"She's right, Marlon," Will noted. "Plus, he'll worry about what did happen to John if he's not in that grave."

"Parker's not the only one wondering that," Miranda said. "If John didn't die in Vietnam, what did happen to him? And how could the Army have made such a terrible mistake? Anyway, John couldn't have come home alive, even if that body isn't his. Or if he did, how in the world could that have happened? And if he did somehow survive, get back to the States, and father a child, we have no idea where he might be. How would that help Parker?"

Marlon held up a hand. "Whoa, Miranda," he said. "I don't have answers to many of those questions, but I can tell you that the Army could make such a mistake. My great-grandfather was shipped home to upstate New York in a coffin after Gettysburg. His family buried him. Six months later, he walked up the lane and knocked on the front door of his house. His wife answered, and promptly fainted dead away."

The lawyers chuckled.

Marlon grinned. "True story," he said. "Listen" he continued, serious tone returning, "I know that was a hundred years before the Vietnam War. But I'm guessing it was still possible in 1973 for the wrong body to have been sent home. I haven't done the research, though, because we don't need to in this case. We have a sealed coffin. John's family never saw the body. And we have Roberta."

"And the dog tags?" Miranda persisted.

"Last seen, according to Parker's decades-old memories, while in shock over his brother's death, in a farmhouse deep in Texas," Marlon answered. "Not in evidence," he continued in the parlance of a trial attorney.

The room fell silent.

"Look," Marlon continued, "you are right, Miranda, that exhuming the body is a far cry from finding Parker's brother. Alive. But why not try? And step one is confirming that John was not buried in Texas in 1973."

Finally, Miranda spoke. "Yes, it will be painful for Parker, in ways I can't even imagine. But I think he'll survive with hope. Even a sliver of it. Without it, he dies in front of our eyes."

Aaron nodded. "I agree," he said. "Let's do it."

CHAPTER 18
THE JUROR'S SON

Saturday

Cassandra, Will, José, and Sue Geller took seats around the table in the small conference room. While the other, larger conference room in Aaron's office suite was furnished to impress, this space was for work. The walls were unadorned. A spare, rectangular table fitted eight upright wooden chairs. A battered credenza graced the far wall. The sole ornament on top of the credenza was a seldom-used office telephone plugged into the wall.

Cassandra had disapproved of Will's plan to include José in the meeting. José needed to rest in the comfort of his home after five grueling days in the courtroom.

He was asking a lot, Will had agreed. Still, whatever Sue had to report, José needed to hear every word, because José would have to make the call on what to do about their new juror.

Sue retrieved a yellow legal pad and pen from a capacious pink bag sporting Winnie-the-Poo, Eeyore, and Roo decals. A diaper bag earlier in its career, Cassandra thought. Cassandra once asked Sue whether it was unusual for a private investigator to dress so showily. Yes, Sue confirmed. That was the point. She was in the perfect camouflage for a PI.

Jim opened the conference room door, walked in, and deposited a white paper bag on the table. "Lunch is served," he said. "Sandwiches from Potbelly."

"Thanks, Jim," Will said, reaching to unpack the bag.

Jim gave a mock salute and walked out, closing the door behind him.

Once everyone was settled with their choice of food, Sue began her report.

"I know I don't need to tell you this," she said, "but I will remind you, anyway. An investigation of a sitting juror must be done with kid gloves. Anything more aggressive would be far too close to jury tampering."

Will leaned back and held up both hands, palms out. "And I would never ask for any improper snooping," he said. "It's only because I trusted you to do this right that I asked you at all."

Sue nodded. "Okay, that's out of the way," she said. "We all understand I was working within strict limitations. Here's what I've got."

"Anna Hinks, forty-two years old, is a widow, with one son. She lives alone in a one-bedroom condominium in a twenty-four-unit building on Belmont Avenue, in the Adams Morgan neighborhood of Northwest D.C."

"Everything Anna said during *voir dire* checked out. She worked as a nurse's aide at Shady Grove Hospital and has been so employed for ten years. Anna has never been a party to a lawsuit in the District, Virginia, or Maryland, nor has she served as a juror in any of those jurisdictions."

"When questioned by the judge, Anna denied knowing any of the parties, the attorneys, or the witnesses in the case. I confirmed that Anna never worked for either of the corporate defendants. She had no recent telephone correspondence with Baylie or any member of his firm and has never been represented by him. I can't be sure about any connections Anna may have with Baylie's witnesses. All of them are from out of town, though, and it seems unlikely that Anna even knew of their existence before the trial."

"On other fronts, Anna has no recent deposits into her checking account other than her salary from Shady Grove. She has never been arrested in D.C. or the neighboring jurisdictions, and she has never been convicted of a crime anywhere in the United States.

"Wow," Cassandra marveled. "How could you know all that?" she asked.

Sue looked up from her notes and glared over the tops of her half-moon, tortoise-shell glasses at Cassandra. "You are not seriously asking me that, are you now, child?"

"No, no," Cassandra assured her. "Rhetorical question."

Sue harrumphed and continued. "The only thing I found that may be problematic is Anna's son. He's a big wig in an activist, anti-immigrant group. America for Americans, it's called. The organization has existed for some time, but its membership has risen dramatically in recent years. Its platform is becoming increasingly zealous. It supported separating parents seeking asylum at the border from their children and calls for cleansing the country from all illegal aliens through mass deportations."

Sue looked over at José. "Sorry, I don't use that term for undocumented persons, José," she explained. "I was quoting from their website."

José nodded his understanding.

"Does America for Americans by chance own a black, stretch limo?" Cassandra asked.

"Yep," Sue answered.

Will sighed. "Anything else?" he asked. When Sue shook her head, no, Will asked the others if they had any questions. None did.

Will stood. "Sue, thanks so much," he said. "You've done a terrific job."

Sue shrugged as she slid her legal pad back into her bag. "I don't know about that," she said dryly. "I found nothing you could use to have her excluded from the jury, but only something about which to worry." Sue took her leave.

"Is she right?" José, who had been sitting quietly, motionless, broke the silence that had fallen on Sue's departure. "That there's nothing we can do?"

"I'm not sure," Will answered. "I'd have to consult with Aaron. He said he has a few tricks up his sleeve that he's used, successfully, in the past, to get rid of a troublesome juror. I'm not sure if any of them would work in this situation, but the bigger question is whether we should even consider it."

"What do you mean?" Cassandra asked. "It seems clear to me that Anna is a problem for us. I mean, lots of people have legitimate concerns about immigration, of course. But her son's positions, which he is advocating in a big way, are so extreme. Isn't it likely she's been influenced by her son?"

"Yeah, probably," Will said. He glanced quickly at José. "Likely, anyway," Will corrected himself, "but Anna was the only alternate. Assume we could come up with a reason to have her stricken. Judge Storer will then have to declare a mistrial unless Baylie agrees to a five-person jury. Baylie has been reasonable enough, but no defense lawyer worth his salt would give up an opportunity to get the case delayed. He won't agree."

The lawyers looked at José's blank face. She had visited José in the hospital the day after his last surgery. José lay strapped to a board on his bed to immobilize his spine. His pain was intense, and his prognosis uncertain. Still, José smiled at her. She had overheard José describing to Will his fears for the future of his son, his father, and his employees. Yet, when she walked into the room where he and Will were talking, José smiled at her. His smiles were gone now.

"I can't wait for another trial," José finally spoke, voice wooden. "The bills I can't pay are piling up. I would sell the company, but J&A is worthless right now. During the last two years, we could keep going because we had existing contracts to fulfill. But I haven't been able to develop any new business since I broke my back. I can't afford more therapy, but if I don't get back to it soon, my back and leg muscles will begin to atrophy. Worst case, I'm bedridden for the rest of my life."

José leaned his head in his hands. Then, he looked up, shifted in his chair, and straightened.

"Look," José said, voice stronger, "I know this was never a sure thing. You were very clear about that, Will. You said the firm had an excellent track record, but there would always be cases you lost. It looks like the chances of winning have gotten slimmer, though. What should I do, Will? Cassandra?"

Cassandra looked steadily at José for several minutes, thoughts racing. What were the chances the delay, if they opted for a second trial, would be a few months only? Slim to none, she thought. More likely they would wait over a year for another chance to try the case.

Anna Hinks might, like her son, despise illegal immigrants. But would she even know José's status had been illegal before he married?

Maybe she missed the point of Baylie's questions on Monday and taken little notice when José took the Fifth. Cassandra did not know.

Should Cassandra talk to Franklin and try to get him to up his offer? To approach him now would be a sure sign of weakness, however, given that she had already rejected the offer. Franklin would be more likely to take the offer off the table than raise it.

Cassandra sighed deeply, out of ideas. She hoped Will had one.

"Have faith in the system, José," Will said firmly. "I do."

"Remember," Will continued, "the jurors took an oath. They swore to decide the case, without fear or favor, based only on the evidence presented. I've talked to dozens of jurors. They all confirmed that they took the oath seriously. They did believe in the crucial role of the jury in the administration of fair and impartial justice. Sure, there are exceptions, have to be, because humans can't completely put aside their passions and prejudices. José, you are playing the odds, but I think it's a good bet."

"I'm listening, Will," José said, "but I've seen the movie, *Twelve Angry Men*, you know. What makes you think I've got a Henry Fonda on my jury if I need one?"

Will smiled. "That was Hollywood and the 1950s," Will answered. "Don't you think people's attitudes have changed a bit since then?" he asked.

"In some quarters," José said. "Not all."

Will's smile disappeared. "You're right," he observed. "One more thing to consider, though. *Twelve Angry Men* was about a criminal trial. The jury had to be unanimous. Not in this civil case. Even if we have no chance with Anna, a vote from her against us won't scuttle us."

"As long as we convince the rest of them to go with our side," Cassandra added.

"You will," José said firmly. "I have doubts about your justice system. But I have faith in you two. Let's try this case."

CHAPTER 19
EXHUMED

Miranda powered down her Kindle and returned it to its protective case. She should have brought her earphones so she could listen to an audiobook. Reading was impossible with the constant noise. How in the world could the players concentrate?

They had planned this trip the previous weekend. Miranda would accompany Chad to his speed chess tournament in Laurel, Maryland. After that, they would head north. Miranda wanted to see the special exhibit at the Baltimore Aquarium. They would have dinner at Phillip's on the Harborplace in Baltimore before returning to D.C.

After the unexpected decision yesterday to launch an exhumation, Miranda thought she might have to bow out.

Miranda had been tasked with contacting Dr. Osborne, the pathologist the firm regularly used as an expert witness. She would see if Osborne could fly to Austin, the city with a major airport closest to Parker's hometown. Osborne would need to find an available lab in which to harvest the tissue samples as soon as the body arrived via ambulance, which could be as early as Sunday morning.

It was late afternoon when Miranda called Osborne. She assumed she would leave a message and, if she were lucky, he would call back the next day. Miranda got through to Osborne right away, however. So, after she made the arrangements with Osborne, Miranda left the office and went home to get ready for the Baltimore trip.

Then, Friday evening, Miranda got the call from Aaron. Having volunteered to talk to Parker about the exhumation, Aaron had stopped by Parker's apartment after work.

"Parker has taken a turn for the worse," Aaron reported tersely.

"Oh, no, I was right the first time," Miranda moaned. "Even the idea of exhuming that body was too much for him."

"No, no, that's not it," Aaron said testily. "Parker understood immediately. And you should have seen the look on his face when it dawned on him that his brother might still be alive today. 'I can't think of anything I'd rather do before I die than see John again,' Parker said."

"Then what's wrong with him?" Miranda asked.

"It's the disease, Miranda," Aaron said gruffly. "I called an ambulance."

"Oh, dear," Miranda said, "is he ..."

"He's alive," Aaron interrupted her. "The ambulance took him to Georgetown because it was the closest hospital. The doctors put Parker on emergency dialysis."

"But that's dangerous, too," Miranda objected. "Parker's blood pressure will soar. If that happens, he could die of a stroke."

"He's sedated," Aaron responded. "I talked to the doctors at Georgetown and insisted they call the VA to get Parker's history. Given Parker's complications with dialysis, they sedated him."

"What's the prognosis?" Miranda asked, ignoring the lump in her throat.

"The doctors will get him back on his feet with dialysis," Aaron explained. "They won't be able to sedate him for ongoing dialysis treatment, though. Sustained sedation is known to cause neurological damage."

"Parker will be back to his dilemma," Miranda said quietly. "He dies of dialysis-induced PTSD or kidney failure. He'll stick with his choice to give up the dialysis, I'm sure, despite this latest scare."

Saturday morning Miranda called the hospital. The nurse told her that Parker was sleeping peacefully, out of danger for the time being.

So, now Miranda sat on a hard, plastic chair parked against the wall of a chilly ballroom in a suburban Holiday Inn. Her ears rang with the arrhythmic clatter of palms slapping chess clocks. Fifty pairs of competitors, positioned across from each other at card tables placed in rows across the ballroom, sped through their one-minute rounds.

Miranda could see Chad's blonde head bent over his board. She smiled. Chad had not promised Miranda that she would enjoy watching the tournament, she told herself. He only said that it would be quick.

Indeed, less than an hour after they had entered the ballroom, the event seemed to be winding down. Players stood, here and there, stretched, and wandered towards the exit. Soon, only a handful of people were still playing. Chad was one of them, Miranda was pleased to see. Finally, with only two other tables still occupied, Chad rose. He walked over to where Miranda sat.

"How'd it go?" Miranda asked.

Chad shrugged. "I've had better days," he answered, "and worse. Do you want the blow-by-blow?"

"No," Miranda blurted. "I mean, no, thank you," she added.

Chad laughed. "Fair enough," he said. "Let's head to the aquarium."

An hour later, Miranda and Chad walked through the entrance of the darkened exhibit hall. Miranda stopped, entranced. The floor-to-ceiling tanks lining the room pulsed with irregular globes of light in a dazzling array of colors: Azure, coral, sky blue, daffodil yellow, lavender, deep purple, each species of jellyfish in a different hue designed for its specific habitat.

"Aren't they gorgeous?" Miranda marveled, taking Chad's hand. They turned to the left, starting their tour around the hall.

At the last tank before the exit, they stopped at the Blue Blubber fish tank. They stood with noses an inch from the glass wall of the tank, Chad's a good six inches above Miranda's. Mesmerized, they watched the creatures drift by, diaphanous bells ballooning in and out, propelling the fish, randomly, it seemed, through their watery, rectangular home.

"Yes," Chad answered, "beautiful creatures. Humbling, too. They look so fragile and helpless. Yet, they've been around an awful lot longer than we have. Notwithstanding our big brains and opposable thumbs, the jellyfish will probably outlast *homo sapiens*, too. If nothing else gets us first, we'll kill ourselves off."

Miranda poked Chad lightly in the waist, where she knew he was ticklish. "Don't be such a party pooper," she teased. "We're on holiday on this lovely spring day. Don't remind me that Armageddon may be right around the corner."

"On holiday?" Chad asked. "With all due respect to the old girl, nobody holidays in Baltimore!"

Miranda laughed. "Okay, that was a stretch. But you get my point."

"Yes, Miranda, got it," Chad said. "Lips sealed on anything gloom and doom. Speaking of lips ..." He leaned down and kissed her. "Yours are so beautiful," he whispered.

Miranda, blushing, reached up and lightly stroked Chad's generous lower lip with her thumb. She rose on tiptoe to return the favor of his kiss when a burst of giggling interrupted her. Miranda turned quickly. Three girls stood at the entrance to the room. Preteens, Miranda surmised, from their t-shirts stretched across flat chests and denim shorts reaching modestly to mid-knee.

The girls, catching Miranda's look, averted their eyes. Then, huddling together, they giggled again.

Their private interlude over, Miranda suggested they leave for the restaurant. The couple opted to walk from the aquarium to Phillip's, Baltimore's iconic seafood restaurant, where their reserved table awaited them.

The Harborplace was not what it used to be, Miranda thought. Twenty years ago, throngs of locals and tourists would have crowded this outdoor urban mall, shopping and dining and circling the magicians and comedians and classical violinists performing for coins and one-dollar bills tossed into a hat. Now, the brick walkways were virtually empty. Shopping online, Miranda supposed.

Chad and Miranda arrived at the restaurant at 6:30 p.m. and were promptly ushered to their table. Their waitress provided menus and drinks. Both ordered the restaurant's signature crab cakes.

As they waited for their food, Miranda asked Chad how his work was going. She knew she would get a stock answer. "Fine," or "slow this week," would be about it. Miranda thought it polite to ask, anyway. Tonight, Chad's response was "good."

Chad had a consulting practice in digital forensics. His clients engaged Chad to detect vulnerabilities in their software systems, avenues for attack by hackers, and patch any potential holes.

The information Chad collected for his clients could not get into the wrong hands. Not to a business competitor or a self-taught Albanian sleuth looking for mission-critical data to steal and hold for ransom. Therefore, Chad was required to sign nondisclosure agreements, the stringent and punitive terms of which rivaled a Mafia family's oath of omertá.

With that topic out of the way, Miranda brought Chad up to date on her week at work. They chatted briefly about local news. Their food arrived, and they began their meal.

Miranda took a bite of her crab. "Hmm, delicious," she crooned. "You know, I should order take-out crab cakes for Parker. He loves them."

"Sure, good idea, honey," Chad responded.

"You know, Marlon was spot on yesterday," Miranda observed, "when he said why not try to find out what happened to John. I had a ton of questions, but only the answers to two of them really matter. Is John still alive? And if he is, can we find him?"

Chad nodded. "And those two questions collapse into one," he said.

Miranda's forehead knotted. Chad got the point.

"We start looking," he continued. "We find him alive, or we find him dead."

Miranda shook her head, suppressing a smile. She was beginning to think she loved this man. Yet, he was a bit of an odd duck. Chad was right, but it was a strange way to put it. No need to go there, though, Miranda thought. Instead, she waved at their waiter, who was conveniently close and with a bottle of wine in his hand. Miranda motioned for him to pour them both another glass.

"I fear John died a long time ago," Miranda said after the waiter left them, "because he never reached out to Parker."

"Or," Chad proposed, "John is alive, but chose not to communicate with his brother because he hated Parker. After all, Parker foiled John's plans to avoid the draft."

"Yeah," Miranda responded, "maybe. On the other hand, John and Parker were close when they were boys, and it's hard to believe John's anger would survive all those decades. Parker was John's only family."

"Don't forget Roberta," Chad added, "assuming John knew he had fathered a child."

"John never contacted her either," Miranda said. She sighed. "But, if by chance John is alive, finding him should be simple, unless he's living off the grid in a cave somewhere. Thanks to you. You can find and follow his digital footprint."

Miranda knew that anyone who used the internet left a data trail that could be harvested and analyzed. A skilled analyst had a decent chance of identifying the person behind the data. Neither Miranda nor anyone else at the firm would have any idea how to go about this. Chad, on the other hand, had demonstrated time and again that anything digital was like an open book to him.

"As you well know, I can't do that, Miranda," Chad said. "I'm under lockdown from the National Security Administration. The consequences of violating that order would be immediate and severe. How could you even think of asking me to take that chance?" he asked, a note of hurt in his voice.

"I'm sorry," Miranda said immediately, reaching over to put her hand over Chad's. "I never would, I swear," she said vehemently. "But I thought you could fish around in the digital waters, without going too deep, and it would be perfectly legal."

Chad nodded, apparently mollified. "That's generally true, Miranda," he said, "but I see a big problem with that route in this case. To fish around, as you call it, and stay well on the right side of the law would take time. Time Parker doesn't have."

Miranda was silent for a moment. "Which all means we'll have to do this the old-fashioned way," she said.

"What do you mean?" Chad asked.

"We find the answers to John the way lawyers find answers to any other question," Miranda replied. "We'll collect the relevant documents and interview the knowledgeable witnesses."

"If there are any," Chad replied. "Any still alive, that is."

CHAPTER 20
ENCODED

Marlon parked his Volvo in the lot under the Kennedy Center, empty now save for a random service vehicle parked here and there. He and Allen had tickets to the Washington Opera Company's production of *Aida* later that evening. Marlon would walk to the nearby Watergate Hotel to join Allen, who had worked late, for a drink before the curtain rose.

Allen had already ordered. The waiter delivered their martinis as Marlon took a seat beside Allen at the bar. Carefully lifting the brimming glasses, the men toasted, then took their first sips.

"The body will be delivered to the morgue in Austin late tonight," Marlon explained. "Dr. Osborne flew to Texas this afternoon. He'll retrieve the tissue samples tomorrow morning."

"Wow, that was fast," Allen commented.

Marlon nodded his agreement. "All the pieces fell into place quickly."

"What do you think happened?" Allen asked. "To John, that is, in Vietnam, if he's not in that grave?"

Marlon shrugged. "It seems to me that John must have abandoned his post," Marlon answered. "Thrown down his gun and run off into the hills. How else can it be that he disappears, never to be seen or heard from again by anybody?"

"Or, he could have gone missing in action," Allen observed.

"Except for the lovely Roberta," Marlon reminded him.

Allen took a sip of his martini. "That's right," he said, "and Roberta grew up in the Philly suburbs. That makes it likely that Roberta was born in the States, if not in Pennsylvania. If the baby was conceived here, John must have come back to the States."

"I think you're right," Marlon responded. "The mother might have met John elsewhere, of course, while traveling. It seems improbable, though, because not many Americans went abroad back then, except for the wealthy and the occasional adventurous hippie. It's most likely that John made it home."

"That must have been quite a journey," Allen noted. "I wonder how he did it?"

"Went to sea, in the dark night of his soul, like Ishmael," Marlon proposed.

"In plain English, Marlon," Allen commanded playfully.

"Found a position as a crewman, no questions asked, and shipped out on a freighter," Marlon rephrased.

"Could have worked, I suppose," Allen said. "Our borders were far less secure back then. John crosses the Pacific on his freighter. He disembarks with the rest of the crew at the port in Oakland. Then, he disappears into the city streets. I wonder what happened to him after that?"

"He stayed hidden, scraping together a living somehow," Marlon answered. "I looked it up. There is no statute of limitations on the prosecution of an active-duty soldier for desertion. If he did desert, John was a criminal, subject to arrest at any time."

"But didn't the draft dodgers get amnesty?" Allen asked. "Not right away, if I remember correctly, but eventually?"

"President Carter gave those who fled to Canada amnesty," Marlon answered. "But not deserters."

"If he was hiding from the law, that might explain why John never got in touch with Parker," Allen said. "John feared the authorities might discover his identity if he corresponded with anyone."

"Maybe," Marlon replied, "although that seems an unreasonable fear. John wasn't exactly on the FBI Most Wanted list. Who would be looking? I think it more likely that John was afraid Parker would turn him in to the military police. Think about it. Parker served his full tour in Vietnam. What was he likely to think about a man who deserted? Even if that man was his brother? Parker was disloyal to his brother once already, remember? Parker told their father about John's plans to evade the draft."

Allen nodded, withdrew an olive on its toothpick from his martini glass, popped it in his mouth, chewed, and swallowed. "If that's how it all happened, John has been in limbo for decades, sadly," Allen said.

Marlon nodded. "For different reasons, but, otherwise, like poor Paco."

"Speaking of Paco," Allen replied, "I wonder why he never got his Mexican passport? John had no choice but to stay underground, I suppose. He was in America and subject to American criminal law. But Paco had committed no crime in Mexico. He could have become a Mexican citizen and end his exile, I would think. I wonder why he never did?"

"I asked him that question," Marlon answered. "Paco looked into it. The only path to Mexican citizenship for him was to marry a Mexican. He never met the right woman. He could have paid a woman to wed him. Even with his teacher's salary, Paco was wealthy compared to so many in the country. Paco chose not to do so. Not again would he take advantage of an innocent person for his own selfish ends, he said."

* * *

Betsy rose from the desk in her apartment's tiny, second bedroom that she used as a home office. She switched on the overhead light as she passed through the doorway and walked through the living room into her kitchen.

She opened the refrigerator door and retrieved a half-empty bottle of white wine. It was Saturday night, the curtains on her opened windows luffed with a warm breeze, and a glass of wine seemed the perfect accompaniment to the evening.

Betsy had been troubled and intrigued by her conversation with Jeff yesterday. Jeff's unexpected and vicious response to her inquiry about Mauricio hurt her feelings, but it also sparked her curiosity. There was a mystery to Jeff's relationship with Mauricio. Jeff had never kept secrets from Betsy. She needed to know why he was now.

Her interest in finding out about Glen Hadley was not so pressing. Still, it would give her pleasure to solve the puzzle of the dead soldier reported missing in action. Also, it would give Jeff peace of mind to know that Glen's remains were ultimately returned to his parents, Betsy thought. At least she had assumed the mistake had been discovered and rectified sometime in the intervening years.

Betsy took the first step in tracking down Glen Hadley during yesterday's lawyers' meeting. She asked Marlon to check with Paco. Would Paco be willing to send Betsy what he had in his library on those missing in action from the Vietnam War?

"Sure, I'd be happy to ask him," Marlon sounded puzzled. "May I ask why, though?"

"I read an article the other day about the recent repatriation from Vietnam of the remains of a soldier who went missing fifty years ago," Betsy answered. "Piqued my interest."

Betsy knew she was more likely to get what she needed from Paco if she asked for information specifically about Glen Hadley. She had discovered the name in Jeff's private files, however. It may not technically have violated her obligation to keep that information to herself by disclosing Glen's name. Still, the thought of doing so made Betsy feel vaguely uneasy. She would try casting a wider net, first.

Betsy took a sip of her wine. She stared out her kitchen window at the tree-lined street four floors below as she pondered what she had learned from the documents Paco had sent her.

Paco's library was truly impressive, or Betsy had gotten lucky. Amid a welter of other information, Betsy found news of Glen Hadley.

Shortly after Glen was reported as missing, in the fall of 1973, his parents joined the National League of Families of American Prisoners and Missing in Southeast Asia. The Hadleys rose to some prominence in the organization.

As a part of their leadership role, Marita and Joséph Hadley provided their contact information in the newsletters circulated to League members. Paco joined the League and subscribed to the newsletter. Paco wrote to the Hadleys, explaining his avocation of cataloging the war, with an eye more towards the personal details than the strategies of generals or movements of armies. The Hadleys agreed to contribute if, and when, they had any news to report.

In 1976, Paco received word from the Hadleys. They had received a letter from a veteran named Jeff Howard. In the letter, Jeff explained who he was and why he was writing. Jeff claimed to have been by Glen's side when he was tragically killed. Glen had died in the middle of an active battlefield, and the fact that he had somehow been reported as MIA was inexplicable.

It was a kind letter, the Hadleys explained to Paco. Jeff extolled their son, a medic, for his courage and dedication to the wounded and dying men. Glen had struggled under impossible conditions yet saved the lives of any number of men. Jeff expressed his sincere condolences.

The Hadleys had no reason to doubt Jeff's good intentions. Still, Marita and Joséph decided Jeff's recollection was not enough. Not enough to convince them that their son was irrevocably gone. They chose hope, instead.

Two years later, the League received an envelope, postmarked in Austin, Texas. The envelope bore no return address. The envelope contained no letter. Instead, it held a grainy, black-and-white photograph of a downed soldier. When the Hadleys saw the picture, their hope died.

The Hadleys remained active in the League, searching for information about their son's body. They prayed that the United States and Hanoi's protracted diplomatic maneuvering would bear fruit, and their son's body would be returned to them for burial.

Joséph died in 2015 with no news of his son and only child. As of Paco's last email correspondence with Marita a year ago, she was still waiting in vain.

Betsy had no doubt that Marita would remember Jeff's letter. Anything to do with her son would have been burned into her mind. So, Betsy would bank on Jeff's kindness to the Hadleys. She would explain her relationship with Jeff and the project on which she was working. It would be tricky to conjure an explanation for exploring the circumstances surrounding Glen's death in that connection, Betsy thought, but she would come up with something.

She returned to her office, wine glass in hand. She opened Outlook, typed in Marita's address, and began to compose.

An hour later, Betsy had a headache and another problem to solve. She had confirmed that Jeff was hiding something about Mauricio. But what?

On a hunch, she had logged into the library of files on Jeff and found the section containing Jeff's correspondence with Vincent. Vincent knew everything, Jeff had told Betsy. Whatever Jeff was not telling Betsy, he would have told Vincent.

The letters and, in the last twenty years, email and texts between Jeff and Vincent were confidential and not accessible to the public. Not even a determined reporter could get in, absent illegal finagling. Betsy's job was digging for dirt that could be used to harm Jeff, and by reading this correspondence, she was straying from her appointed task.

Betsy had to know why Jeff did not trust her, for the first time ever. She had to clear the air, one way or another. She set aside her guilt. Jeff had forced her into this.

Jeff and Vincent's correspondence began when Jeff started law school. The timing made sense. The two were roommates as undergraduates at the University of Virginia. They had no need to correspond in writing until both moved on.

Betsy read quickly through the limited number of letters written as the two men began building their careers and families. Betsy knew Jeff's story well, and Vincent's was straightforward. He had gone into politics right out of college, landing a job as a staffer on the Hill with a junior representative from Virginia, and there he stayed. Vincent never married.

The men wrote little about their war experiences. Betsy supposed that was to be expected. Vincent had a cushy war with his job at the Pentagon. Jeff, although he apparently came through unscathed, no doubt wanted nothing more than to put his year in the jungle behind him.

The one exception to this silence involved Company 19. Jeff reported to Vincent that he took the train from Charlottesville to D.C. to attend his company's first reunion in 1976. More news of the men from Jeff's unit followed.

Betsy was offended, then amused that she could be offended after all these years, as she read the correspondence about her and her parents. Vincent advised Jeff not to take the Thornhills' case. He also warned against Jeff's taking Betsy in. Vincent feared that the little girl would be an unnecessary distraction. Jeff needed to focus on his work and his relationship with his wife. Helen, longing for a baby and taking so long to conceive, was unhappy, Vincent had written. Jeff needed to be there for Helen, not rearing a stranger's child.

The first anomaly appeared in a letter from Jeff to Vincent in September 1983. Two paragraphs were undecipherable. The strings of letters, separated by spaces and punctuation marks, had the appearance of the English language. Yet the words, if that is what they were, made no sense. Betsy was no expert, but whatever Jeff had written, it was in code.

Huh, Betsy thought. Was this a joke of some kind? Somehow, though, the scrambled letters did not elicit a humorous feeling. Jeff was intentionally hiding something. The content on either side of the unreadable passages gave no clue what that something might be. And why, she wondered, would Jeff be going to such lengths in private correspondence?

Betsy scrolled down. During the two months after the first encoded section, the correspondence was more frequent than normal, and every letter contained an encoded block. Then, fewer letters and none with messages in code. Finally, she found one more, ten years after the first, then nothing for two more years.

Betsy thought for a minute, then scrolled quickly to the file for last week's correspondence. It contained dozens of email messages. Three included a section in code. Why had the code been resurrected, she wondered? What happened last week?

Intrigued, Betsy returned to her new mantra. Vincent knew everything. She composed her last email for the night.

CHAPTER 21
AN OLD BUDDY

Sunday

Will glanced at his watch. He would have to leave soon to be on time for his meeting with Betsy. He had decided to walk rather than take a cab. It was a bit of a hike, twenty minutes or so, but he needed the exercise.

"Let me read you back that last question," Will said into the phone on his desk, which was on speaker.

Will had come into the office earlier that morning to finalize his cross-examination of the witness, Ralph Stallman, whom Baylie would call first thing Monday morning. Stallman, a general contractor, would testify regarding the industry's standard of care for protecting persons working on multistory sites from falls.

Stallman had worked as an inspector for the Federal Occupational Health and Safety Administration before turning to private industry. His affiliation with the agency overseeing the safety of the entire workforce would impress the jury, Will thought. Will was, therefore, particularly exacting in crafting his cross and had asked José to review his draft. Will could have consulted his own expert on the standard of care issue. José was equally expert, however, and José's advice would be free of charge.

The men came to an agreement on the wording of the questions. Will was preparing to ring off when José raised another topic.

"I talked to Dad," José said. "I understand you convinced him it was a good idea to explore the possibility of regularizing his immigration status. Dad also reluctantly agreed to let you approach Jeff Howard, a senator from Virginia, about it."

"Yeah," Will replied. "Howard and Betsy are very close. He took her in, practically adopted Betsy, when her parents got in trouble. Long story. Anyway, Howard has clout, and he may soon have even more. He's running for the U.S. Senate. And he served in the same unit as Mauricio in Vietnam."

"I understand your reasoning," José said. "But to make that connection work, you'll have to name names. You'll be admitting to a stranger that Dad is here illegally. I don't like it."

"Mauricio balked, too," Will responded. "More so than I would have thought. 'Don't you trust a comrade-in-arms?' I asked him. He hemmed and hawed. 'It's too much to ask,' Mauricio finally said."

"It's a lot, anyway," José replied, "to go out on a limb for an undocumented person. Especially now, given that Howard's in a high-profile election."

"Jeff could do it through behind-the-scenes maneuvering and not anything public," Will responded. "Anyway, if he can't or won't, he'll say so. And remember, I'm running this by Betsy, first. If she thinks there's any risk to Mauricio, she'll tell me."

Will did not vocalize his next thought. He hoped he could count on Betsy. Where her loyalties lay was not yet clear.

José's sigh came through the speaker loud and clear. "I trust your judgment, Will," José said, "but be very careful. Sleeping dogs, you know."

Will powered down his computer and rose from his desk. "Yes, I know the expression," he said. "Here's another one. Nothing ventured, nothing gained."

Will breathed a sigh of relief when he heard the chuckle for which he had been angling. The tension in the air eased.

"Fair enough," José conceded. "Anyway, if you have another minute, there was something else I wanted to run by you."

"Yeah, go ahead," Will answered. "I'm meeting Betsy at noon, to talk about Mauricio, in fact, and need to get going. But I can walk and talk and even chew gum at the same time."

José laughed. "A man of many talents," he responded.

A memory had come to him the day before, José explained. It was an unusually warm day for April. Benjy persuaded his father and Mauricio, who had joined them for lunch, to inflate Benjy's plastic wading pool. Mauricio was filling the pool, remarking that Benjy had outgrown the toy and needed to be taught to swim in a real pool. The hose sprang a leak. Mauricio, jeans soaked, emptied his pockets.

Mauricio had set his wallet on the patio wall. His father had to have replaced his wallet many times over the years. Yet, to José, this version looked exactly like the one Mauricio carried when José was a boy. Mauricio had few vanities, but he did buy himself a quality leather wallet, hand-tooled in Mexico, and always the same deep copper shade. The wallet. Suddenly, that episode from long ago sprang into José's mind.

* * *

It was in 1994. José remembered because it happened shortly after his twelfth birthday. His mother was serving José breakfast when his father, dressed for work, entered the kitchen. José could not follow all the quick words in Spanish his father and mother exchanged, but he understood his father had lost a document. An important document.

Mauricio had to go to work, but José's mother got up from the kitchen table and started turning the house upside down. When José returned from school that afternoon, he found his dad sorting through the trash in the bin outside their back door. Later, on his hands and knees, Mauricio crawled across every inch of their small yard, peering into the shorn grass.

After José had finished his homework in his bedroom, he wandered out into the kitchen. His mother stood on a chair, hauling pots she rarely used from the topmost shelves. She handed a cast-iron skillet down to José's waiting hands.

"Careful," Berta said. "It's heavy. You can help us look now, too. Papá has lost his social security card."

José knew what his mother was talking about. He had seen his dad retrieve bills from his open wallet and noticed the social security card tucked behind its clear, plastic sleeve. José had only a vague notion of the card's function. He knew only that it was from the government, and that the government had replaced his father's driver's license when it went missing last year.

"Why the big fuss?" José asked. "Why not just get another one?"

Berta frowned. "It's not that easy, son," she answered. "Trust me on this. We must find this card. And don't tell anybody. This stays in the family."

José, bewildered, nodded. "Okay, momma," he agreed.

"We'll start again in the morning," Mauricio said that evening at dinner, white-faced and grim.

The next day, a Saturday, Mauricio returned to the construction site where he was employed. Mauricio had told his boss, the day before, that he feared he had lost his wedding ring at work. The boss had given Mauricio permission to return to the site on his day off to search for it. The security guard had been alerted. Mauricio left the house at dawn and returned after dark, empty-handed. The search went on at home.

By the following Saturday, José was bored with the routine. Each day after school, homework finished, his job was to find a new place to search for the card, somewhere out-of-the-way they might have missed in the first sweeps. He had run out of ideas, though. By now, he was drifting aimlessly around the house, wishing he were out playing with his friends. José was determined not to complain, though. With the hunt for the card added to her housekeeping job in Bethesda and her daily work in their home, his mother looked increasingly exhausted. His dad's expression fell from worried but determined to pale and haunted as the days went by.

"It's not here," José said as the family sat at the remnants of the lunch his mother had prepared. "There's nowhere else to look. Are you sure it's not at the site?"

"I never thought the card would be there," Mauricio said, "because I never take it out of the house unless I absolutely need it. I looked everywhere, anyway. I also told some of the guys to keep an eye out for my missing ring. If any of them had come across my card, they would have brought it to me. It's not there, either."

"So, what are you going to do?" José asked.

His father sat silently, staring at his only child. Then, he looked over at his wife, who managed a faint smile.

"I'm going into the city," Mauricio said, in a tone José had never heard before. Mauricio pushed himself back from the table, rose, and marched out of the room without another word.

***

Will stopped at the crossing light on Constitution Avenue. He forced his wandering attention back to José's voice.

"José, I think you lost me," Will said. "Why are you telling me all of this?" he asked.

José explained. His mother finally told her confused and worried son that his dad had gone into D.C. to the Library of Congress. There, he would find the phone number he needed. Then, with some luck, his old Army buddy would help him out again.

"Dad received a replacement card in the mail a month later," José continued. "He kept that card in a fireproof safe in the house."

"My parents would not have been worried about losing a counterfeit social security card," José concluded. "I think it was a real card they lost, and it was replaced with another real card by that Army buddy. That's why E-Verify confirms the number on it as legitimate. I don't know the 'how' or 'why' of any of this, but I know the social security card issue was bugging you, and I'm passing on what I remember."

Will thanked José and ended the call. How Mauricio had acquired his almost-genuine card was still a puzzle. The only thing Will knew was that a friend of Mauricio's from his stint in the Army had something to do with it.

Will picked up his pace. Betsy would be waiting for him.

***

Betsy sat on the top step of the Lincoln Memorial. Spread before her, dozens of others also found the steps of the Memorial a comfortable perch. From here, they could enjoy the expansive view east across the reflecting pool, the Washington Monument, and the Mall to the Capitol.

She glanced back at Lincoln's massive head towering behind her. Betsy had stood in front of that statue countless times. Its gaunt, lined face; prominent nose; wide, thin-lipped mouth; and deep-set eyes exuded a grim determination but also weariness, sorrow, and compassion. As she did with every viewing, Betsy marveled at the talent of the sculptor and the character of the great man.

She spotted Will, climbing up towards her. She waved as he approached.

Greetings over, they descended the steps. As they strolled around the block-long, rectangular reflecting pool, Will explained his purpose.

"As you discovered, Mauricio Marquez and Jeff Howard served in the same unit in Vietnam. I don't know if Jeff remembers Mauricio, but I don't think it would matter. Surely Jeff would do what he could to remedy Mauricio's undocumented status, don't you think, Betsy? After all, Mauricio earned his citizenship."

Betsy glanced up sharply. Will's passionate tone surprised her.

She had been with Aaron's firm for more than a year now. Betsy chided herself for not socializing with her associates as much as they did with each other. Still, she had spent enough time with them to know something about her colleagues' characters. Practical, level-headed, mild-mannered Will was a stickler for following the rules. His plea on behalf of Mauricio took her aback.

Dismay replaced her initial reaction. Will's implication was clear. He wanted Betsy to enlist Jeff's support. Jeff had told Betsy in no uncertain terms that he wanted nothing to do with Mauricio Marquez.

Betsy did not want to turn Will down cold. Finesse was in order, she decided. She would try to open Will's eyes to the hopelessness of what he was trying to accomplish.

"You are talking about something that happened decades ago, Will," Betsy began. "Whether it was Mauricio or some clerk at the Pentagon who screwed up, it's way too late to figure it out and fix it."

Will waved her off impatiently. "I don't see it that way at all," he argued. "Someone only needs to confirm Mauricio's service record. He was entitled to citizenship. End of story."

"You're ignoring the fact that Mauricio's presence here is illegal," Betsy retorted. "He may have been entitled to citizenship, but the fact is that he didn't get it. Mauricio won't get his citizenship handed to him now after fifty years of violating immigration law."

They reached 17th Street and stopped at the light. White tents crowded the green expanse of the National Mall in front of them. Each offered different events for the entertainment or edification of D.C. denizens and tourists alike. Choices included church services, yoga classes, a food tasting sponsored by a handful of local restaurants, speeches by political activists, and try-outs for open mic night at a new comedy club on H Street. Hundreds of people wandered through the maze of activities and jogged or strolled down the broad pathways flanking the Mall.

When the "walk" light flashed, Betsy and Will crossed onto the Mall. They headed north, then turned east toward the Capitol.

"I empathize with Mauricio, I really do," Betsy said. "But he made his decision. The decision to break the law. I don't see rewarding him for that, and I would have thought you would see it the same way, Will."

They stopped suddenly as a child ran across the sidewalk in front of them. The little boy clutched the string at the end of which a bright, red balloon bobbed. Hard behind him trotted his mother, presumably, a young woman in a polo shirt and jeans, hair clutched under a blue bandana. She called out an apology. Will smiled and waved her on.

"People break the law all the time," Will began, resuming the conversation. "Have you ever exceeded the speed limit? How many people cheat on their income taxes? Did you know," Will continued, warming to his subject, "that the maximum penalty for illegal entry is six months in prison? Impeding the delivery of the mail carries the same penalty. For crossing a state line with the intent to sell a denture not made by a licensed dentist, you can get up to a year in prison."

Betsy laughed. "Anyone who's gone to law school knows that the criminal code contains some real oddballs," she said.

Will smiled. "That's true, but the point is that, according to the letter of the law, Mauricio's crime was minor. A misdemeanor."

"Jaywalking is a misdemeanor, too," Betsy responded, "but doing it doesn't hurt anybody. A lot of people think illegal immigrants take jobs away from lawful citizens. Also, too much money, taxpayer dollars, is spent to provide those people public services."

"That's one side of the story," Will said, "and both may be true under some circumstances. I put my money on the other side of the argument, however. I'm convinced by the data produced by economists and sociologists showing that immigration, legal or not, is a boon to the U.S. economy."

As they passed by, the young couple sitting on a bench rose and departed. "Let's snag it, shall we?" Will asked.

"Sure," Betsy said.

As Will and Betsy took their seats, a stilt walker in a red, white, and blue Uncle Sam costume strode by their bench. Will tipped his head back to get a full view of the entertainer's top hat swaying to and fro, twenty feet above the ground. "I don't understand how they can do that," he marveled, before returning to the topic at hand.

"Remember, we're not talking about some generality," Will continued. "This is not 'the immigration issue' on a list of talking points for a political rally. We're talking about a friend, a man who contributed far more than he took. Mauricio and his son started a business, creating jobs. Mauricio pays taxes owed and contributes to the social security fund. That's why he bought a fake social security card when he didn't get his citizenship, you know. Yet, he'll never see a penny of it back."

"I'm sure Mauricio would have been a model citizen, if he were a citizen," Betsy conceded. "But you can't get around the fact that he's not. Therefore, he has no right to be here."

Will touched Betsy's shoulder lightly. She turned to face him.

"I'm a rule follower, too, Betsy," he said. "I don't even speed, ever. I have never cheated on my income taxes. But when my wife's life was threatened, I would have broken any law to save her. Without any hesitation."

"I might do the same," Betsy admitted. "Commit a crime out of love, that is. I finally figured out that's what my mother did. She didn't accompany my father to the neo-Nazi bar that day because she was politically inspired. She did it for my father."

Will nodded.

"I would expect to be punished, though, regardless of my motivation," Betsy continued. "It's a lifelong regret that I grew up with my mother in prison, but I don't begrudge the system for that."

"Bah, humbug," Will said, following up on the note of uncertainty he detected in Betsy's voice. "Your mother didn't deserve prison for life. Nor your father. They didn't intend that man to die. The system I believe in dispenses a just punishment, tempered with mercy, not an eye for an eye."

"And Mauricio's just punishment?" Betsy asked. "What did he pay for his crime?"

"A lifetime of fear and uncertainty," Will answered promptly. "Of jumping up, heart in throat, when there came a knock at the door. Of living in the rigidly circumscribed space where secrets were safe, making few friends, staying in the neighborhood. Of knowing you'd gain no respect, no matter how hard you worked, because you were disposable. As José Antonio Vargas put it in *Dear America, Notes of an Undocumented Citizen*, of being treated like a thing, not a human being."

Betsy stared at Will. She was out of arguments. She could lie, or put Will off, for now. Maybe something would happen to change Jeff's mind.

"I'll think about it," she said.

CHAPTER 22
A GENEROUS GESTURE

"Remember, cup to lip, not lip to cup," Parker cautioned Lydia, who was sitting across from Parker at their kitchen table, eating a bowl of soup. "It goes down better that way," Parker said, nodding his encouragement.

Miranda, leaning against the kitchen doorframe, watching Parker tend his roommate, smiled fondly.

Miranda had come by at 5:00 p.m. to find Parker preparing an early supper for Lydia. Miranda offered to run out and get Chinese from the take-out place around the corner. Parker thanked her but declined the offer. Unless Miranda wanted to join them, he and Lydia would be fine with what they had at home. Miranda demurred. She would dine later.

Parker reached across the table for the paper napkin he had placed beside Lydia's plate. He carefully wiped off the dribble of soup running down her chin. Lydia looked up from her bowl and smiled at him. Parker beamed.

He glanced over at Miranda. "Thank goodness for Campbell's tomato soup," Parker said. "On a bad day, Lydia has little appetite. But she'll always eat at least half a bowl of her favorite soup."

Lydia finished her lunch. Parker accompanied her to the living room, Miranda following. Miranda noticed how closely Parker hovered over Lydia. She wondered if Lydia had taken another fall recently.

Parker helped Lydia settle into the wooden rocking chair Parker had found at Goodwill and refinished, thinking its gentle motion would soothe her. He turned the radio on the mantle to the classical music station and smiled with satisfaction as Lydia began rocking gently, eyes closed.

Parker motioned for Miranda, and they returned to the kitchen.

"Are you sure I can't make you a sandwich?" Parker asked.

"No, thanks," Miranda answered, "but you go ahead and eat. You know, I just realized it's been over a month since I've visited. I've been too busy, I guess. Anyway, how's Lydia doing?"

"She has more bad days, I'm afraid," Parker answered. He paused to open the refrigerator door, pull out a loaf of white bread and a package of bologna, and fix his sandwich. Miranda sat across the kitchen table from Parker as he ate.

"What happens on a bad day?" Miranda asked.

"On a bad day, Lydia can't do everyday things," Parker said, sighing heavily. "Once, I turned from the counter to see her staring at the fork in her hand, rotating the tines slowly. She'd forgotten what she was supposed to do with it."

"Oh, dear," Miranda said.

"On bad days, I help her into the kitchen, get her seated, and put a plate of food in front of her. With every bite, she slumps lower in her chair, until she's practically eating off the plate. I understand why she does that. Her hand shakes. The food falls off the spoon before she can get it all the way to her mouth. But I'm terrified she's going to choke while eating all bent over like that."

"Do you know how to do the Heimlich maneuver on her if she does choke?" Miranda asked.

"Well, I took a first aid course at the YMCA," Parker answered. "So, yes, theoretically. But I pray I never have to try to save Lydia from choking to death in front of me."

Miranda stared fixedly at Parker. All this on top of his own failing health was too much for the man, she thought.

"You need some help around here, Parker," Miranda said. "I can call …"

"Oh, I have plenty of help," Parker interrupted. "We're doing fine. Home health comes in once a week to bathe Lydia. Thank goodness for Medicare, which pays for the service. Then there's Mrs. Lopez down the hall. She stays with Lydia when I'm in the hospital. Says she's glad to do it."

Miranda had met Parker's elderly neighbor who, like Parker, hailed from Texas. Parker had befriended Mrs. Lopez after her husband died. Parker fixed Mrs. Lopez's leaky faucet and changed the bulbs in her ceiling fan.

"When Mrs. Lopez found out Lydia was coming to stay," Parker continued, "she said she would be happy to help when I needed her, provided I took care of her plumbing. She was kidding. Mrs. Lopez likes Lydia. And she's lonely."

"Speaking of hospital," Miranda said, "I think you should reconsider your decision not to get treatment. You were so sick Friday. I'm ..." Blinking hard, Miranda told herself to get a grip.

Parker, rising, came around the table and put his arm around Miranda. "Don't cry, sugar," Parker said. "I may be sick, but I'd rather be sick than crazy with PTSD. I'm no good for you or Lydia in that condition. And everybody's got to die sometime."

Miranda took a deep breath. "But not yet. Not if we find John."

Her phone rang. Marlon's number appeared in the display. Miranda answered.

"Hi, Miranda, is this a bad time to talk?"

"Not the best. I'm at Parker's."

Marlon softened his tone, apparently hearing the tremble in her voice.

"I've got good news, though," Marlon said. "About the exhumation. Why don't you put me on speaker so you can both hear what I have to say."

Miranda complied.

"Dr. Osborne flew back from Austin this morning," Marlon's voice filled the small room. "Jim met him at the airport and retrieved the tissue samples. Jim will take them and those from Parker and Roberta to the lab. We should know by tomorrow morning whether the body is John's."

***

By Sunday, mid-morning, Vincent had not responded to Betsy's email. Irritated, she texted him. First, Jeff bit her head off when she mentioned

Mauricio. Now, she was getting the cold shoulder from Vincent. Why had Betsy inexplicably become *persona non grata* with those two?

Betsy was on her way to the subway stop, having just left Will at the Mall, when Vincent finally called. He began with a perfunctory apology.

"Betsy, sorry for the delay in getting back to you, but we have a serious situation here. It's taken all our attention."

"What do you mean by 'a situation?'" Betsy asked. "Should I be concerned? Can I help in any way?"

"No, we're on it," Vincent replied curtly. "Why did you need to talk? I presume it's about your project for Jeff. Did you find anything?"

"Sort of," Betsy answered, "although I guess it's my own curiosity as much as anything. Why is Jeff so touchy about a soldier with whom he served in Vietnam named Mauricio Marquez?"

Vincent responded promptly, initially surprising Betsy. But, as Vincent talked, Betsy realized he and Jeff had planned this.

"Look," Vincent said, "Jeff hasn't wanted to tell you about it, but now's the time."

Ten years after the war, Mauricio, out of the blue, called Jeff. Mauricio told Jeff that he had not gotten his citizenship papers. Mauricio had been flying under the radar, but with the Reagan administration cracking down on undocumented immigrants, Mauricio feared he would be caught and deported. Mauricio had a wife and a baby son and the life he had created for all of them in the States. Would Jeff help him?

"Jeff was torn," Vincent explained. "It was unfair that Mauricio hadn't gotten the citizenship he deserved. However, his staying in the States illegally was still a crime. Yet, we decided to do something."

"I knew a guy who knew a guy in the right place in the Social Security Administration," Vincent continued. "A 'clerical error,' so to speak, got Mauricio a card with a number that was, for most intents and purposes, legitimate. Only scrutiny by a qualified expert would expose the card as fraudulent."

"Why did Jeff feel it necessary to keep this from me?" Betsy asked. "It was a kind and generous thing to do."

"Think again, Betsy," Vincent's voice had sharpened. "We committed criminal fraud getting that card. You can't say a word to anyone about this. And that's why you can't mention Jeff's name to Mauricio. Jeff must avoid any connection between them. Otherwise, Jeff's role in getting that card could be exposed."

Betsy thought for a minute. Vincent's reasoning was not making sense. Mauricio would be the last person to spill the beans on Jeff. So, what was the risk in her talking to him?

Yet, Vincent was right. Getting that card may have been a generous gesture, but it was also a crime. Betsy could not imagine why Jeff would go so far out on a limb, even for a fellow veteran. Something else was going on here. Vincent had delivered his lines, though. He was not going to tell her anything more.

"One other thing," Betsy said into her phone. "It'll take only a minute. Why did you and Jeff encode your private correspondence?"

If Vincent was surprised at the question, he hid it well. He laughed.

"It was a habit we picked up, almost as a joke," he said. "Whenever we were discussing women or affairs of the heart, we camouflaged the subject to keep it safe from any prying eyes, even if no other person was ever likely to see it."

"What cipher did you use?" Betsy asked. "A book cipher? One-time pad?"

"You never fail to surprise me, Betsy," Vincent said, chuckling. "In what class at MIT did you learn about ciphers?"

Betsy laughed. "I know no more about ciphers than what I've read in John Le Carré novels," she protested. "I presume I can learn, though, just as you and Jeff apparently did. I would enjoy trying my hand at deciphering if you would tell me what you used."

"Back off," Vincent barked.

Betsy stopped in her tracks. Another rebuke.

"Dig all you want, elsewhere," Vincent said tersely, "but our love lives are none of your business." He ended the call.

Betsy had reached the Farragut North Metro stop. The train arrived, crowded with tourists sporting Washington Redskin caps, backpacks, khaki shorts, and sneakers. Betsy boarded, her thoughts turning to Vincent's contrived explanation for the code.

Betsy had known pragmatic, hard-headed Vincent for a very long time. She could not imagine him being concerned if information about his love life was leaked, if he even had a love life. Vincent was wedded to politics. For different reasons, she thought Jeff would not be terribly bothered, either. Another secret.

An idea came to her.

Betsy knew Miranda's boyfriend, Chad, was a software sleuth whose job was breaking into computer networks. Betsy suspected that Chad possessed a range of edgy skills, which might include codebreaking. She would call Miranda when she got home.

After exchanging pleasantries, Betsy explained the ostensible reason for her call. A friend who worked in a tech firm needed assistance on a sensitive data security matter. Betsy considered recommending Chad, but she wanted to check with Miranda first.

"Is he trustworthy, do you think?" Betsy asked. "Can Chad keep a secret?"

Miranda laughed out loud. "For a lifetime," she answered, "safe from anyone, even the best-trained ones in the business."

"What do you mean," Betsy asked.

"Not even the federal agencies looking for Russian hackers in the interests of protecting our nation's security could get to Chad's secrets," Miranda assured her, "unless and until he was ready to disclose them."

CHAPTER 23
IF THE BOOT FITS

Trial Day 6

"All rise," intoned the bailiff as Judge Storer bustled into the courtroom. She took her seat on the dais.

The bailiff opened the door to the jury room. The jurors filed in, faces impassive. Will wondered, for a moment, how they had spent their weekend break. Had the jurors obeyed the Judge's admonition that they were forbidden to Google anything about the case, the parties, or the witnesses, or talk to anybody about the case?

Or had the thirty-six-year-old hair stylist complained on her Facebook page about her tedious days in the courtroom last week? Did the oldest woman on the jury, with the close-cropped, gray hair, retired from her job as a secretary at the Department of Housing and Urban Development, look up forecasts on prospects for the construction industry in the D.C. metropolitan area? Perhaps Anna Hinks told her son that the plaintiff in the case was named José Marquez and then listened to him railing about immigrants ruining the country.

On a strategic level, had their tactic of aiming for an all-female jury been a mistake? They made this decision based on the mock trials the firm conducted a month ago.

Three faux juries, eighteen people, were solicited with an offer of a modest stipend. Announcements were posted on local college websites and bulletin boards in church basements. In addition, the associates and staff passed word-of-mouth requests for volunteers to friends and family.

Will presented a stripped-down version of the case to his mock jurors. He called no witnesses but, instead, summarized the expected testimony. Cassandra argued for the defense. At the conclusion, each "juror" was polled with a list of questions ranging from the simple, "who won?" to their impressions of the persuasiveness of specific evidence.

The lawyers expected that the middle-aged, blue-collar, male workers in these mock juries would likely side with José and award him the most money. These men, like José, engaged in hard, physical labor. They faced physical risks in doing so. They should be sympathetic. Instead, these male jurors unanimously found for the defense.

Later, when the lawyers discussed the results of the mock trials, Marlon observed that, on second thought, the reaction of those men made sense. They had to believe that nothing terrible would happen to them on the job if they took due care. Otherwise, if maiming or death could result from some other fool's mistake or just bad luck, the risk would be too high to bear. So, José must not have been careful enough.

Will would try for an all-female jury.

He could not reject a jury candidate solely because he was male, of course, for that would get him a Batson challenge from Baylie. After all, a lawyer could not use his peremptory strikes to eliminate jurors based on their sex, race, religion, or ethnicity. Will got lucky, however, with the line-up of the jury pool and the striking of jurors for cause. He had his female jury, and now he had his doubts.

"Mr. Baylie, you may call your first witness," Judge Storer said, launching the sixth day of the trial.

"Thank you, Your Honor," Baylie responded, rising. "I call Ralph Stallman."

An hour and a half later, Stallman's direct and cross concluded, Judge Storer called a fifteen-minute break. The jury filed out.

Will swiveled in his chair to face Cassandra and, leaning in, spoke softly: "I think that went well."

"I agree," Cassandra whispered back. "Stallman was good, but we expected that. I think you limited any damage on cross."

Will nodded. He knew Cassandra would not be anything but encouraging in the middle of a grueling day of trial. Still, the pat on the back was welcome, particularly given the convincing performance the remainder of the morning would require of him.

Baylie's next witness was Ken Bloom, an accident reconstruction expert.

Will did not hold the pseudo-science, as he thought of it, of accident reconstruction in high regard. As far as Will knew, no university offered a degree in accident reconstruction. Textbooks, to be distinguished from how-to manuals, were not published in the field, let alone scholarly articles.

The conclusions these people reached were not based on any recognized scientific principles—not engineering, physics, or math—but instead from on-the-job training. Many of them worked for insurance companies, investigating car accident claims, before turning to the more lucrative litigation work. Denying liability was an ingrained habit.

Will had not seen an accident reconstructionist on opposing counsel's witness list for years. The firm handled primarily medical malpractice cases, not car accidents or slip-and-falls. Yet when Bloom's name appeared on Baylie's list, Will knew how to respond. He objected that Bloom had no education or training qualifying him to testify as to expert opinions.

The lawyers briefed the point. At the hearing on Will's motion to disqualify, Judge Storer expressed a healthy skepticism about Bloom's credentials. She overruled the motion in the end, based on precedent. The accident reconstructionist had been a fixture of litigation, both civil and criminal, for decades. He was not ready to fade away just yet.

After taking Bloom's deposition, Will thought Bloom's testimony at trial would be as unimpressive as his credentials. When Will saw Baylie's exhibit list, however, he realized how Baylie would grab the jury's attention and enhance Bloom's credibility. Will revised his strategy accordingly.

Baylie walked Bloom through his background and experience. Then the witness explained the methodology he had used to formulate his opinions on how the accident had happened.

Will tuned out Bloom's recitation of the measurements he took and the force-displacement vectors and other obscure phenomena he supposedly calculated. Will was all ears, though, when Bloom answered Baylie's next set of questions.

Baylie began by asking Bloom what he discovered when he closely examined a shard of the plywood sheet through which José had fallen.

A:To the unaided eye, it would have been easy to miss, but, under the microscope, it was clear.

Q:And what was it that you saw clearly through the microscope?

A:Cleat marks.

Q:Where on the plywood fragment were those cleat marks?

A:Skirting the edge. In fact, the outsole was almost off the edge of the plywood sheet.

Juror Number 1 caught Will's eye. She must remember the testimony of Baylie's safety expert. He had opined that it was unsafe to step anywhere but squarely in the center of anything covering an open duct.

Q:How, if at all, did the position of the cleat marks affect the opinion you have in this case as to how the accident occurred?

Baylie's voice had risen dramatically, Will noted.

A:Confirmed it. Mr. Marquez had to have stepped on the edge and not squarely on the center.

"Objection, Your Honor," Will jumped up. He knew Bloom would simply rephrase his answer. Bloom had testified enough times to realize where he had gone wrong. Still, Will was not going to let Bloom's error slip by without a challenge.

"Sustained," Judge Storer ruled, almost before Will had finished speaking.

A:Sorry, Your Honor. I should have said it is my opinion that Mr. Marquez stepped on the edge of the plywood. His weight and position caused the plywood to flip out of place. Mr. Marquez then quickly shifted forward to catch himself. With the sudden force on the cantilevered board it shattered, sending both the man and the broken plywood crashing down through the ductwork.

Will glanced back at the jury. Juror Number 1 again. She was frowning slightly as Baylie brought into focus the image he had projected onto the whiteboard to the jury's left.

An artist had reconstructed the plywood sheet covering the duct on the construction site. The shapes of the fragments, recovered from the first floor of the building, below the terminus of the duct in the roof, were delineated with white lines. On one of the fragments, at the outer edge, pocked depressions formed an outline in the shape of a boot.

"May I approach the witness, Your Honor?" Baylie asked.

Judge Storer nodded. They had previewed what was to come in the pretrial conference, so the judge already knew Will had no objections. Instead, Will was gleefully anticipating what Baylie was about to do with his witness.

Bloom reached down into the witness box and drew out a dark brown, cleated, leather work boot. Will knew the boot was a men's size 10. To the casual eye, the boot, neither overly large nor small, would appear to fit an average size man. A man José's size.

Bloom carried his exhibit with him as he walked to the whiteboard, hoisted the boot, and set it, sole down, on the drawing. The boot fit.

Baylie thanked his witness and sat down. Bloom was excused.

Will rose. "I call my rebuttal witness, Your Honor," he said. "José Marquez."

Baylie objected, but only for the record. At the pretrial conference, Baylie argued that Will's rebuttal testimony should be deferred until Baylie concluded his case. The timing of rebuttal was at the discretion of the judge, however. Judge Storer had sided with Will on this one.

It was José's turn to reach down to his right, rise, and walk to the witness stand with a work boot in his hand. Judge Storer reminded José that he was still under oath. After José was settled, Will began questioning him.

Q: What do you have in your hand?

A: My work boot. The right foot of a pair, to be exact.

Q: When is the last time you wore that boot?

A: April 4, 2017.

Q: How is it that you remember the exact date?

A: Because I'll never forget it. That was the day of my accident.

Q: Had you worn that boot, or that pair of boots I should say, before the day of the accident?

A: Oh, sure. I'd been wearing 'em for months. I wear the same pair of work boots every day. I replace them every six months or so.

Q:Mr. Marquez, please approach the exhibit displayed on the whiteboard and place the boot you are holding on the image.

Will glanced back at opposing counsel. Baylie was peering closely at the shoe in José's hand. Baylie finally realizes where this is going, Will thought with satisfaction.

José's shoe, a size 6, lay a good two inches within the outline of the boot on the drawing.

To nail the point, Will had José confirm that he did not on that day and would never risk stepping anywhere but squarely in the middle of a plywood duct cover.

Will concluded the rebuttal by asking José the size of the dress shoes he was wearing in court that day. José replied that his polished dress shoes were a size 10. José explained, sheepishly, that he used inserts to wear a size more appropriate for a man of his height when he was out in public. At work, José needed more stability than the inserts allowed. On the construction site, he had to use boots that properly fit the tiny feet he had inherited from his father.

Having only seen José in a suit, tie, and dress shoes, Baylie had been fooled into thinking his "generic" boot would do the trick. Will had been confident that he was not obligated to disabuse Baylie of his notion. O.J. Simpson's defense team did not tell Marcia Clark that the gloves found at the scene of Nicole Brown's murder would, infamously, not fit.

CHAPTER 24
THE UNKNOWN SOLDIER

Judge Storer adjourned for the day at 4:00 p.m. From the courthouse, Will called the office to check in. All quiet, Marlon reported.

"Let's make this an early one, for once," Will told Cassandra. "Go on home. Enjoy your evening."

Norma looked up, concern on her face, when Will walked into their kitchen.

"Is something wrong?" she asked, after they greeted each other and kissed.

He laughed. "It must seem like it, but all is well. We're ahead of schedule in the trial, so we ended early today. Are you finished with work for the day, too?"

Norma nodded. Will grinned. As he reached for her hand, his phone, sitting on the kitchen table, rang.

"I'm tempted to ignore it," Will claimed.

Norma giggled. "Not a good idea," she said. "You are in trial, after all. Go ahead and take it, sweetheart. We have plenty of time."

Will smiled, blew Norma a kiss, and picked up his phone. From the caller ID, he knew it was Cassandra.

"What's up?" Will asked, phone to his ear, walking into the living room to take the call.

"That creepy adjuster called a few minutes ago," Cassandra answered. "I wish he wouldn't call me at home."

"Franklin wouldn't know if you were home or at the office," Will said. "Besides, what better time to call? I presume he's aware of what's going on in the courtroom. He would know you'd be free right now."

Cassandra knew why Will was placating her. Settlement discussions were fraught enough without letting emotions into the mix. "Don't worry, Will," she replied, "I'll be nice to him. As nice as I can be, anyway. But between you and me, I still think he's a creep."

"Fair enough," Will said. "What did Franklin have to say?"

"He's made a real offer," Cassandra answered. "Not close to where we want to be, but the first indication of good faith in the negotiations, I'd say."

Will laughed. "Maybe they are getting serious because of Baylie's boot debacle," he said.

"Or maybe they were relying on our alternate juror, Anna, for something, and she's reneging," Cassandra proposed.

"Could be," Will said, "but, for some reason, she never worried me as much as she has you. Anyway, what are they offering?"

"Two hundred K," Cassandra said.

"Not bad, given where they started, and a big jump from the last offer," Will responded. "Definitely worth a counter-offer this time. What do you think?"

They discussed it and decided on five million. Cassandra rang off to call Franklin. Will turned his attention back to his wife.

***

"Lawyers, lawyers, the meeting will start in nine minutes, lawyers," Aaron's voice sounded over the intercom.

Miranda started down the corridor, heeding the summons. She wondered why the boss had called another meeting this late in the afternoon. They had already had the daily briefing that morning.

Jim emerged from Aaron's office just as Miranda entered. Now she knew. She could tell from the look on Jim's face. He had delivered the results of the DNA tests to Aaron.

Miranda took her seat in the semi-circle of chairs in front of Aaron's desk. Marlon and Betsy were already in their places. All waited expectantly as Aaron extracted a document from a manila envelope, unfolded the report, scanned it quickly, and looked up at his associates.

"The body we exhumed is almost certainly not John Evans," Aaron said. "We don't know if Parker's brother is alive today, of course, but John was not buried in that grave."

"Where do we start?" Miranda asked the room. "Start looking for John, that is," she said, excited.

Aaron interrupted Marlon as he started to answer her.

"What you do with your free time is for you to decide, of course," Aaron began, "but I remind you all that this is a law firm. I've had second thoughts since I approved paying for the exhumation. I don't think any of this is worth the effort."

"But it's Parker!" Miranda objected.

Aaron scowled. "You don't need to state the obvious," he harrumphed, "and I am, you know ..." Aaron paused, clearing his throat. "I'm quite fond of Parker. I wish things were otherwise. But I fear it's too late. Parker is too far gone. He wouldn't survive a transplant, assuming his surgical team would still operate. Even if, by some miracle, we found his brother alive, well, and willing."

"A miracle would be lovely," Marlon retorted, "but I'm not convinced we need it. We only need to be smart."

Miranda took a deep breath. She rarely argued with the boss.

"Look," Miranda leaned forward, eye to eye with Aaron. "Forget the kidney transplant for the moment. Parker hoped for a donor. He longed to find a family tie. He's been searching forever, you know, convinced he wasn't alone in the world. Parker found Roberta, but we don't know how she's going to react. She might decide to keep her distance. We probably won't find John. But knowing we're looking will mean the world to Parker."

Aaron shifted in his chair as if the padded seat had suddenly become uncomfortable.

"None of us is going to miss a deadline by spending some time looking for John," Marlon said. "This is a quiet week for us anyway, and that's all the time we have, given Parker's state."

"If that," Miranda added. From the look on his face, Miranda could not tell whether Aaron was convinced, but she decided to take the chance. "So, I repeat," she said. "Where do we start?"

"From the beginning," Marlon answered. "We follow his journey until we find John. Here's what we do."

CHAPTER 25
UNEXCUSED ABSENCE

Trial Day 7

At 9:00 a.m., as scheduled, Judge Storer gaveled the trial into session.

The jury filed into their box. The lawyers took their seats at counsel table.

"Where's José?" Will, frowning, whispered harshly.

Cassandra knew Will's irritation was not directed at her, and she responded calmly. "I have no idea. He didn't call you?" she asked.

Will shook his head. "Slip out and call the office, will you, Cassandra?" Will asked. "See if anyone there has heard anything."

Cassandra knew the office would have called or texted if José had been in touch. So did Will. Nonetheless, she did as Will asked. Baylie had not called his witness yet, and Cassandra's departure raised no stir.

Having made her call, Cassandra peered from the corridor through the glass panel of the courtroom door. Baylie's economist was on the stand. Cassandra would have to wait until the break.

At 10:25, Baylie completed his direct examination. Judge Storer told the jury that they would have a fifteen-minute break. When they returned, the trial would resume and continue until 1:00 p.m.

"I know that's later than your usual lunch hour," Judge Storer continued, smiling warmly, always solicitous of her jury. "So, be sure to have your snack, if you've brought one, during the break. The long morning will be worth your while because you'll have the afternoon free."

After the courtroom cleared, Cassandra pushed open the courtroom door. She walked down the aisle to the well and their counsel table. Will looked up as Cassandra sat beside him, eyebrows raised, questioning.

"Aaron was on the verge of texting me when I called," Cassandra answered his look. "José had just contacted the office. No details, but something came up at work. Something serious enough that José had to deal with it immediately. He told Aaron he'd try to get to the courthouse for the afternoon session. I reminded Aaron we're off this afternoon. He'll let José know and tell him to come to the office, instead, as soon as he can."

Will's eyes widened. "José well knew that his presence in court is critical to his case. It would be different if he had a medical emergency. Of course, he would be excused for that. But what could have been so critical at work? And why couldn't Mauricio take care of it?"

Cassandra had no answers.

Back at the office, Marlon and Jim commandeered the small conference room. For the next week, this would be the associates' common workspace in the hunt for John Evans.

Marlon pulled the chairs out from under the table and lined them up against the walls. Jim brought in a six-foot-square whiteboard and hoisted it onto its sturdy, aluminum base. Jim left briefly and returned with a laptop under each arm. Marlon connected the electronics while Jim retrieved a pile of yellow legal pads and a box of pens from the supply closet.

"Now what?" Jim asked.

"We'll start with a timeline," Marlon answered.

Fifteen minutes later, Marlon stepped back to inspect his handiwork.

Date Fact Source
04/72 John graduates HS Parker
07/17/73 John disappears in Vietnam Buford ("Buzz") Kowalski
09/06/77 Roberta born Roberta

Betsy walked into the conference room.

"Lamentably few entries," she observed.

"I'm just getting started," Marlon demurred. "We'll have more entries after Miranda talks with Lydia. At least," Marlon corrected himself, "if Lydia's recall is intact, and she's willing to share what she knows."

"Who's Buford Kowalski?" Betsy asked.

"He's a Vietnam veteran from John's unit whom I interviewed yesterday evening."

"What a coincidence!" Betsy exclaimed. "You happened to interview someone who served with John?"

"Not a coincidence at all," Marlon replied. "I was intrigued by something Parker said during his interview. John died because he had the bad luck to be in the wrong place at the wrong time, according to Parker. John had gotten separated from his own unit. I followed up on the soldiers in John's unit who are still alive and located Kowalski."

"And, fortunately, he agreed to talk to you," Betsy said.

Marlon smiled. "Buzz, as he's called, was delighted. He's a retired insurance salesman. His wife died two years ago, and his children all live on the West Coast. Buzz happily told me all about his seven grandchildren. After that, I was able to get him to talk about the war."

"So," Betsy said, "Buzz is a nice man with a nice family, but does he also have an extraordinary memory?"

"You mean, did I believe Buzz when he told me the exact date John disappeared?" Marlon responded. When Betsy nodded, Marlon explained.

"Buzz remembers the date because he got his ticket out the same day. He took a bullet to the thigh. The shot nicked his femoral artery. Buzz almost bled to death. The medic saved his life. The wound saved him from the war."

"Buzz remembers thinking, right before he was shot, that John was gone," Marlon continued. "Buzz said he kept an eye on John because the man was absent-minded. The only thing John seemed to focus on was his pictures, according to Buzz."

"What pictures?" Betsy asked. "Of his family? A girlfriend?"

"No, his own pictures," Marlon replied. "John was a shutterbug. He carried a camera slung around his neck and was always snapping pictures."

"What was John's attitude towards the war?" Betsy asked.

"John hated every minute of it," Marlon answered. "That wasn't unusual, though, Buzz said. Except for the career soldiers, the gung-ho hotheads who had wanted to be in the Marines but didn't pass muster, and the occasional crazy guy, everybody wanted out."

Betsy was quiet a moment. Then, she asked: "How badly did he want it? Out of the war, that is."

Ah, Marlon thought, Betsy had come to the same conclusion as had he. There was only one logical explanation for the presence of John's tags on the body that the Evans family buried. John removed the tags from a soldier killed in action and replaced them with his own.

And why? To get out. "John Evans" is accounted for as killed in action. The real John runs away.

And somehow, he evaded both friend and enemy to avoid a court martial, if captured by the former, or torture and death if found by the latter. A monumental task, Marlon thought, but John succeeded. He sired Roberta, after all.

John's deception would cause deep heartache to his brother and girlfriend as they grieved for the wrong man. The family of the dead soldier would suffer the anguish of not knowing what had happened to their son.

Had John been so mentally deranged by Vietnam that he could not anticipate these consequences? Or had he simply not cared about anything but his own skin?

"Well?" Betsy's impatient voice interrupted Marlon's thoughts.

"Sorry," Marlon answered. "I was thinking. Anyway, Buzz said John might not have wanted to, but he did his duty. He didn't even shirk it. John didn't malinger or abuse sick-bay privileges or even complain about taking point, as so many guys did. John was no coward, either. John once volunteered to hold an exposed flank as the unit was moving out, risking his own life in doing so."

"The man Buzz remembers does not sound like the kind of person who would do the tag switch," Betsy said.

She had figured it out, Marlon thought.

"No," Marlon responded, "but people are complicated. We make rash, split-second decisions. John wanders off from his unit. He sees a body, a man he doesn't know. The dog tag around the corpse's neck catches John's eye. A way for him to escape from the madness of the war flashes through John's mind. He removes the dead man's tags, tossing them into the jungle. He puts his own tags around the corpse's neck. Voilà."

Betsy shook her head. "The picture you've painted is not quite right," she said. "When John came upon it, the body bore no dog tags."

Before Marlon had a chance to unravel that statement, the familiar voice boomed over the intercom.

"Lawyers, all lawyers, to my office immediately," Aaron commanded.

CHAPTER 26
NO MATCH

Will had returned from the courthouse to find José and Mauricio waiting for him. José quickly explained why he had not been at the trial that morning. Will realized he needed advice from his colleagues and asked Aaron to call them in.

Waiting for the others to arrive, Will paced by the east window of Aaron's office. José, who sat directly in front of Aaron, looked misplaced, Will thought, in his jeans and work shirt instead of his usual suit. Mauricio, attired like his son, almost hidden in his high-backed chair, sat next to José.

In a few minutes, Marlon followed Betsy in, closed the office door, and sat down.

"Okay, everybody, listen up," Aaron said sharply. "Will has another problem with this trial. Let's figure it out."

José muttered something in Spanish to Mauricio. Will had a good guess as to what José had said. Aaron did care about the Marquezes as individuals, not only as his clients, but his clinical description of the situation must have stung.

"It's a problem for the trial but a disaster for José and his dad, of course," Will said to the room.

"What's happened?" Marlon asked.

"I received a no-match letter from the Social Security Administration," José answered, "for Dad."

"What's a no-match letter?" asked Marlon.

José explained. Periodically, at intervals consistent with changes in the political winds, the Social Security Administration notified employers of their employees whose names and reported social security numbers did not match. The purpose was to "out" undocumented employees using counterfeit social security cards to get jobs.

"The letter came in the mail to the office yesterday," José continued. "The office manager opened it, as she does all the company's mail. I don't know if she missed the significance or what, but she didn't let me know about it until I stopped by the office early this morning."

"I had to warn Dad, but I couldn't get him on his cell. I forgot he went to Grandparents' Day at Benjy's school today and had to turn off his phone. I went looking for him, and that's why I wasn't in court."

"So, what happens now?" Betsy asked.

"As the employer, I will be fined if I don't remedy the situation," José answered. "I have to fire the employee or prove the no-match was a mistake. Sometimes the employee misspelled his name on a form, for example."

"If I don't do one or the other, the immigration authorities will come snooping around. We don't know for sure if the Social Security Administration corresponds with Immigration and Customs Enforcement, but we suspect they do."

"What do you mean by 'we?'" Will asked, looking over at Mauricio, who was sitting quietly, eyes down. "You and Mauricio?"

"No, I'm talking about the construction industry," José replied. "As I said, these no-match campaigns happen occasionally, and they tend to target specific industries. The construction industry, I suppose for obvious reasons, is often in the bull's eye."

"We owners discuss how best to manage the situation. We can't afford to lose good help, but neither can we afford to pay a hefty fine. Anyway, this time, I can't exercise either of the usual options."

"Why not?" Marlon asked. "You could officially terminate Mauricio's employment. He could still help you on the side, of course."

"That won't work," José said. "Everybody in the company would figure out why I let Dad go. The office manager knows about the no-match letter, remember. People would talk. Someone might talk to the wrong person."

"Don't you trust your own crew?" Cassandra asked.

"Mostly," José answered, "but I don't know the political views of every one of my guys. Anyway, even if my employees keep mum, immigration could pursue the matter if Dad is suddenly off payroll."

"Well," Will said, "you have that other option. Fix the mistake. Given that Mauricio's card passes E-Verify, that's what the no-match must have been."

José shook his head. "I don't think so," he said, "because this is like no other no-match program I've seen or heard about. When it happens, the Social Security Administration sends out hundreds, or even thousands, of letters in one sweep. A small company might get a single no-match notification for only one employee, but J&A is not that small."

"I've asked around. Nobody else has gotten any letters. No, this looks like a one-shot war. Somebody took aim and fired at Dad, and only Dad."

The silence that ensued was broken by Mauricio. "Will you help us?" he asked, accent deepened by the strain, looking directly at Aaron.

Aaron frowned, fiddling with a pen. As he opened his mouth to respond, his phone rang. Aaron peered at the caller ID, lifted the receiver, and swiveled his chair a quarter turn to gain some privacy to take the call.

Marlon, seated in his chair, leaned towards Will's. "What providential timing for Lorraine's call," Marlon spoke quietly. "He was on the verge of saying no, but a chat with his wife will improve Aaron's outlook considerably."

Will nodded his agreement. He was not going to rely on Aaron's decision, however. Instead, he would move matters along on his own.

Will stood. "I'll be right back," he called as he strode towards the office door. He walked out and trotted down the corridor to his office. Kneeling in front of the three-drawer file cabinet to the left of his desk, he opened the bottom drawer. Flipping through tabbed files, he extracted the document he needed and hurried back to Aaron's office. Luckily, Aaron was just hanging up the phone.

"We need to get to the bottom of that mysterious social security card," Will proclaimed as he resumed his seat in front of Aaron's desk. "The card that is almost, but not quite legitimate."

Will looked directly at Mauricio. It would not be easy to get his secret source out of this man.

"Look, whoever got it for you must be behind the no-match letter," Will continued. "Who else would know that a card which passes E-Verify could still be fake?"

"Wait a minute!" Betsy blurted.

"What is it?" Will asked, annoyed at the interruption.

"Nothing, sorry," Betsy replied.

"If we're going to try to help you, you have to tell us who got you the card," Will said.

Mauricio nodded. Now, Will had to convince Aaron. Will turned towards his boss.

"Mauricio can't tell unless he can be sure the information will remain confidential," Will continued. "He has to be our client. Our usual contingency fee won't do in this case because we won't investigate or try a case for him. So, I grabbed a standard retainer agreement for you to sign, Aaron."

Aaron did not respond immediately. Will feared Aaron was taking a minute to conjure a reason to refuse that would not devastate the Marquezes, dishearten Will, and jeopardize a successful conclusion to the trial. Guessing what that excuse might be, Will made a preemptive move.

"It won't be malpractice," Will argued. "We're not qualified to and will not be giving Mauricio advice on his immigration status. We'll only find out what happened and do what we can, based on what we discover, to get Mauricio to someone better equipped to help him."

"Fine," Aaron capitulated in a surprisingly cheerful tone. "You and Mauricio go to your office and talk. Find out who gave him the card. Report back here. We'll get other work done while you're gone."

Mauricio helped José to his feet, and they followed Will out of Aaron's office.

Half an hour later, Will returned. José and Mauricio, exhausted from the ordeal of the morning, had gone home. Somehow, they would try to prepare for the dreaded arrival of an ICE agent at their door.

"Jeff Howard secured the social security card for Mauricio," Will announced.

A babble of voices rose. Everyone looked at Betsy. She shrugged her shoulders and said nothing.

Betsy must have known, Will thought, given her unconcerned response to the news. What else did Betsy know that she was not telling her colleagues?

"Explain, Will," Aaron commanded.

It was ten years after the war. Mauricio managed to find enough day work in construction to get by. Berta took care of one-year-old José.

Life was decent, but Mauricio was tired of hiding, of keeping secrets, of constantly looking over his shoulder. He was tired of the petty difficulties posed by his status, as well. He hated having to rise at 4:00 a.m. to ride the bus for an hour to get to work because he could not get a driver's license.

He and Berta argued about which course was better for José. In the end, they came to an agreement. They would go home. Back to Mexico.

Soon after they had made their decision, a knock sounded on the door to their apartment, startling them both. Mauricio was even more surprised, looking out through the peephole in the door, to see the familiar face of a comrade from Vietnam, Jeff Howard.

Mauricio opened the door, shook hands with Jeff, and invited him in. While Berta made coffee, Jeff succinctly explained his purpose. Jeff could not fix Mauricio's problem entirely. What Jeff could do was make it possible for Mauricio to stay in the States with a high degree of confidence that his undocumented status would not be detected.

"How did Jeff know Mauricio hadn't gotten his citizenship?" Cassandra asked, interrupting Will's tale. "And how did he find Mauricio?"

"Mauricio had the same questions, of course," Will answered, "but the first thing he did was deny that he had the 'problem' to which Jeff seemed to be referring."

Mauricio could not produce any papers, however. In addition, Jeff seemed to have come with good intentions. Mauricio eventually admitted that his citizenship application had unaccountably been denied.

Jeff explained that he presumed as much when Mauricio made no appearance in Company 19's alumni network for so many years. Mauricio had seemed particularly attached to his comrades while they were in Vietnam. His conspicuous absence afterward made Jeff wonder what had gone wrong.

Jeff had no idea how to find Mauricio until the notice appeared in the alumni newsletter that Mauricio lived in the D.C. area. Jeff tracked down the veteran, Billy Wrangle, who reported Mauricio's appearance. By pure happenstance, Billy had run into "Mouse," as they all called Mauricio, in a hardware store. One thing led to another, and Jeff was able to track Mauricio to his home.

"Jeff didn't explain how he was going to get the card, and Mauricio didn't ask. Mauricio accepted the deal he was offered. Jeff would procure him a government-issued social security card. In exchange, Mauricio would never tell a soul how he got it. Nor would Mauricio have any contact with Jeff ever again. He broke that last promise once."

Will related José's story about Mauricio losing his card. "When Mauricio called his 'Army buddy' for a replacement, that was Jeff," Will concluded.

"Why would Jeff go out on a limb like that?" Marlon asked. "I could understand Jeff doing a favor for a former comrade-in-arms, but committing a crime for him?"

"Beats me," Will answered. He shifted his gaze to the person in the room most likely to know. "Betsy?"

"Jeff is loyal, certainly, and he, like Mauricio, felt a strong connection to his company and Vietnam veterans in general. I'm also sure he would have been appalled that Mauricio had not been rewarded, as he should have been, for his service."

Not much of an answer, Will thought.

"Mauricio didn't think that was it," Will said. "That is, Mauricio never had the feeling that Jeff's offer came from a sense of camaraderie or duty. Instead, although Jeff didn't say anything directly, Mauricio got the impression that Jeff wanted Mauricio to be in his debt."

"Okay, enough history," Aaron said. "These are the facts we have now. Jeff Howard got Mauricio the card. Mauricio didn't turn himself into the authorities. So, it must have been Jeff."

"But why?" Marlon asked.

"I asked Mauricio that question," Will answered. "He hasn't a clue."

CHAPTER 27
AN OPEN WINDOW

All eyes locked on Betsy. Again.

Her colleagues expected an answer, but she did not have one. Only Jeff did.

She had to talk to him. Could Jeff have ratted on Mauricio? If so, which Betsy had a hard time believing, why? For now, she needed to buy time.

"Why would Jeff do that?" Betsy broke the expectant silence. "That is, assuming Mauricio's explanation is true. Why would Jeff renege on a decades-old bargain with Mauricio?"

"Will," Betsy continued, "you said Mauricio has had no contact with Jeff since that one phone call more than twenty years ago. So, what could have triggered such a response from Jeff?"

She had almost convinced herself. The sticking point was Jeff's dramatic reaction when Betsy first mentioned Mauricio's name. She would get to the bottom of this.

"But you'll ask him, right?" Will asked.

"Of course," she said, although she was wary of what Jeff's answer might be.

"What Betsy says makes sense," Marlon observed, "and there is an alternative explanation for the no-match letter. A simple one. The Social Security Administration finally detected the fact that Mauricio's card was not genuine without a tipoff from Jeff or anyone else, for that matter. That card had fooled a lot of people for a long time. Still, after all, it was fake."

"But why now?" Will asked. "And why was Mauricio and only Mauricio the target of what appears to be a one-shot investigation?"

"I don't know," Aaron spoke up. "But it seems to me that we are back to where we were last week. You convinced Mauricio to let us explore avenues for regularizing his status. We put that task on the back burner. Now, the matter is urgent. Get to work."

"I expect it will be soon," Marlon rejoined. He turned to Betsy. "Give me an hour to make these calls about Mauricio to the politicians to whom Aaron has ties. Then, I'll join you back in the small conference room."

"Okay," Betsy agreed. She proceeded down the corridor to her office. Betsy sat at her desk, aimlessly opening a browser. Staring at the familiar logo, she tried to sort through Jeff's strategy here.

She did not think it plausible that a random check at the Social Security Administration led to the discovery of a problem with Mauricio's social security card. Instead, someone, apparently anonymously, alerted the authorities.

As Will had said, the most likely culprit was the person who got Mauricio the card in the first place. That person, as they all now knew, was Jeff.

But, if that were the case, why did Vincent tell Betsy, just yesterday, that Jeff got the card for Mauricio? Jeff had to know that Betsy would suspect Jeff as soon as she got wind of the no-match letter. Would Jeff deny his involvement in that? Or would he confess to that, as well, and then expect Betsy to do nothing while he destroyed an innocent man?

Betsy shook her head. None of this was making any sense.

What was it about making sense that rang a bell?

Then, it came to her. She would enlist Chad to decrypt the coded messages between Jeff and Vincent that she had found. She suspected she would find something useful in that correspondence, some evidence with which to confront Jeff about the no-match letter.

Betsy opened the website and accessed Jeff's files. The correspondence was read-only. She would have to copy the encoded sections by hand. Betsy glanced at the clock on her computer screen. She had forty-five minutes before she was to join Marlon to work on John's timeline. She might just finish before then.

At 2:00 p.m., right on schedule, Marlon appeared at the door to Betsy's office. "I could use some fresh air before we head back to the conference room. Want to take a walk?"

"Sure," Betsy answered. "Let's go."

"Any luck with your calls?" Betsy asked as they walked past the reception desk towards the elevator.

Marlon pursed his lips. "It's Tuesday afternoon and those names on Aaron's list represent busy people," he responded. "For the most part, I left messages. We'll be right back," Marlon interrupted himself to inform Beebe, their receptionist. He pushed open the glass door to the office suite, waving Betsy through in front of him.

The elevator chimed. The door opened to reveal a young man in a suit. Marlon smiled politely as he and Betsy entered the car. The three passengers rode silently down the four floors to the lobby.

Betsy and Marlon exited the building and turned right towards the Connecticut Avenue crossing to Farragut Park. Midafternoon, passersby were sporadic. Marlon and Betsy had privacy again.

"Back to John," Marlon said. "Why did you say the soldier's dog tags were not on his body when John came upon it?"

"Because I received a picture of the dead man this morning. His name is Glen Hadley. His was the body buried as John Evans. In the picture, Glen has no dog tags around his neck."

Marlon stopped abruptly. "Whoa, wait! How do you know all this?"

"From Paco," Betsy answered.

"Paco?" Marlon asked, brow furrowed.

"Yeah," Betsy replied. "Last week, I asked you to contact Paco about documents he had in his files about MIA from Vietnam. Remember?"

"Oh, yes, now I do," Marlon answered.

When the light turned, they trotted across Connecticut and started their circuit around the park.

Betsy told Marlon what she had learned from Paco's documents.

"I contacted Glen's mother, Marita," Betsy continued. "I asked her to send me a copy of the photograph of her son that she got from the

National League of Families of American Prisoners and Missing in Southeast Asia."

"You can see in the picture that Glen was blasted or burned by whatever hit him," Betsy continued, "leaving his clothing in tatters. His chest is bare. The absence of the tags is very clear."

"Poor Glen," Marlon responded. "Go on."

"Marita knew it was her son in the picture," Betsy responded, "but Glen was MIA according to the Army's records. So, Marita sent a copy to the Pentagon. She was informed that the image of the face was too distorted. They could not use the picture to confirm a match with the photograph of Glen they had on file. Marita's picture was insufficient evidence for them to change Glen's status. He remains MIA."

"I don't suppose it likely," Marlon said, "because she is his mother. But is there any chance Marita is mistaken?"

"No," Betsy answered firmly. "She's correct. Glen died in Vietnam. Glen was killed on July 17, 1973."

"How do you know the date when Glen died?" Marlon asked.

"Jeff told me," Betsy answered. "Jeff was by Glen's side when Glen was hit. Jeff knows the date because it was during his company's last major engagement, which was on July 17, 1973.

"So, Jeff took the picture?" Marlon asked.

"No," Betsy answered. "I don't think so, anyway. I just got the picture this morning and haven't talked to Jeff. But Jeff would have told me, if he had photographed Glen, when we talked about his death."

Marlon was quiet a moment. "July 17," he said. "The same day John disappeared, according to Buzz. So, I was right. John did put his tags on Glen's body, although he didn't steal Glen's first, as I had thought."

"Yep," Betsy agreed, "and took the picture."

John?" Marlon asked.

"Who else?" Betsy answered. "How likely is it that someone else was on that spot between the time Jeff saw Glen get killed and John switched the tags?"

"I don't know," Marlon answered. "It depends on how much time elapsed, I would think."

"Fair enough," Betsy countered, "but, if another soldier found the body, why would he have taken a picture? Why not do whatever needed to be done to recover the body?"

"Good point," Marlon answered. "Speaking of which, why did Jeff leave him?"

"I asked him that," Betsy said. "Jeff said if Glen had been wounded, he would have gotten help and dragged Glen out of there. It was not Jeff's job to bring in the dead in the middle of a firefight, however."

They reached the northwest corner of Farragut Park. Turning south, they passed the row of food trucks emblazoned, respectively, with colorful pictures of fajitas, hummus and pita, crepes, and dishes from dozens of other cuisines.

Marlon stopped in front of a smoothie stand, with an apology for the interruption. He had missed lunch, he said. Marlon purchased his drink, and the lawyers strolled on.

"John could have taken the picture," Marlon said, returning to the topic. "According to Buzz, John always carried a camera. Why would he, though?"

"Remember, in the picture, the body wears no tags," Betsy answered. "I think John took the picture as proof, of sorts, that he didn't steal the tags."

"Makes sense," Marlon admitted. "A burglar wouldn't photograph the window of a house he was about to smash in. But if the window were wide open, maybe yes."

"That's what I envision," Betsy concluded. "Glen's tags go missing. John appears and snaps the picture. He takes off his tags and puts them on Glen."

"But tags don't just 'go missing' in the middle of a battle," Marlon responded. "Somebody took Glen's tags. But if not John, then who?"

CHAPTER 28
RETURN FROM THE DEAD

Miranda knocked on Parker's apartment door at 2:30 p.m. Parker had told her midafternoon was usually Lydia's best time. Miranda's stomach fluttered. What was taking Parker so long?

Miranda had been tasked with talking to Lydia about John. The lawyers suspected John would have tried to find Lydia, his high school girlfriend, when he returned to the States. As a deserter, John was a wanted man. Who else could he trust? Maybe Lydia was Roberta's mother. Maybe Lydia even knew if John was still alive.

If any of this were so, Lydia had never said a word to Parker or anyone else. Miranda would be trying to wrest closely held secrets and from a woman with dementia. Miranda needed help. She turned to a person she had consulted before on cases involving neurological injury, Katherine Hammock, M.D.

Kathy, now in her sixties, was only the third female pediatric neurologist in the country to be board certified. She treated children, not persons of Lydia's age suffering from dementia. Still, Kathy read a wide array of professional journals in neurology specialties not her own. Miranda trusted that Kathy would provide sound advice for the delicate matter of probing Lydia's memory.

Miranda told Kathy about Parker, Roberta, the exhumation, and the search for the resurrected John. Miranda emphasized that time was of the essence. Nobody knew when Parker's kidneys would fail completely, but it would be any day.

The lawyers believed Lydia would reveal the truth once she understood Parker's dire situation. Parker had not yet told Lydia that he was dying.

The tricky part was how to ask the questions. Lydia's mind was so fragile. A misguided attempt to raise ghosts from her past might push Lydia deeper into dementia.

Kathy, quickly grasping the situation, had rattled off a list of dos and don'ts for the interview. Miranda also sought Kathy's advice on whether Parker should be present for all or part of her visit with Lydia.

The door opened. "Come on in, Miranda," Parker said, a smile on his face.

Miranda followed Parker into the kitchen. Lydia, sitting at the table, greeted Miranda. The three sat at the kitchen table chatting while Parker made coffee and served a plate of cookies.

Miranda was relieved to find Lydia to be calm and, thankfully, lucid.

As planned, after a half hour or so, Parker excused himself to take his medications. Miranda broke the difficult news to Lydia about Parker's deteriorating health. Lydia knew Parker was sick, of course, but not that the illness had abruptly become life-threatening.

When Parker returned to the kitchen, he dropped to his knees beside Lydia's chair and wrapped his arms around her. Miranda left Parker alone to comfort Lydia.

Later, Lydia and Parker joined Miranda in the living room. Miranda shared with Lydia what she had already told Parker. Aaron would ensure that Lydia was well cared for and had all she needed when Parker was no longer there for her. Lydia's tears, this time, were of relief.

As soon as Lydia calmed, Parker told her what the lawyers had learned about John. And Roberta.

Miranda knew, even before Lydia opened her mouth, what was coming. Lydia's initial look of mild surprise had quickly been replaced with a serene smile.

"I want to meet our daughter," Lydia said.

After that, Lydia spoke freely about John's return from the dead.

John came back to his hometown, after ostensibly being buried there, to find a shocked and bewildered Lydia. John did not explain much about his odyssey back to the States. He wanted to put that behind him.

The pair quickly fell back into their old relationship. John would come and go, never telling Lydia where he was living. It was too dangerous, he said. The consequences of any slip of the tongue would be disastrous for both.

Lydia discovered she was pregnant. She wanted to run away with John. Eventually, though, she agreed with John that his was no life for a couple with a child.

She believed her parents would see her through the initial months of her pregnancy after telling them a story about the bronco rider who seduced Lydia the second night of the county fair. Lydia would be allowed to live at home until she started to show.

Then, she would be shipped off to her Aunt Pauline in Austin for the delivery. Her father could live with that plan. Everybody knew the banker's daughter had been pregnant when she left town for a lengthy "vacation" the previous summer.

After that, Lydia would be on her own. Her father could not bear the shame of having a daughter under his roof who had born a child out of wedlock with a man who had so obviously abandoned her.

Lydia had no money, nor did John. Lydia could scarcely support herself, let alone a child. She and John could think of no viable alternative other than putting the baby up for adoption.

In the two years after the baby was born, John's visits became less frequent. It was becoming harder to make the trip undetected, he had said. Once again, Lydia thought about abandoning everything and going to wherever John disappeared. In the end, she could not do it. Lydia deeply loved John, but she was getting older. Comfort and safety won out over John, and a lifetime of uncertainty.

"I wasn't in contact with John for years," Lydia explained, "until six years ago. Out of the blue, I received an email from him. I was happy to know he was still alive. We exchanged a dozen or so messages. Then, John disappeared again, with no explanation."

"Did he tell you where he was living?" Miranda asked.

"No," Lydia replied.

Miranda asked a few more questions and answered those of Lydia's that she could. Miranda promised to be in touch with Roberta right away.

"She was reluctant to meet Parker," Miranda said, glancing at him ruefully, "but I think she'll want to see her mother."

Miranda thanked Lydia, told Parker to stay in touch, and took her leave. She caught a Lyft downtown.

Back at the office, Miranda found Betsy and Marlon in the small conference room. Miranda reported on her conversation with Lydia.

"In all that time, Lydia never told Parker his brother was alive," Betsy said, shaking her head. "That seems cruel."

Miranda shrugged. "Depends on how you look at it," she countered. "Lydia swore to John that she would never tell. She didn't see how it would help Parker to know, in any event. During the years in which Lydia had no contact with John, she didn't even know if he was still alive. Then, shortly after Lydia heard from John again, and might have told Parker, she started having problems with her memory. She wasn't always sure whether John had been real or only a dream."

"And now, Lydia sees that it might save Parker's life to know," Marlon observed, "so she talks."

"Plus, she kept her promise," Miranda said. "Lydia didn't tell. The DNA did."

"So, what do we do now?" Betsy asked. "We know John was alive as of six years ago, but that's about it. How do we track him down?"

"We find a priest," Miranda answered.

CHAPTER 29
THE OTHER CANDIDATE

"That's my line," Marlon protested.

Miranda and Betsy laughed. It had been Marlon's idea to call in a priest for assistance when the firm was helping Will extricate his wife, Norma, from the immigration authorities the previous year.

"Father Brennan might be able to help again," Miranda said. "I'll tell you why later. Right now, I've got to catch Will about contacting Father Brennan. Will knows him best."

Miranda turned and left the room.

"By the way," Betsy said as she and Marlon turned back to their whiteboard, "you did email Paco, didn't you? To see if he has anything in his files on John?"

"Of course," Marlon answered. "Yesterday, right after we read the DNA report. Paco responded immediately, saying he'd get right on it. He also asked if we had any pictures of John."

"Why a picture?" Betsy asked.

"Paco has a trove of photos from Vietnam," Marlon answered. "Paco thinks a picture with John in it might hold a clue as to where John is today. Maybe John hung out with someone in his unit whom we can locate and contact, for example. Paco needs to know what John looked like to find his image."

"Lydia probably has pictures of John," Betsy observed.

"She did," Marlon responded, "according to Parker. I called him after I read the email from Paco. Unfortunately, Lydia lost them long ago. She lived in a basement apartment when she first moved to D.C. After a heavy rainfall, her apartment flooded. Lydia's photo albums, still unpacked in a box on the floor, were ruined."

"Parker?" Betsy asked.

"Not one," Marlon answered. "Parker burned the few family photographs they had in the house during the worst of his PTSD when he first got back from the war."

"How about a high school yearbook?" Betsy asked.

"The family couldn't afford to buy one," Marlon answered. "I asked Parker to contact the high school he and John attended. Parker will ask the archivist to send John's picture from his senior year as soon as possible."

While they were talking, Marlon updated their timeline.

Date Fact Source
May 1972 John graduates HS Parker
07/17/73 John gets separated from his unit Buford ("Buzz") Kowalski
07/17/73 Glen Hadley killed in action Jeff Howard
07/17/73 GH dog tags missing Marita Hadley's photo
Fall 1973 Glen Hadley, MIADOD
09/30/73 Glen/John buried Parker
09/06/1976 John returns to Texas Lydia
09/06/77 Roberta born Roberta
Circa 1979 John disappears Lydia
TBD/2013 John emails Lydia
TBD/2013 John disappears Lydia

"TBD?" Betsy asked.

"To be determined," Marlon answered. "If Lydia is still using the same email service provider, she can request her records. If they've been retained that far back, Chad can recover the email for us, and we can check those dates. Another thing to put on the 'to-do' list. We need to follow up on every clue we have, no matter how faint, because we don't know which one will turn out to be the key to finding John."

"You're right," Betsy said. "And along those lines, I'll ask Marita when she received the photograph of her son."

"You did tell her about the exhumation, didn't you?" Marlon asked.

"Yes, I called her," Betsy answered. "I also told her we had arranged to have the remains sent to the POW/MIA Accounting Agency. Marita will be in contact with them. The identification should go quickly once Marita tells them the body is likely her son, Glen."

Marlon studied the whiteboard for a moment, then turned towards Betsy. "When Jeff told you about Glen's death, did he say anything about Glen's dog tags?"

"No, he didn't," Betsy answered.

"Don't you think he would have mentioned it if ...?"

"I've thought of that," Betsy interrupted, "and the answer has to be, yes. If, for some reason, Glen wore no tags when he died, Jeff would have noticed. He would have mentioned it to me."

"Which means," Marlon said, "that we're back to John removing Glen's tags, as illogical as that seems."

Betsy was convinced that another candidate was far more likely. Who had been by Glen's side when he fell? Mauricio and Jeff. But which of them would take such a risk, and why?

"Heh," Miranda said, stepping through the conference room door.

Chad followed Miranda into the room. He leaned his long frame against the wall across from the whiteboard.

"Will called Father Brennan and has arranged to see him this evening," Miranda continued.

"That's great," Betsy responded absently. Miranda's reappearance turned Betsy's attention back to John.

Betsy tried to imagine John as a young man on the run, stealing into his hometown at night to find Lydia, desperate to make amends and get his life back. A thought occurred to her.

"Miranda," Betsy began, "Lydia must have asked John how he could have done that to her. That is, maybe she could try to understand John wanting the Army to think he was dead, but what about her?"

"This is what John told Lydia," Miranda responded. "'By chance, I happened upon an opportunity to get out of Vietnam. In the split second of my decision, the only person I thought would pay the consequences was me. I was willing to pay the cost. I was wrong on all counts.'"

The room fell silent. After a few minutes, Betsy rose from her chair and walked over to the whiteboard.

"Give me the marker for a minute, Marlon," she said. Marlon handed it over.

"Who did pay, in addition to John?" Betsy asked rhetorically. She circled the names on the board: Marita, Lydia, and Parker. "John's father, too, of course, but he died soon after John's funeral." She drew an x across Marita's name. "John tried to make it up to Marita and her husband by sending the photograph of their son's body."

"We believe John sent the picture," Marlon interrupted.

"Bear with me here," Betsy said impatiently. She x'ed out Lydia's name. "John returned to Lydia, and they resumed what was apparently a close and loving relationship. That leaves only Parker. Wouldn't John have tried to make amends to his own brother, as well as the others?"

"But how?" Miranda asked. "John let Lydia know he was still alive, but not Parker. As far as Parker knew, until the exhumation, John was dead."

Betsy grimaced. "I don't know," she replied. "Maybe anonymously? What I do know is that we aren't anywhere close to finding John, and we're running out of time."

The three lawyers agreed that each would draft a list of questions to ask Parker. Betsy and Marlon would email theirs to Miranda, who would try to meet with Parker again in the morning. The objective of that conversation would be to uncover interventions by John in Parker's life, of which Parker was unaware.

"No easy task," Betsy observed wryly.

"No harder than Will's," Marlon replied. "He's trying to wrest secrets from a priest. I'm going back to my office, team, to work on my list and email Paco with some thoughts."

"I'll work on mine, too," Miranda responded, "but only until 5:00 p.m. After that, Chad and I are going to get a drink. Do you guys want to join us?"

Marlon agreed. Betsy demurred, saying she had too much work to finish.

Chad pushed himself upright and started to follow Miranda out of the conference room.

"Can I talk to you a minute, Chad?" Betsy asked.

Chad turned back into the room. "Sure," he said. "What's up?"

Betsy motioned Chad to join her at the conference room table. He took a seat.

Betsy explained the project she was working on for Jeff. Chad nodded, as though he already knew about it. Of course, Miranda told Chad everything, Betsy thought.

Betsy asked if she could engage Chad as her agent. She needed help in understanding some documents in Jeff's files. Complete confidentiality was expected. Chad agreed. Betsy showed Chad the encrypted passages she had copied from Jeff and Vincent's correspondence and asked Chad if he could decrypt them.

Chad sat, staring at the passages for several minutes. Then, he grabbed one of the legal pads on the table and reassembled the letters in various combinations.

"This is not amateur work," he finally said. "One of those two men had serious training in encryption."

Betsy shrugged. "Jeff's a lawyer, you know," she replied. "We didn't have a class in encryption at my law school, and I doubt Jeff's did, either."

Chad smiled. "And Vincent's been a politico all his life, right?" he asked.

"Yes," Betsy answered, "but Vincent was at the Pentagon during his Vietnam service. I don't know that he was in Intelligence, but I suppose it's possible."

"This is better than Army Intelligence," Chad replied. "I'm guessing Vincent was seconded to the Department of Defense from the CIA. Anyway, can you give me a clue as to what this might be about? I could use a leg up on trying to figure this out."

Betsy hesitated, but only for a moment. Miranda had assured Betsy that she could rely on Chad to keep secrets.

"I suspect the coded passages have something to do with Mauricio Marquez," she blurted.

Chad said nothing but only returned to his work. He pulled out his phone, checked a couple of websites, and performed some calculations. He rechecked his sources.

Fifteen minutes later, Chad broke the silence.

"Is this job time-sensitive?" he asked.

"Most definitely," Betsy responded. If Betsy had guessed right, breaking the code might help her solve the mystery of the no-match letter. Getting to the bottom of that was the first step towards helping Mauricio out of the mess he was in.

"Then I need to consult someone with more expertise than I have," Chad said. "With your permission, I'll call my friend and ex-partner, Ed Dante. Ed is the only chance we have of cracking the cipher quickly. Between the two of us, Ed would always beat me in code-breaking."

Chad promised that Ed was the soul of discretion. Jeff's secrets would be for Betsy's eyes only.

CHAPTER 30
CONFESSION

As Chad was contacting Ed Dante, Will rang the doorbell of a four-story row house on the eastern edge of the Capitol Hill area of D.C. Father Brennan, who lived in the home for retired priests comprising the top three floors of the building, was expecting him.

Earlier, Will called José to ask what the family had decided to do about the no-match letter. As José began to answer, Will, belatedly, realized his mistake. If the Marquezes had decided Mauricio would go into hiding, Will should not know about it. If the authorities questioned him, it would be best if Will could honestly say he did not know, rather than argue about the scope of the attorney-client privilege.

Before Will could retract his question, however, José answered it.

"Do you remember what St. Francis said when asked what he would do if the world came to an end?" José asked.

Will grinned on his end of the connection. José knew Will had been raised a Catholic and would understand immediately.

"Keep hoeing his garden," Will answered.

José chuckled. "Right," he said, "and that's what Dad decided to do. He'll be at work in the morning, as usual."

"Hoping the end doesn't come, I'm sure," Will responded. "Which reminds me, did you speak to the office manager?"

"Yes," José answered. "I told her the no-match had to be a mistake and that I'll work it out. I hope that's the story that circulates in the office."

Will returned his attention to the matter at hand when the door to the row house opened. A tall, thin man with a pronounced stoop, wearing a black shirt and pants, white collar around his neck, extended his hand.

"Greetings, Will," Father Brennan said in a strong baritone as the men shook hands. "It's good to see you again."

"Good afternoon, Father," Will said, bowing his head slightly. "You look well."

The lines worn into the octogenarian's face deepened further as the priest laughed, rubbing his hand across the pate of his bald head. "Still alive, thank the Lord," Father Brennan responded. "Come in, and how's Norma?" he asked, beckoning Will into the house.

Will followed Father Brennan through the vestibule and into a long, rectangular room, empty but for an irregular stack of phone books piled against the left wall. "What happened to Justice for Immigrants?" Will asked. The last time Will had been in this room, the immigrant advocacy group's headquarters held rows of desks laden with phones, papers, magazines, coffee mugs, and the other detritus of a busy working day.

"Ran out of funds," Father Brennan answered. "A shame, really. They did good work. They packed up everything and moved out, leaving," Father Brennan pointed towards the rear of the room, "only their best furniture."

Will laughed. He recognized the faded burgundy sofa with sagging cushions languishing against the wall. Will had sat there the last time he conferred with Father Brennan.

After the men settled in on opposite ends of the sofa, Will finished the story he had begun when he called Father Brennan to arrange this meeting.

"Lydia can't remember exactly when," Will began, "but it was soon after his first, surprise visit to her. John made an odd request. Lydia was surprised because John's family was Baptist. Moreover, John had not gone to church at all since he turned thirteen, and his dad said it was time for John to make up his own mind about his religion. Anyway, John wanted to see a priest."

"When Lydia asked him why, John evaded the question. When she pressed him, John said that he would trust his secrets only with Lydia or a priest, and the deepest, darkest ones were for the ears of the priest only."

"The nearest Catholic church to their hometown was St. Rose of Lima's in the county seat forty miles away. John thought it too risky for him to make the journey. He didn't know the roads well. He wouldn't have a safe place to wait if he arrived at the church, it was locked, and the priest was away. John feared the priest would brush him off if he, a stranger, called on the telephone out of the blue."

"Lydia journeyed to St. Rose's and found the priest. The priest agreed to meet John at Lydia's house. After that first time, the priest visited John often."

"More than a decade later, Lydia was lonely," Will continued. "They had given their daughter up for adoption. She and John drifted apart. Lydia had second thoughts about losing touch with him, but had no idea where John was. On a whim, she called the priest. Father Del Porto."

"The priest knew where John was, but wouldn't tell Lydia, I assume," Father Brennan said. "And that's why you want me to see if I can track down Father Del Porto and see if we can change his mind."

Chad opened the revolving glass door of the Daily Grill. Miranda and Marlon preceded him inside. They took a high-top table on the M Street side of the restaurant. Through the windows, Miranda watched the pedestrians pass by while Chad and Marlon ordered their drinks at the bar.

Miranda smiled and thanked Chad when he set two wineglasses on the table. Marlon settled into his seat with his martini.

The friends engaged in small talk, but only for a moment. The conversation turned to the timeline on the whiteboard.

"Chad, what information can you glean about John from the email he sent Lydia?" Miranda asked. "Legally, that is," she added.

"The IP address of the computer he was using," Chad answered.

"But that's simple," Marlon observed. "Anybody can do that."

"Not if the sender camouflaged the address," Chad replied. "It's not terribly difficult to do."

"Why hide his IP address?" Miranda asked.

"As an irrational response to living life as a wanted man," Marlon proposed. "I say 'irrational' because the military police rarely search for deserters, period, let alone one from so long ago. I looked it up. John could easily have done so, too. Still, he could be paranoid about being found."

"Either way, it doesn't matter," Chad said. "That is, I'm confident I can uncover the IP address even if John tried to hide it." Chad looked at Miranda and smiled. "Legally."

"Okay, we start with the IP address, then what?" Miranda asked.

"From the IP address, we could determine the general location of the device used to send the email," Chad answered. "That won't help much unless John was living in a sparsely populated location. Even if he was, and we could do a door-to-door search for him, he sent those emails six years ago. Wherever John was then doesn't mean he's still there now."

"Yeah, but he might be," Miranda responded. "I've been in my house for ten years."

"Well, I agree we should follow the IP address to wherever it takes us," Chad said. "I'll do that as soon as you get me the carrier records, assuming you can."

"Any other ideas, guys?" Miranda asked.

"Canvass everyone we can think of with whom John may have been in contact," Chad responded. "Human beings are social animals, you know. We are hard-wired to make connections with other people. Over the years, I've seen men knowingly risk their livelihoods and even their lives, driven by the need to communicate."

"John reached out to Lydia and a priest," Miranda said, pausing, "and maybe Parker."

"We hope so, but I have my doubts," Marlon replied. "Remember, we can't be sure of John's feelings for his brother."

"John would have needed somebody in whom to confide," Chad said. "Someone to whom he could tell his story."

"And that would be the priest at St. Rose of Lima's," Miranda confirmed.

"Yes, but maybe somebody else, too," Chad said. "Not for forgiveness. For understanding. Appreciation."

"What do you mean?" Miranda asked.

"Early in my career," Chad began, "I worked in industrial espionage. With Ed Dante. I well remember our first client engagement."

"The company's general counsel walked Ed and me through the contract. He highlighted the terms prohibiting any illegal conduct on our part. Ed and I wondered how we would acquire useful information from our client's competitors without offering bribes or snooping for dirt to use as blackmail."

"We quickly discovered," Chad continued, "that we didn't need bribes. People talked. Employees spilled the beans because of a fight with the boss, or they didn't feel valued. Most often, useful information came in the form of a confession. A manager had inflated sales for the last two quarters. A purchasing agent altered a sell-by date."

Miranda chuckled. "That sounds familiar," she said. "I always felt guilty when I flouted one of my mom's rules. I didn't always tell her about it, but, if not, I'd confess to Aunt Judy."

"I don't mean a confession of guilt," Chad explained. "Our informants told their stories to be admired. They expected us to be impressed by their cleverness, or power, or the justness of their conduct. Anyway," Chad said, reaching across the table to clasp Miranda's hand, raise it, and kiss the palm gently, "John told his story to someone whose opinion of him John valued."

Miranda smiled at Chad, momentarily distracted. She looked up at Marlon's next words.

"Something about what you just said, Chad, is ringing a bell," Marlon softly drummed the fingers of his right hand on the tabletop as he spoke. "But it's not quite coming to me. Oh, well," Marlon lifted his glass, "a toast to success. To finding John."

CHAPTER 31
THE THREAT

Trial Day 8

Will pulled open the door to the courtroom, holding it open for Cassandra. She bustled through. Will followed immediately behind her.

He glanced up at the clock hanging on the wall behind the judge's dais. Ten minutes remained until showtime, but he'd arrived twenty minutes later than planned. Will, who inherited his early bird habits from his mother, told himself to relax. Still, his stomach, which had been clenched since their cab got stuck behind a fender-bender, stayed knotted.

As he walked into the well, Will stopped. He laid his hand on José's left shoulder, patting gently, cognizant of the body cast beneath José's dark suit coat.

"How're you doing?" Will asked quietly. José smiled and said he was fine. Will thought José looked paler than usual this morning, however.

As he squared his notebooks on counsel table, Will glanced over and nodded at Baylie, who responded in kind. Behind Baylie and his co-counsel sat a middle-aged man with thinning brown hair. Will had not seen him in court before now. He must be the mid-level manager shanghaied into spending hours sitting through a trial about which he knew nothing. He was the representative of Baylie's corporate client for the day, in other words.

The courtroom was otherwise empty. The judge's clerk and the court reporter should be seated by now, Will thought. Just then, the door to the jury room swung wide, banging sharply against the wall.

"Everybody out!" the bailiff boomed. "Out of the courthouse, now. There's been a bomb scare."

* * *

Betsy slid her silver Toyota Corolla next to the curb on the street in front of her apartment building. She would shower and have the cup of coffee she had not taken the time to brew before she left for Richmond. She could still make it to the office before 10:00 a.m., so no need to call to explain her absence.

As her coffee perked, Betsy thought back to her dawn meeting with Jeff. Jeff had been honest. Betsy had to figure out how to deal with the facts he had disclosed.

Yesterday afternoon, Betsy told Chad he could call any time before midnight if he heard from Dante. Shortly after eleven, Chad called. Dante had cracked the code.

The transcribed version of the correspondence between Jeff and Vincent was in Betsy's inbox. Ed had encrypted it, for security's sake, but arranged for the document to open automatically in word format once the email hit Betsy's IP address.

Betsy opened her laptop and clicked on the attachment from Dante. The encoded messages between Jeff and Vincent, although now in readable English, were nonetheless cryptic. A casual reader lacking the background and context would be unlikely to understand the conversation.

Betsy knew enough to ferret out what had happened, but not why the two men went to such lengths to hide what they had done. She had a hunch, though.

Betsy had to talk to Jeff face-to-face. So, she decided to drive to Richmond the next morning. She planned to arrive at 6:30 a.m. The demands of the campaign may have disrupted his other routines, but Jeff had been rising at that hour for as long as Betsy had known him. She was confident she would catch him at his home.

Betsy had slept fitfully but rose refreshed. She dressed in jeans and a t-shirt for the two-hour, dawn trek to the capital city of the Commonwealth of Virginia.

Traffic was blessedly light on I-95, and Betsy arrived on time. Jeff opened the front door of his two-story Colonial when Betsy rang the bell. His look of concern turned to irritation when she assured him nothing was wrong with her, but that she needed to talk to him. He led her into the den, without offering her coffee.

Betsy had decided to come clean. On a basic level, she trusted Jeff. He had been acting strangely lately. Still, Jeff was a good man who would ultimately do the right thing, she believed.

Betsy recounted what she had learned about Jeff and Mauricio and explained Ed's translation of the coded email. She half expected Jeff to explode when he understood how deeply Betsy had pried into his private files. The old Jeff would have thought it clever and entirely in keeping with Betsy's attention to detail. As for the new Jeff, Betsy was not sure. Jeff said nothing, however, and his expression, neutral, concentrated, did not change.

"It was you, wasn't it?" Betsy asked. "But why? Why get Mauricio the card all those years ago and then take it away now?"

"Marquez threatened me," Jeff answered, "in an email I received on Saturday."

Betsy's eyes widened. "Mauricio? With what?"

"He threatened to disclose something that happened during the war," Jeff said.

"You did take Glen's tags," Betsy said, keeping her voice level.

His response relieved her. Jeff did not deny the accusation angrily and demand that Betsy leave, immediately. Instead, he sighed, sank back into his chair, and ran his fingers through his hair.

"I should have admitted it years ago," Jeff said, "when I first found out that Glen was reported as MIA. I'm ashamed I didn't tell the story to the Hadleys. My silence in the face of their pain kept me up at night for a long time."

"I was young and scared, though. I looked it up, and I had committed serious crimes in taking that tag. I can't be prosecuted anymore because it happened too long ago. But my run for the Senate is dead in the water if the public finds out what I did. My reputation will be ruined."

Jeff did not ask how she knew about the tags. It was as though Jeff expected her or someone else to discover the truth, or he was relieved to confess, Betsy thought.

"Why did you do it?" she asked.

Jeff took her back to that day. He was three weeks from shipping out. Those first, bewildering days after a soldier stepped out on the tarmac in Vietnam for the first time were bad. The end was even worse, and the most terrifying part of the tour. With each day that passed, the fear of dying, so close to escaping, grew. Plus, Company 19 had a new commanding officer, a green lieutenant gunning for medals. Jeff was sure the officer was going to get them all killed in a very short time.

"The firefighting was fierce that morning," Jeff had continued. "Mauricio, Glen, and I sought cover together under a tree. A round of enemy fire caught Glen. I knew right away that he was dead."

"Glen was a medic, you know. His medical bag lay beside his dead body. I suddenly realized the bag was a ticket out. I would grab it, run off, and link up temporarily with a different unit. I would explain that my own had fallen apart, which was true. Everybody knew the seams were unraveling in the U.S. Army all over Vietnam."

"But why take the bag?" Betsy had interrupted.

"As a medic, I would be welcomed," Jeff replied. "No questions asked."

"Just as I reached to grab the bag, another thought flashed through my mind. I should be a real medic in case some officer checked. I needed Glen's tags, as well as his bag."

"I took the tags off Glen's neck. With my other hand, I removed mine. I intended to pocket my tags, keeping them until it was safe to become Jeff again. But when a bomb exploded right behind me, I dropped my tags. It wasn't worth risking my life looking for them. I ran."

"A body missing a tag was not unusual, you know," Jeff continued. "Guys were always taking off their tags. It was against orders. But it was worth a reprimand to get the chain off a dirty, sweaty neck."

"So, finding bodies without identification was not uncommon. The remains would be sent to Graves Registration for identification. It never occurred to me that Glen would turn up MIA. I can't imagine how that happened."

Jeff paused and closed his eyes. "Mauricio was right there. He saw everything. He's threatening to go public with it."

"Mauricio doesn't strike me as the kind of man who would threaten somebody without a good reason," Betsy said. "Why now?"

Jeff threw up his hands. "I have no idea," he said, exasperated. "Over twenty years without any contact, then this, out of the blue."

"Mauricio said he had no idea who or why anybody would have been out to get him," Betsy replied. "I suppose he could have been lying. But are you sure the email came from Mauricio?"

"I didn't have anybody on my tech support staff confirm it, if that's what you're asking," Jeff answered testily. "Mauricio was the 'sender,' though, and, more importantly, nobody else could have known about the tags. Nobody else was near Glen's body."

Betsy, on the verge of telling Jeff about John, bit her tongue. So far, Jeff had been candid with her, but she had more questions.

"Vincent told me that Mauricio came to you," Betsy said. "Mauricio said you found him. Which is the true story?"

Jeff grimaced. "That was Vincent's idea," he answered. "Vincent thought that if we told you the truth, you would wonder why I went to such lengths. It would make no sense unless I wanted something in exchange. Your suspicions would have been aroused, and you would have wanted answers."

So far, Betsy was satisfied with Jeff's answers. His actions were justified by the facts as Jeff knew them, except for one.

"Whoever sent the email, I don't see it as particularly threatening," Betsy said. "Your story is sympathetic enough. Understandable, even. Nobody should have been hurt by what you did. Surely your people could have spun this away to nothing."

"I couldn't take the risk," Jeff said, shaking his head. "Not at this stage of the game."

"So, instead, you are ruining Mauricio's life?" Betsy had asked, voice shaking.

Betsy brought her thoughts back to the present. She absently rinsed her coffee cup and placed it on the rack.

Jeff had explained about the no-match letter, and she believed him. Jeff's was the most plausible version of events. But how could she use this information without breaching Jeff's trust?

CHAPTER 32
LUNGE AND PARRY

Betsy arrived at the office a few minutes after 10:00 a.m. She greeted Beebe and started down the corridor toward her office. Betsy heard what sounded like Will's voice behind her. Startled, she turned to see Will and Cassandra walking into Aaron's office. Betsy pivoted and followed her colleagues.

"What's going on?" Betsy asked as she joined the trial team, Marlon, and Miranda in the semi-circle of chairs in front of Aaron's desk, which was empty. "Why aren't you at court?"

"A bomb scare at the courthouse," Will answered, surprising no one. Every office building in downtown D.C. had been emptied, at least once, by a similar threatening call, usually from a disgruntled crank.

"The jury has been excused for the day," Will continued. "Judge Storer didn't want to make them hang around until the police clear the building. It could take all day. José went home, and the lawyers are on call. We'll go back this afternoon, if it's safe, and conference with the judge on jury instructions and a couple of pending motions."

"One more in the series of unexpected events in this trial," Marlon said dryly.

"Tell me about it," Will responded, shaking his head.

"But," Marlon continued, "at least you can see the light at the end of the tunnel of your trial. We, on the other hand, are completely in the dark concerning both John and Mauricio, unless somebody else has good news."

Marlon told his colleagues that Parker had gotten John's senior picture from their high school administrator. In the photograph, John's hair, fashionably long for that time, hung low over his brow, obscuring his eyes. A straggly mustache had the same effect on his lips. The contour of John's lower face, propped on the back of his palm, consciously or unconsciously emulating Rodin's "the thinker," was contorted.

"I sent it to Paco," Marlon concluded, "but that picture could have been any eighteen-year-old, hippie 'wanna-be.'"

"Father Del Potro is a dead end, too," Will chimed in. "I got an email from Father Brennan early this morning. He easily tracked down his fellow priest, who was also retired from an active ministry and living in Santa Fe."

"Father Del Potro did recall, from his time at St. Rose of Lima's, a young man whom the priest agreed to meet at the girlfriend's house. Father Del Potro remembered this man, from among the thousands of penitents whose confessions he had heard over the years, because of the unusual sin to which he had professed."

"Father Del Potro could not disclose what he heard in the confessional, of course," Will continued. "He would say that the man, whose name Father Del Potro could not remember, was sincerely contrite for succumbing to the temptation."

"Father Del Potro saw the man at mass, off and on, until he was transferred to another parish in New Mexico. Unfortunately, he has had no contact with John since then."

"Bah, humbug," Marlon stood. He walked to the corner of the office behind and to the right of Aaron's desk. He reached around behind the human skeleton guarding the room and retrieved the office rainstick from where it had been propped against the wall. Marlon shook the stick fiercely. The pellets inside rattled and clattered.

The rainstick had been an office holiday party gift brought by some long-gone secretary. The three-foot plastic, putty-colored tube was not the genuine article. Still, the lawyers brought it out, over Aaron's objection, to clear the air. When a brainstorming session ran dry or an argument became tense, one of the associates would grab the stick.

Usually, laughter followed the ceremonial shaking. Not today.

"Do tell us your news isn't bad, too, Miranda," Marlon said.

"It's bad," Miranda said. "I'm sorry."

Marlon sighed. "Well, I tried for a better vibe," he said.

"Parker was asleep when I arrived," Miranda continued. "Lydia, though, was sprightly and alert. I think the prospect of meeting her daughter has sharpened her mind. Certainly, her spirits."

"Anyway, Lydia apologized for not having Parker up and dressed, but he had a bad night. When he did wake up, Parker was disoriented. After a cup of tea, he said he was ready. I walked him through our list of questions."

"Parker tried so hard," Miranda's voice cracked, "but we came up with nothing. Parker could not remember anything in his adult life that could, even remotely, have a connection with John. Except for Lydia, of course."

"The email?" Marlon asked after a minute.

"Lydia terminated her email account two years ago when her dementia worsened," Miranda answered. "She hadn't been able to write a coherent email for days on end."

"We could initiate an ancillary proceeding and issue a subpoena to her old provider," Cassandra suggested.

Marlon shook his head. "The provider would move to quash," he said, "and I doubt we could convince a judge to deny the motion. We are, after all, on the proverbial witch hunt. Besides, all that would take far longer than the time Parker has left."

"It was always a very long shot," Miranda said, voice shaking. "Parker knew it, too, guys. He said to thank you all so much for trying so hard, and for being his best friends."

Miranda sobbed audibly. Betsy, glancing around the room at her colleagues, saw downcast faces and glistening eyes. She so wanted to cast a ray of hope. Betsy waited for the impact of what may have been Parker's last words to subside.

"I'm afraid I don't have anything helpful on that front," Betsy said, "but I do have an idea about the no-match letter."

"And?" Will asked.

"Maybe it wasn't from the Social Security Administration at all," Betsy answered. "Maybe it was fake."

Betsy knew it was fake because Jeff told her so earlier in the day.

Jeff was surprised Betsy thought otherwise. Surely, it would have been madness for Vincent to tamper with the inner workings of the

Social Security Administration again, trying to undo what had been done decades earlier. Pilfering an official letterhead had been simple.

Jeff had also been surprised at Mauricio's silence. Jeff expected Mauricio to make contact as soon as he got the no-match letter. Mauricio had to know the letter came from Jeff. Jeff was the only one who knew Mauricio's card was fake. Mauricio also had to know that Jeff sent it because of the threat.

Mauricio lunged, for some reason unknown to Jeff. Jeff parried. It should have been time for the men to lay down their épées and figure out what had gone so wrong. Jeff, baffled, did not know what his next move should be. So far, he had done nothing after the no-match letter was dispatched.

"A fake?" Will echoed. "That seems as far-fetched as the other options we discussed yesterday. Or, now that I think about it, maybe not. I suppose any determined person could get his hands on a sheet of government stationery. Somebody with a grudge against Mauricio."

"If true, that's a huge relief," Cassandra noted. "The immigration authorities are not on to Mauricio. Instead, somebody pulled a dirty trick."

"Maybe, maybe not," Marlon replied. "A relief, that is," he continued. "It depends on who that 'somebody' is and what he wants."

Marlon looked pointedly at Betsy. She met his eyes, detecting not quite a warning, but a caution.

Marlon had most of the information he needed to solve the puzzle of Mauricio, Betsy thought. He knew Mauricio and Jeff served in the same unit in Vietnam. During the last major engagement of that unit, Glen Hadley was killed, Jeff at his side. Glen's dog tags disappeared from his corpse. After the war, Mauricio got an almost-authentic social security card from an "Army buddy." Years later, with the no-match letter, somebody challenged the authenticity of that card.

All the signs pointed to Jeff as that "somebody." But Marlon could not be sure. Or, not sure enough to challenge the *bona fides* of a well-respected, sitting senator, unless Betsy confirmed Marlon's theory.

Mauricio, meanwhile, perched on the edge of a dangerous cliff. If nobody in authority followed up on the no-match letter, Mauricio would remain on solid ground. Alternatively, he might be shoved over the edge.

If Marlon saw disaster coming, he would do all he could to save Mauricio. If that required sacrificing Jeff and her relationship with Jeff, Betsy had no doubt which side Marlon would choose.

Betsy had to find a solution. Some way to salvage them all.

She excused herself and left Aaron's office. She needed to talk to Mauricio. Alone.

By noon, Betsy had gotten through to Mauricio on his cell. She arranged to speak with Jeff at 4:00 p.m. Jeff seemed more amenable to making himself available once their morning's conversation had cleared the air between them.

Betsy sat at her desk, thinking. Marlon appeared at her door.

"Need a break?" Marlon asked. "I'm heading down to the Mall," he continued. "The cherry trees are finally in full bloom."

Betsy hesitated. The invitation tempted her. Like most Washingtonians, and every tourist who happened to be in town at the right time, she made the annual trek. Spring was not complete without an hour basking in the ineffable beauty of the capitol's famous cherry blossoms ringing the Tidal Basin.

Noon on the first day of full bloom, delayed this year because of the long, chilly spring, was not the time to make the trip. The place would swarm with people.

Plus, Marlon's motive for asking her to go was suspect. Marlon did not need a companion to run down to the Mall. No, if Betsy went with him, Marlon would use the opportunity to push for an answer. Where had Betsy gotten that theory about the fake no-match letter?

The gist of her thoughts must have been evident to Marlon.

"I don't want to talk shop," Marlon said, "and I'm not going around the Basin. It will be a zoo down there. We'll stop east of the Washington Monument on 15th Street, at that isolated grove known only to the cherry blossom cognoscenti."

Betsy laughed and agreed to go. Twenty minutes later, staring up at the blue sky through an enveloping bower of delicate flowers, she thought of the first time she had seen the cherry trees blossoming in D.C.

* * *

A soft knock sounded on her bedroom door. Betsy was awake, but not because of the dawn's light glowing behind the curtains at the window. She had spent most of the night staring into the unfamiliar darkness. Betsy had stayed in bed, not yet sure whether she should await a summons to leave her room in the morning.

"Come in," Betsy said as the door swung open. Mrs. Friedlander, Betsy's new foster mother, stood in the doorway, smiling.

"Good morning, Betsy," she said. "Did you sleep well?"

Betsy nodded politely.

"I have a surprise for you," Mrs. Friedlander said as she pushed the bedroom door fully open and stood to the side.

"Get up, sleepy-head," Jeff said as he stepped into the room, holding his arms wide.

Betsy leaped out of bed, lunged across the room, and flung herself into Jeff's enveloping hug.

"Come on, get dressed, honey," Jeff said as he ruffled Betsy's hair. "We're going on an early morning picnic."

Jeff drove them into the city. Betsy chattered excitedly, eager to share everything that had happened in the week since Jeff drove her to Mr. and Mrs. Friedlander's home. Jeff nodded, smiling.

As Betsy and Jeff walked around the Tidal Basin, hand in hand, Jeff told her the story of the cherry trees. The mayor of Tokyo sent the trees to Washington to commemorate the friendship between Japan and the United States. Betsy listened intently, although she was perfectly capable of reading the explanatory plaques spaced at frequent intervals on their path.

"We fought against Japan during W.W.II, you know, Betsy," Jeff said, nodding approvingly when Betsy indicated that she did. "Someone chopped down a number of the cherry trees because they were a gift from the enemy," Jeff continued. "Well, I guess it was never proven," he continued, "but I believe it."

Betsy frowned. "That's stupid," she said. "It wasn't the trees' fault."

"No, of course it wasn't," Jeff responded. "That's one of our human failings. When anything goes wrong in the world, we have to find something or someone to blame. Too often, those we blame are innocent. Too often, the problem is largely of our own making."

Jeff paused, looking out across the Tidal Basin to the Jefferson Memorial.

"Bear witness to your mistakes, Betsy," he continued. "Don't blame others for your own failings. Instead, see your mistakes clearly, make amends for those you've wronged, and try to do better next time. You'll be a better person. At least, you'll be an honest one."

* * *

Will stepped back. He raised both arms and smacked the bag with his right gloved fist, protecting his face with his left. The bag rocked gently backward, then forward.

"The left, now," Jim commanded.

Will's left punch hit off-center. The punching bag swung wildly off to the left. Jim caught it in his upstretched hand.

"Get in with the left quicker next time," Jim advised.

"I knew there was a good reason I always give up on this," Will complained. "It's hard!"

Will, confined to the office by the Judge's instructions to be available, had fidgeted and paced for an hour. He pulled out a deposition transcript to read, but he could not focus.

Will had wandered down the corridor. Jim was in his office. Will asked if he could go a few rounds on the punching bag hanging from the ceiling behind Jim's desk. Hitting the bag for a few minutes would be a welcome diversion.

Cassandra stuck her head in as Will was pulling off his boxing gloves.

"There you are," Cassandra said. "I've been looking for you. Franklin called."

"Did he raise his offer again?" Will asked idly, mind elsewhere.

"Nope," Cassandra said glumly. "Quite the opposite."

Will looked up sharply. Cassandra had his attention now.

"Franklin took his offer off the table. He gave no explanation. We're back to a no offer case.

"What the heck ..." Will began, interrupted by Beebe's voice over the intercom.

"Will, pick up on line 3," Beebe said. "It's Judge Storer's clerk."

"Hi, this is Will McCarty," Will said into the receiver.

"Are we heading to court?" Cassandra asked a few minutes later, unable to decipher Will's one-sided conversation on the phone.

"Yes, right now," Will answered. "Judge Storer is having the lawyers in for an emergency hearing. The clerk wouldn't tell me the details, but, apparently, we have a big problem with one of our witnesses."

CHAPTER 33
DISAPPEARED

Will and Cassandra caught a cab for the trip to the courthouse. Wrapped in their thoughts, neither spoke.

Will's phone rang, breaking the silence. It was José. Their terse conversation alerted Will to what he could expect at this hearing.

Heart pounding, Will's thoughts whirled. Focus, he told himself.

He needed help. Will gave Cassandra her instructions.

When they arrived at the courthouse, Cassandra immediately caught a cab back to the office. She was to round up whoever was around to brainstorm. Interrupt the hearing with a text message, if necessary, Will told Cassandra.

Will took the escalator up to the judges' chambers.

The clerk motioned Will towards Judge Storer's office door. Will knocked. The judge bade him enter. The pitch of her voice—low, steely—confirmed his suspicions. Will squared his shoulders, opened the door, and walked in.

"Sit down, Will," Judge Storer said sharply, skipping her usual polite greeting.

Baylie, sitting on one of the two chairs in front of the judge's desk, swiveled his head to look at Will. Eyes narrowed, face mottled red, chin thrust forward, Baylie mouthed, "you little shit."

Will took a chance. "What's wrong with you, Baylie?" he asked.

"I know about the ICE visit," Baylie growled, "and I now know Mauricio is illegal. You must have known all along. Yet, last Thursday, you told me Mauricio's social security card was valid."

"I did not lie to you," Will said, directing his remark to Baylie.

"How is that not a lie?" Baylie barely kept his voice below a shout. "You lied to keep me from grilling Mauricio about his status!"

"I repeat," Will shouted. "I did not lie."

"Counselors," Judge Storer barked, "stop it. I'll tell you when I want you to speak. Will, Taylor has asked for a mistrial on the grounds that your professional misconduct prejudiced his ability to represent his client. What is your argument against his motion?"

"How prejudiced?" Will asked. "He wouldn't have gotten anything from Mauricio about his status, anyway. I would have had Mauricio plead the Fifth, as José did."

"Taylor?" the Judge said, asking for his response.

"Apples and oranges," Baylie replied. "I knew José is a U.S. citizen. I had to tread carefully with him. Had I known Mauricio was undocumented, I would have asked my question differently. 'Are you an illegal Mexican?' That would have gotten the jury's attention, even if I got no answer to my question."

"Now that I think about it, why didn't you know Mauricio's status?" Judge Storer asked. "Didn't you depose him?"

Baylie grimaced. "One of my greener associates took Mauricio's deposition," he said. "He asked Mauricio the question and Will objected. My associate stupidly backed off. By the time I noticed that the answer was missing, it was the Sunday before the trial. It was too late to do anything about it."

Judge Storer turned her attention to Will. "Replay your conversation with Taylor, and in the exact words."

Will recounted his conversation with Baylie on the morning before Mauricio testified. Baylie confirmed the accuracy of Will's rendition.

"Will," Judge Storer said, "you will find my next question offensive. But for the unusual circumstances here, I would never ask it of you."

Will, confused, paled. What else could be coming?

"Did you pressure José's human resources director into testifying that Mauricio's social security card was legitimate?" the Judge asked.

"Of course not!" Will forced away his furious wave of anger, the display of which would only worsen matters. "I would never do such a thing, period," Will said in as calm a voice as he could muster. "But you don't have to rely on my word. His deposition was taken a year ago. At that time, I had no inkling of any of the immigration issues that have emerged in this case."

Baylie snorted. "Fat chance," he said. "My office spotted those mismatched social security numbers on José's work records immediately. Are you telling me you didn't?"

"That's exactly what I'm saying," Will answered. "It was obvious that I was surprised when you asked José about the numbers while he was on the stand."

Will knew he was right. The judge had to have noticed that Will was unprepared to defend his client at that moment.

Judge Storer fiddled with her pen. Will felt sweat beading on his forehead as he waited for her to announce her decision.

"I am missing parts of this picture, but I don't see any way to fill in the blanks, given the attorney-client privilege," Judge Storer finally said. "From the facts I do have, I don't think that Will's conduct is sanctionable."

Will surreptitiously pulled his handkerchief from his suit coat pocket and wiped his brow.

"It's a close call, however," Judge Storer continued, "and I would be tempted to call a mistrial, except we have a solution. Taylor can simply recall Mauricio to the stand. Then, whatever misperception your little ploy may have created in the jurors' minds can be dispelled."

Judge Storer directed her gaze at Baylie. "Counselor?" she asked, seeking his satisfaction with her decision. He nodded. "Will?"

Will fidgeted in his chair. "I'd be fine with that outcome," Will said, "except we can't get Mauricio back to the courthouse. He's disappeared."

In the momentary silence that followed his words, Will breathed a quiet sigh of relief. Thankfully, that was all Will knew.

During their brief conversation in the cab, José told Will that ICE agents showed up at J&A's office an hour earlier, looking for Mauricio. Luckily, Mauricio was out, working on one of the construction sites. One of José's employees, who had stopped by the office to retrieve a batch of change orders, saw the ICE agents on his way out and alerted José, who was at home resting.

José followed the instructions Will had given him yesterday after Will made the mistake of asking what Mauricio would do about the no-match letter. José told Will his father was gone, but José did not know his location.

Will did not know whether that statement was true or not, but it did not matter. If asked, Will could honestly say that he could not produce Mauricio.

At the rap on the partially opened door to her office, Betsy looked up. Marlon stepped in.

"You bought Jeff some time with that story about the fake no-match letter," Marlon said, voice taut. "I wasn't sure where the sick bastard was going," he continued. "But now this."

"What are you talking about?" Betsy asked.

"Cassandra's back from court," Marlon answered, "and she told us ICE showed up for Mauricio. I know Jeff is responsible." Marlon reached into his shirt pocket and pulled out the photograph of Glen Hadley's body. "So, this," he held out the picture for Betsy to see, "is going to the Washington Post."

"I know this picture isn't a smoking gun," Marlon continued. "But with everything else I know, it's enough for me. I'm sure it will be enough for Lily Chen, too. She's an investigative reporter at the Post and a friend of Miranda's. Lily will be delighted to start digging. A candidate for the U.S. Senate is the target, after all."

"No, Marlon, please," said Betsy. Rising in haste, she banged her shin against her desk as she struggled around the barrier between her and her colleague.

Marlon, both hands raised, palms out, stopped her. "I thought you were on our side," he said, "but I should have known better."

Betsy thought furiously. Jeff sincerely believed that it was Mauricio who threatened him. Of that Betsy had no doubt. Yet, Mauricio denied doing it. To Betsy, this could only mean that somebody else made the threat, although she had no idea who that could be. But Marlon would think Jeff was lying to save his skin, and that Betsy was protecting Jeff.

She would figure this out.

"Jeff did not contact ICE," Betsy began. "I'm sure of it."

"I have no reason to believe you," Marlon said stiffly, turning on his heel, heading out of her office.

"Wait, trust me for a moment, Marlon," Betsy said as she extricated herself from her desk. Ignoring his harsh words, Betsy approached Marlon and placed a tentative hand on his shoulder. He stopped and turned to face her, to Betsy's relief.

"Assume the no-match letter was fake," Betsy continued, "and assume, for the moment, that Jeff sent it. Why? Why not go directly to ICE if Jeff aimed to out Mauricio? Isn't the logical answer that he must have had another reason for sending the letter?"

Marlon stared at her, face expressionless. "I don't see that Jeff's motive matters a whit," he finally said. "The no-match letter arrives. ICE is alerted that Mauricio is undocumented and turns up on Mauricio's doorstep. If the ICE agents can find Mauricio, and they most likely will, Mauricio will be deported. To make matters worse, if that's even possible, suppose Baylie somehow gets a whiff of what has happened. If he does, José's case goes down the tubes. And this is all Jeff's fault."

Betsy sighed heavily. "Not entirely," she began, but stopped herself. An explanation would do no good. Instead, she needed a solution.

"Give me until the end of today," Betsy said. "Please."

Marlon turned away. Not enough, Betsy thought.

"I have an idea for a last-ditch effort to find John," Betsy added.

"John?" Marlon shook his head. "We're talking about Mauricio and ICE. How does John fit into this picture?"

"And if it works," Betsy continued, "it'll give José and Will a fighting chance in the trial, too."

Marlon walked out.

CHAPTER 34
A CHARACTER WITNESS

Cassandra returned to the large conference room with an armful of legal pads. She set their supplies on the table just as Will walked in, returning alone from the courthouse.

Will dropped his battered leather briefcase on one chair and sank into its neighbor. He looked as though he had gone ten rounds, Cassandra thought, against somebody who could actually box.

"Am I correct in assuming our 'problem' witness is Mauricio?" Cassandra asked.

"Yep," Will answered.

"Meaning," Cassandra continued, "that Baylie found out Mauricio is undocumented?"

"Worse than that," Will said. "He knows everything."

"What's going on?" asked Marlon, who had wandered in. "Cassandra looks like she's seen a ghost."

"I have, in a way," Cassandra said absently. "The specter of disaster."

"You mean Mauricio," Marlon replied.

"Well, that too, but this is another," Will said. "You're not going to believe it. I hardly do myself. Remember José said his office manager opened the no-match letter. The woman, Holly Bradford, has access to all of José's files. Holly found Baylie's contact information in a case document. She called Baylie to tell him ICE had come looking for Mauricio."

"Oh, man, Baylie must have been furious," Marlon said.

"To put it mildly," Will replied.

"Did Judge Storer order a mistrial?" Cassandra asked.

"No," Will answered, "although I considered consenting to Baylie's motion for one. I couldn't decide which would be worse."

"With a mistrial, we'd retry the case in a year or so, but José can't wait that long," Will continued. "If we try this case to the end, I'm afraid we're bound to lose it once all this about Mauricio comes out. It would have been one thing if I'd called an undocumented witness. But now, Baylie will also make it clear that we were hiding that fact."

"Tough call," Cassandra said.

"A very tough call," Will agreed. "Anyway, I decided to argue against the mistrial. I think that's what José would have wanted. I won that fight. No mistrial. I lost the second one, though."

"After the Judge ruled against him on the mistrial," Will explained, "Baylie requested leave to call Holly Bradford as a witness. Baylie said that if he couldn't confront Mauricio himself with his irregular status, he was entitled to demonstrate that fact through Holly."

"And?" Cassandra asked. "What was your response?"

"I argued that Mauricio's status is not relevant to any of the issues in the case. Accordingly, Holly's testimony would simply confuse the jury."

"And Baylie countered by claiming Mauricio's status is relevant to his credibility, right?" Marlon asked.

"Yep," Will answered. "Judge Storer said that, personally, she thought immigration status was irrelevant to credibility. She had to follow precedent in her jurisdiction, though, which holds that it is. Holly will testify. Tomorrow."

"You know, I wonder why Holly called Baylie?" Cassandra asked. "She didn't even let José know about the no-match letter until the day after it arrived."

"Why call opposing counsel instead of her boss?" Marlon responded. "Apparently Holly wanted to hurt José, or Mauricio, or both men badly. What we don't know is why she wanted to do that."

"Not yet," Will said, "but I'll find out. I hope. Judge Storer ordered Baylie to make Holly available for a videoconference deposition at 5:00 p.m."

"Now that," Marlon observed drily, "should be interesting."

"I totally screwed this up," Will said, shaking his head. "I should have put Mauricio on the stand and have him take the Fifth. Whatever Baylie could have squeezed out from behind that barrier, it would have been far less damaging than this."

His colleagues could only, silently, agree. Now, it only looked like José's side had been hiding the facts.

"The only thing I did right today," Will continued, "was to convince Judge Storer to allow me a rebuttal witness."

"And exactly what part of Holly's testimony are we going to be able to rebut?" Cassandra asked dubiously. "The facts are the facts."

"We refute the implication that Mauricio is a bad man," Will said, "by calling a character witness."

"Who?" Cassandra asked.

"I don't know yet," Will answered. "You two can think about that one and find out anything you can about Holly Bradford. I have to get ready for Holly's deposition."

"I have a question to add to your list," Marlon said. "Ask Holly if she contacted ICE."

Jeff had told Betsy to call him if she uncovered anything about the mysterious threat he had received. She did have something to share, although it would not be what Jeff was expecting.

The last thing Betsy wanted to do was drive back to Richmond, but she was not confident that a phone conversation would convince Jeff. So, Betsy returned to Richmond, anticipating that she would find Jeff in his Senate office.

She was in luck.

Betsy told Jeff what had happened, what she wanted of him, and what she would give him in return. He showed surprise only at the last part.

"Tell me now, Betsy," Jeff urged. "We can get started."

"Look what happened to Mauricio," was Betsy's response. "I know you didn't intend to ruin his life, but that's what's happening. I need proof that John Doe won't be harmed if he's found. If you do what I ask, I'll have that proof."

"You choose them over me?" Jeff asked, equal parts anger and hurt in his voice.

"No," Betsy answered. "The choice is yours."

CHAPTER 35
SURPRISE WITNESS

Trial Day 9

"All rise," called the bailiff, promptly at 9:30 a.m.

Cassandra, standing at counsel table, felt unduly exposed without Will beside her. She turned and smiled at José, sitting behind her, reassuring herself as much as their client.

"Good morning," Judge Storer said as she took her place on the bench. She peered at Cassandra. "Are we waiting on Mr. McCarty?"

"No, Your Honor," Cassandra answered. "He'll be here after the lunch break." After he had prepared their new witness and revised his closing, Cassandra thought. Will had a lot to do between now and the afternoon session when Holly Bradford would testify.

Baylie called his last expert witness, to be followed by his client's operations manager. Baylie was saving his big guns for last. It was going to be a long morning, Cassandra knew.

Judge Storer released the jury for lunch at noon. Cassandra hurried downstairs to the courthouse cafeteria to meet Will.

"How'd it go?" Cassandra asked as she slid into a chair next to Will.

He shrugged. "He'll be a powerful presence on the stand," Will said, "but I'm not sure how helpful his testimony will be."

Cassandra pulled two power bars from her bag and handed one to Will. "I'm guessing you haven't had lunch," she said.

Will smiled crookedly. His facial muscles had almost forgotten how to look happy, Cassandra reflected.

"You guessed that right," he said. Will peeled the wrapper off the bar and took a bite. "Let's go over my cross-examination again," Will said after a minute, "and see if anything else comes to mind."

Cassandra had sat through Holly's deposition the evening before. As she listened to Will recite his questions for the cross, Cassandra recalled what they had learned about this new witness.

Holly, a short, plump, moon-faced twenty-six-year-old, grew up in rural Wisconsin. Her high school boyfriend joined the Marines after graduation. Holly followed him to Virginia when he was stationed at Quantico. She found a job in nearby Manassas as a secretary with a fellow Badger who owned a small construction company.

Shortly after she got settled, Holly's Marine dumped her. Holly considered returning home. Her family encouraged her to stay where she had a good job, though. Wisconsin was rebounding from the Great Recession more slowly than Northern Virginia.

Holly stayed with her company for seven years. She was proud when she was promoted to office manager, even though it was a one-person office. When her boss suddenly died of a stroke, she had to find another job.

José hired Holly to fill the position of office manager for J&A Builders. The previous manager, who had been with José since his company's inception, had recently retired. Holly had been with J&A for six months when the no-match letter arrived in the mail.

During her deposition, Holly freely admitted to contacting ICE and calling Baylie's office. She denied involvement in the long list of politically charged organizations and movements that Will had prepared, however. Nor was Will able to identify anything else that he could confidently predict would undermine her expected testimony at the trial.

The one thing Will did get from Holly was, at best, a double-edged sword.

"What do you think?" Will asked. "Should I ask her that last question, or not?"

Cassandra opened her mouth to answer when Will's phone rang. Cassandra overheard the voice of the caller.

"Hi, it's Jim. He's in the witness room."

"And José?" Will asked.

"In his regular spot," Jim answered.

Will thanked Jim and ended the call.

They had debated whether to have José in the courtroom during Holly's testimony until José made the decision. He was not ashamed of his father. José feared his absence would suggest otherwise to the jury.

"Well?" Will asked, returning to his cross-examination.

"I vote yes," Cassandra replied, "but, as always, you will read your jury and decide on the fly."

Will grimaced. "This jury doesn't read," he said. "Well, it is what it is," he continued, "and time to get going."

He and Cassandra gathered their papers and briefcases and headed towards the escalators.

Twenty minutes later, all parties in their places, Baylie called his last witness. In fifteen minutes, Baylie walked Holly through her background and association with J&A, quickly getting to the gist of her testimony.

Q: Did J&A Builder receive a letter from the Social Security Administration this past Monday?

A: Yes.

Q: Did you, in your capacity as office manager, open and read the letter?

A: Yes.

Q: Do you have a copy of that letter with you here today?

A: Yes.

Baylie had the court reporter mark the letter as an exhibit. Baylie then handed copies to Will and the judge's clerk, who handed it up to Judge Storer. Will knew the contents of the letter by heart, but he pretended to read it through, anyway.

Q: Will you please read what has been marked as Defendant's Exhibit EE to the jury.

Will stood and objected. "The document speaks for itself," he said.

"Overruled," Judge Storer responded. "I have considerable discretion on that rule of evidence, as you know, counselor," she continued, "and I'm allowing the testimony. You may instruct your witness to proceed, Mr. Baylie."

As instructed, Holly began reading:

A: "The Social Security Administration is committed to ensuring the accuracy of earnings records ..."

Holly confirmed, when Baylie asked, that she brought the letter to the attention of José. Will objected when Baylie then asked about José's response. Baylie came up with an exception to the rule excluding hearsay, and Judge Storer allowed the answer.

A: José said it was a mistake and he would fix it.
Q: And what was your response to what he said?
A: I ... I wasn't comfortable.
Q: Why not?
A: Well, it was his father who was in trouble, so I had my doubts. I trust the authorities, so I called ICE, and they came. So, I was right.

Cassandra stole a glance at the jury. Had the pride in Holly's voice sounded vindictive? Or was Holly coming off as a good citizen who had done the right thing? No way to know, she concluded. Yet.

Q: Did you call my office to bring these matters to my attention?
A: You mean the no-match letter and ICE matters?
Q: Yes, sorry if I wasn't clear.
A: I did call you.
Q: Why?
A: I knew Mauricio testified at the trial because he told me so. I was sure that Mauricio, as an illegal alien, was not qualified to testify in a court in America. But José's lawyer snuck Mauricio in, anyway. It was not right. I didn't know anyone else to call. So, I called you, Mr. Baylie.

"Your witness," Baylie said as he stepped back from the podium from which he had questioned Holly.

Will glanced at Cassandra. She gave him an encouraging smile. Will rose from counsel table, yellow legal pad in hand. He crossed the well of the courtroom, stopping ten feet from the witness box.

"Good afternoon, Ms. Bradford," Will said.

Cassandra, surprised, glanced at the jury. Had they noticed? Will never addressed a witness in that combative tone of voice. Will had chosen to send a clear signal to the jury. Cassandra hoped his decision did not backfire on them.

Q: Why did you take the position at J&A?

Holly shifted in her seat. She looked uncomfortable, for the first time, on the stand, Cassandra thought.

A: I looked a long time before applying to J&A. I couldn't find anything else. Seems like even secretaries have to be college graduates these days. I'm not.

Will had Holly admit that her job at J&A was a good one. She was well paid, and the company provided a generous benefits package. Her office was comfortable.

Holly confirmed that José was a good boss: fair, reasonable, always pleasant to her. Mauricio, who was often in the office, was always polite and respectful of her. Holly left work at 5:00 p.m., but she knew the Marquezes often worked long into the evening. She also knew, from having seen them together, that both men adored Benjy, and the child was well-behaved.

Q: Is it fair to say that, from what you know about him, José is a good man?

A: Yes, that's fair.

Q: You would say the same thing about Mauricio, correct?

Holly agreed, as Cassandra expected. Will had asked Holly these questions during her deposition.

Q: Did you ever observe José do or say anything untruthful?

A: No.

Q: So, why did you distrust José when he said the no-match letter was a mistake?

A: As I said a few minutes ago, I just had my doubts. José might have been protecting his father.

Q: What's the other reason, Holly?

A: It's those people. You read such terrible things about them in the news.

Q: And by "those people," you mean persons of Mexican descent, correct?

A: Mexicans, that's right. Thieves and rapists, and they come here illegally to take jobs from hard-working Americans.

"That's all I have, Your Honor," Will said. He turned and walked back towards counsel table.

Will remained standing as Holly left the witness box. He turned and watched her walk down the center aisle and out of the courtroom. Then, he motioned to Jim, who was sitting on a bench at the rear of the room.

"We'll call our character witness now, Your Honor," Will said. "I call Senator Jeff Howard."

CHAPTER 36
THE RIGHT PATH

Betsy jumped out of her cab. She trotted to the courthouse's main entrance on 4th Street as she spied Jeff striding out. Betsy raised a hand in greeting as Jeff's eyes caught hers.

"How did it go?" Betsy asked.

"I did the best I could for him," Jeff answered.

"Okay, here's what we know," Betsy began, completing her side of the bargain. "His name is John Evans."

Jeff called Vincent before Betsy finished her story. Vincent concocted a preliminary search plan on the spot. Jeff bade Betsy goodbye and hurried off.

All along, Betsy was convinced that Jeff was far more likely to find John than she and her colleagues. As a long-time state senator on a campaign for the U.S. Senate, Jeff's network was enormous. Jeff's dedicated and talented staff were skilled in tracking down and analyzing information. Perhaps most importantly, Jeff had his chief of staff. Vincent demonstrated time and again that he could overcome any barrier to Jeff's political success.

Yet Jeff would not distract his people from the campaign to try to find a kidney donor for Parker, a stranger to him.

After her talk with Jeff early yesterday morning, Betsy mulled through all she had discovered. She realized Jeff had a powerful motive for finding John.

John must have made the threat. Mauricio denied seeing Jeff do anything to the corpse after Glen Hadley was shot. The only other person in the vicinity was John. He had taken Glen's picture, after all. John must have been close enough to see Jeff steal the tags.

But Jeff had not seen John. In fact, Jeff knew nothing about John at all.

Betsy was tempted to call and disclose everything to Jeff. She wanted Jeff to find John before the story was leaked. The disclosure would embarrass and humiliate Jeff, at a minimum, and could well end his senatorial campaign. Betsy believed Jeff was entitled to take measures to prevent the disclosure of a wrong done by him decades ago in the heat of battle.

She would not tell Jeff, however, if doing so would risk irreparable harm to John. John had made his own bad decision during the war. Yet, as far as Betsy was concerned, John should not be punished for his crime while Jeff got off scot-free.

The risk was real. After all, Jeff lashed out at Mauricio by sending the no-match letter. Jeff tried to downplay the sting of his reaction, explaining that he believed the consequences would be benign. Mauricio was supposed to react to the letter by reaching out to Jeff and explaining the reasons for his threat. The two men would work it all out.

Jeff's plan had gone terribly awry.

Betsy needed to know that the same thing would not happen to John. She wanted assurance from Jeff that he would not turn John over to the military police, even if Jeff thought that was the only way to silence John. Betsy made her second trip out to Richmond yesterday to exact Jeff's promise.

None of that would help Mauricio, but she could ask something more of Jeff.

Betsy did not think even a state senator could stop the immigration authorities from investigating Mauricio. But if Jeff testified in court on Mauricio's behalf, Jeff might prevent an almost-certain jury verdict against Mauricio's son.

Betsy had known it would not be an easy decision for Jeff. Jeff had taken a hard stance against illegal immigration in his campaign. He had no choice if he wanted the support of his party and his most loyal voters. Jeff's about-face in testifying on Mauricio's behalf would not sit well. Indeed, it could be the death knell of Jeff's campaign.

Betsy smiled as she waved down another cab for the return trip to the office. Jeff told her those many years ago under the cherry blossoms what it meant to be a good person. She believed Jeff would do as he had counseled her. He had justified her faith in him.

Betsy arrived back at her office at 5:00 p.m. She dropped her briefcase and plopped into her chair. Marlon rapped on her door jamb.

"I heard what happened at court," Marlon said. He grinned. "You were on our side. Great job."

Betsy nodded, hiding the swell of relief, pride, and sense of belonging in a slight smile.

"On another front," Marlon continued, "breaking news."

He walked over to her desk, leaned over, and held out his phone. Betsy read the email displayed on the screen.

Marlon:
Get me Jeff's personal cell number. Now. I have a different deal to offer him than I originally had in mind. Years ago, I followed Jeff down the wrong path. Today, he chose the right one. I will follow him again.
John Paul Evans

Betsy jumped to her feet. "John Evans," she said, wonderingly. "You found John!"

"Not exactly," Marlon responded. "He found me."

CHAPTER 37
WITHOUT FEAR OR FAVOR

At 4:00 p.m., after Jeff's testimony, closing arguments, and instructions, Judge Storer sent the jury back to begin deliberations. They would only have an hour this afternoon, the Judge told the jurors. Still, they could elect their foreperson and get started.

If this had been an ordinary trial, the lawyers would have packed up and gone back to their offices as soon as Judge Storer left the bench. The evidence was technical and complex. The witnesses presented conflicting stories on how the accident happened. The experts disagreed on why it occurred. No jury could sort all this out in an hour.

In this case, the lawyers stayed put. This verdict could come without any discussion of the accident or its aftermath. Instead, the jury might decide against José based on one quick, up-or-down vote because of Mauricio's undocumented status.

Baylie moved to a bench near the back of the courtroom, where he sat reading a brief. José went out into the hallway to take a walk and stretch his back.

Will and Cassandra stayed at counsel table, talking softly. Voices in the courtroom echoed, and this conversation was for their ears only.

"Jeff did a great job," Cassandra said. "The jury had to have been impressed with his long record of public service."

"Yes," Will agreed, "and Jeff spoke eloquently of Mauricio's service in Vietnam. Jeff's indignation at the bureaucratic error that prevented Mauricio from getting the citizenship he deserved sounded sincere."

"I don't think he only sounded sincere," Cassandra protested. "I think Jeff meant every word. He's got charisma, too. People are drawn to Jeff and want to be on his side."

"Oh, so he has your vote now, too," Will teased.

Cassandra snorted and flapped her hand at Will. "I'm not that gullible," she said. "By the way, that last question was risky. 'Do you know that it is a federal crime for an undocumented person to stay in the States?' What if Jeff had simply said, 'yes.' What a lousy way to end the questioning!"

"What do you take me for?" Will feigned disgust. "A young lawyer still wet behind the ears? I asked that question in advance and knew what Jeff's answer would be. 'Yes, but I've seen elected officials commit more heinous crimes.'"

"Brilliant," Cassandra observed.

"Yeah, it worked well," Will replied. "But we still don't know whether Jeff's efforts blunted Holly's damning testimony. Our alternate jury probably has allies by now. I wonder how many?"

José returned to his post behind Will just as Judge Storer's clerk walked through the door behind the dais. She took her place at the table beside the judge's desk.

Startled, Cassandra and Will exchanged nervous glances.

Cassandra felt a hand on her shoulder. She turned towards José.

"What's going on?" José asked, voice hushed.

"Surely not our jury," Cassandra whispered back. At least, I hope not, she said to herself. "Probably a last-minute hearing on another case," she continued.

Cassandra hauled her litigation bag up from the floor and set it on counsel table. "Let's get ready to go. The Judge will clear the courtroom for the hearing."

Will did not move.

Baylie slipped into the well and sat at his table.

Judge Storer entered the courtroom. The lawyers automatically rose, although the bailiff was not present to call the command.

"Juror Number 2, the jury foreperson, sent out a note," Judge Storer said as she took her seat. "They've reached a verdict."

Cassandra dropped her bag on the table with a thud.

The jurors filed into their box.

"Madame Foreperson," Judge Storer began, "what is the jury's verdict?"

Juror Number 2 rose from her seat, squaring her shoulders. "We find for the plaintiff, on all counts," she announced.

Cassandra blinked hard, holding back tears. She turned to grasp Will's hand and saw that his eyes, too, were wet. José wept openly. Wide grins creased all three faces when the foreperson announced the generous amount the jury had awarded in damages.

The jurors, having been released from the constraints of their official role, trickled out of the jury box. They talked among themselves, stopping to extract cell phones from bags to exchange contact information.

José asked Will if it would be appropriate for him to approach and thank the jurors. Will said yes.

José walked stiffly over, Will and Cassandra flanking him. Juror Number 1 had taken her leave, but the five remaining women crowded around.

"Oh, honey, I went home every night and cried my eyes out," said Juror Number 5, a bosomy, late-middle-aged woman in a snugly fitting floral print dress. "It was just awful what happened to you, and I worried about your poor little boy. He's adorable," she said, voice warm.

"We took a vote right away," said Juror Number 2. "We were all agreed on the first vote."

"We all had our minds made up on liability," said Juror Number 6, Anna Hinks. "We took a little more time deciding on damages."

"You have saved my life," José said, voice thick. "I mean that sincerely. I can't thank you enough."

With final "best wishes" and "take cares" to José and each other, the jurors left the courtroom. Cassandra, with a nod to Will, followed. She caught up with Anna at the top of the escalator. Anna stood, alone, the other jurors having taken the elevator.

"Excuse me, Ms. Hinks," Cassandra said. "Do you have a minute for a quick question?"

"It's Anna," she said, smiling, "and sure."

Cassandra first told Anna that she was under no obligation to talk to her. Anna was entitled to keep her thoughts about the case to herself.

"Go ahead," Anna responded. "Being a juror was a fascinating experience, and I'm happy to talk about it."

"We," Cassandra hesitated, "we know about your son," she continued. "That is, we discovered he's strongly anti-immigrant. Yet, Juror Number 2 said the verdict was unanimous. Was all that testimony about no-match letters and an ICE investigation just confusing? Or, anyway, I don't get it," Cassandra said, stumbling to express her thoughts.

Anna snorted. "Not confusing at all," she said. "It was clear as a bell. Mauricio is undocumented, as was José before he married his American wife."

"That didn't bother you?" Cassandra asked.

Anna's eyes had gone steely. "I took an oath to decide the case based on the evidence, without passion or prejudice," Anna said coldly.

Cassandra blushed. "Sorry," she said. "I'm sorry I offended you."

Anna's face softened. "Well, I suppose you are justified in your concerns. Too many people are so angry these days that they can't see straight anymore. My son is one of those people."

"Do his views affect yours," Cassandra asked, "when you're not in a jury box? I'm curious."

"Good grief, no," Anna replied. "He's my son, and I love him, but he's an idiot. We're Roma. I emigrated here from Romania after my parents were killed in a rampage against our village. So, you see, Mauricio and I, we are the same. I was lucky, though. I received asylum and became a citizen. Mauricio was, unfortunately, unlucky."

CHAPTER 38
CAMOUFLAGE

The sun sat low in the western sky, but Marlon did not yet need the patio lights. He sank into the cushion of the wicker chair and sipped from the glass of wine he had brought from the kitchen.

He should have known, Marlon thought. At least his suspicions should have been aroused.

He knew Paco's tale of renouncing his citizenship smelled fishy. Marlon had too readily explained away his doubts. Similarly, Marlon did not question Paco's fixation on the Vietnam War. Instead, he wrongly assumed Paco's obsession was the natural consequence of the fact that the war upended Paco's life. Marlon had not considered that what drove Paco were guilt and a thirst for retribution.

Paco's stories had been the clincher, if only Marlon had been paying more attention. What was it that Chad had said at the bar? Everybody had to tell their story. To confess.

Marlon opened the laptop he had set on the glass-topped table beside his chair. He selected the file, opened the first story Paco had sent, and reread it.

The old car bumped roughly over the worn tracks in the dirt road. The broiling sun was directly overhead. Mark's stomach clenched. He swiped the beads of sweat off his brow with the faded red bandanna he gripped in his right fist. Mark was accustomed to the heat and the rutted roads by now. The source of his discomfort lay elsewhere.

"When will we cross the border, Antonio?" Mark asked his driver, voice thick.

Antonio, a short, stocky man about Mark's age, glanced over and grinned widely, his teeth gleaming white in his swarthy face. "Cálmate, Mark," he said. "Already happened. You're back in the U.S. of A."

Antonio had told him the risk was low. This section of the border was quiet and rarely patrolled, he said. Although Antonio had no documents authorizing entry into the U.S., he crossed here regularly to bring brightly colored woolen sarapes, embroidered by his mama, his aunts, and other women in the village, to the markets in one or another of the American towns close to the border. Only once had Antonio been stopped—by a Texas Ranger according to his badge—and unceremoniously ordered back to Mexico.

The consequences of being caught for Mark, he knew, would be far worse. Mark was a deserter from the Army. He had managed to get out of Vietnam and across the Pacific into Mexico, the borders of which were porous. If caught in the United States, he would be court-martialed and probably spend the rest of his life in a military prison, he figured. The lonely bleakness of his future outweighed his fear. He had to knock a chink in the dark tunnel surrounding him. He was going home to find Dee.

It had taken Mark three years from the time he arrived in Mexico to create a semblance of a life. He crossed the mountains to Mexico City, where he slept in parks and begged for bread on the streets. The economy was booming because Mexico had become a global oil exporter. People were generous, and Mark managed not to starve. He was always scared and alone, however.

One sunny morning, Mark wandered the cobbled streets of a neighborhood he had not passed through before. Somewhere off to his right, a bell gonged once. After a short pause, the bell pealed again, the first note of a slow, stately rhythm. The churches in Mark's hometown were all Baptist or Lutheran, and protestants did not believe in bells. Still, Mark knew that a Catholic mass was about to begin.

Mark turned his steps towards the source of the call to service. After a few minutes, he came upon a stucco building topped by a steeple, which housed the bell, suddenly gone silent. Atop the steeple stood a wooden cross. The door to the church, reached from the street by a brick stairway, stood open to the darkness within.

Mark had one foot on the bottom step of the stairway when he spied, out of the corner of his eye, a man in a flowing, shiny white robe hurrying from around the side of the building. Mark leaped back, almost tumbling in his hurry. The man, who otherwise would not stand out in any crowd in Mexico City, wore a thin, solid black collar around his neck. Mark was poised to turn and run when the priest smiled at him, reached out, and gently touched his shoulder.

"Mi hijo," the priest said. "Come," he continued, switching to English, "come to mass, my son. You look like you could use it."

Father Pedro saved him. Truly saved Mark's life, for he had been hanging on to a rapidly raveling thread.

After that first mass, the priest took Mark into the rectory across the street from the church and introduced him to the housekeeper, Miriam. Tiny Miriam, her age and lifetime of hard work etched into her deeply wrinkled face and worn hands, twisted by arthritis. A village girl brought to the city decades ago by her father, who had secured for her the safe and honorable job of serving the series of priests assigned by the diocese bishop to this congregation, she nodded at Mark, silently acknowledging his presence.

"Miriam will clean you up and feed you," Father Pedro said. "Then, we'll talk."

Over the next few months, the priest and Miriam got Mark back on his feet. Father Pedro enlisted a parishioner who let Mark sleep in a dilapidated but dry and reasonably clean lean-to on his property. The priest gave Mark odd jobs around the church and rectory, at first, then found Mark a part-time job with another parishioner who laundered clothes for the wealthier residents in the neighboring barrio.

During the occasional evening when the priest was not occupied with parish duties or clerical obligations to study and pray, he and Mark talked—about religion, of course, but also political events in both their native countries and the world, war and peace, their respective pasts, and hopes for the future. Mark had spoken a handful of words for months. His evenings with Father Pedro made him feel human again.

Miriam was as important to Mark's recovery as the priest. She fed him, patched his worn clothes, and made sure there was a bucket, a bar of soap, and a towel on the stool beside the water spigot in the patio behind the rectory.

Despite the kindness of Miriam and Father Pedro, Mark wanted to leave the city. He felt claustrophobic among all the people and the cars and the crowded-together houses. Besides, Father Pedro would be assigned elsewhere in due time. The next priest would likely not be as accommodating to the young, American man.

Father Pedro knew the cities and many of the villages in Mexico reasonably well, at least by repute. He was young, newly a priest, and had not traveled the country himself. However, his many friends from the seminary came from all over Mexico. From them he had learned much. Father Pedro also had a good map, which he and Mark explored.

Eventually, Mark settled on a village to the north, not far from the U.S. border. He pledged his eternal gratitude to Father Pedro and Miriam, the priest blessed him, and Mark left Mexico City on a rusty, dented bus.

Father Pedro must have seen something worth saving in the tattered vagabond, Mark thought later. Mark was not sure he could live up to whatever version of himself the priest had discerned, but he would give it a try.

Marlon, having finished the story, sat back. His eyes wandered to his wine glass, thoughts elsewhere. He opened the second installment of Paco's story.

Having crossed the border without incident, Mark could breathe again. In the long ride still ahead of them, he would figure out how to approach Dee.

She might already have moved on, of course, but Mark strongly doubted it. Someday, he was confident, Dee would spread her wings. She would have needed to recover, first, from the events of the last few years.

He could not leave a note under the moss-covered birdbath in her parents' backyard, as he used to do. The heavy old stone, the concave center of which was filled with water only when it rained, which was rarely, would no doubt still be in its place. A note from him would *instantly propel her, screaming, back into the house, however. Anyway, he thought, no good for another reason: She would not be looking there anymore. Whatever he did, it had to be quick. He could not, for anything, be seen by anyone else.*

In the end, it was dumb luck.

Antonio dropped Mark off, at dusk, on the outskirts of town, where the road from the south emerged from a wide, shallow arroyo. Antonio, who would be staying the night with a distant cousin living in the town, would come back for Mark after he had been to the market early the next morning.

Mark, crouching beside the dirt road, peered up over the rise. Twenty yards in front of him, a woman pedaled her bike down the road, towards Mark's hiding place. A pale, round face emerged from the gloaming. Dee.

When he thought of that first meeting, later in life, Mark would remember the joy and immense relief they had both felt deeply. Their encounter had not begun with those emotions, though, but with shock, disbelief, furious anger, guilt, and bewilderment.

Mark's lucky charm was strong that night. Not only had he found Dee, but he also had a safe place to spend the night. Dee's parents were in Austin, spending the night while visiting Dee's maternal aunt. In the hours before dawn, Mark and Dee argued, and cried, and talked, and eventually fell into a brief sleep in each other's arms.

The next morning, Antonio's wagon rolled over the rise into the arroyo, where Mark crouched, concealed in a scruff of tall, dusty weeds just off the road. Mark had a plan for relying less on luck during his next visit, a handful of mail addressed to him, delivered by the postal carrier in Mark's absence to Dee, and a full heart.

Marlon took another sip of his wine. John had not even camouflaged his characters that well. Dee, a common diminutive of Lydia. Paco, a variant of Paul, John's middle name.

CHAPTER 39
ALL IN

Trial Day 10

By noon, Will was not yet back from his post-trial motions hearing. Marlon, at work in his office, considered texting Will to make sure nothing unexpected had happened. He decided against it. Will had probably taken a much-needed respite and gone to the gym.

Marlon turned back to the brief on which he was working. He looked up again only when Betsy appeared at his door.

"What time does John get in?" she asked.

"Six o'clock this evening," Marlon answered. "I'll pick him up at Dulles."

"It'll be a close call," Betsy responded. "Chad and Miranda are already at the hospital."

"Yes, I know," Marlon said, "but it was the best we could do under the circumstances. By the way, I'm curious. Did you think Jeff would find John in time?"

"A fifty-fifty chance, maybe," Betsy answered, "but it was the only shot we had. Until John came in from the cold on his own."

"Have you had a chance to talk to Jeff," Marlon asked, "since we got the email?"

"No," Betsy responded, "so I'm still at a loss as to why John wanted to talk to him."

Marlon laughed. "And you're dying to find out, right? Well, I had a long talk with Paco this morning when we made the flight arrangements. Let's grab lunch, and I'll interpret that email for you."

Fifteen minutes later, the two colleagues had a table at Firehook Bakery and their sandwiches and coffee.

"Okay," Betsy said, "what's the 'deal' John has for Jeff?"

"'Different deal,' is what John offered in the email," Marlon responded. "To understand that we have to go back to the beginning. John's original plan was that Jeff would get John a pardon. In exchange, John buries Jeff's story for good. John gives Jeff the evidence he had collected demonstrating that Jeff stole Glen's tags."

Marlon paused to eat the last bite of his sandwich. The fact of Jeff's theft had not yet been verbalized between them. Marlon intended to keep it that way.

"What happens in Vegas ..." Marlon began. Betsy nodded. Marlon did not have to say more. Betsy knew she had earned their loyalty. Jeff's secret was safe with the firm.

"Why didn't John contact Jeff, tell him what he discovered, and propose the deal?" Betsy asked. "And why did John wait so long to make his move?"

"John didn't think he had enough proof," Marlon answered. "John's evidence was circumstantial. He feared Jeff would explain it all away. John believed he also needed the eyewitness. He needed Mauricio."

"But Mauricio didn't see anything," Betsy protested. "He ..."

"John thought he did," Marlon interrupted. "Our shutterbug took a picture of Jeff and Mauricio as they were leaving the site where Glen was killed. John waited so long because he never found Mauricio until I emailed to tell him that Mauricio was one of Will's witnesses."

"Okay, so now John knows how to contact Mauricio," Betsy replied. "Why not do just that? What was the point of sending Jeff a threatening email disguised as one from Mauricio?"

"John didn't know how to approach Mauricio," Marlon answered. "Remember, John believed that Mauricio had kept Jeff's secret for decades. Why would Mauricio suddenly reveal the truth to John, a total stranger?"

"John's solution was to send the threat to Jeff," Marlon continued. "John anticipated, reasonably enough, that Jeff would hit back."

"And Jeff did," Betsy said, "by sending that fake no-match letter."

"Right," Marlon replied, "which completely surprised John. John had no idea Mauricio was undocumented. John expected, instead, that

Jeff would warn Mauricio of some dire consequence if Mauricio went public with Jeff's secret."

"I'm following you so far," Betsy commented, "but how would any of that advance John's goal of getting a pardon for his desertion?"

"Bear with me a minute, Betsy," Marlon said. "I'm getting there. Imagine how Mauricio would have felt if all this played out as John had planned. Confused. Scared. A powerful man who knows Mauricio's status is angry at him, and Mauricio has no idea why. Mauricio turns to the firm for help."

"Ah, I see," Betsy said, nodding. "Mauricio tells us everything that happened when Glen died. John then comes forward with the documentary proof he has. Given the combination of their evidence, Jeff's goose is cooked, unless he makes a deal. Jeff's secret will be kept if he arranges for John to come home safely."

"That was the plan," Marlon confirmed. "It worked, too, if not exactly the way John intended."

"What do you mean?" Betsy asked.

"Mauricio did come to us," Marlon answered. "He did disclose his secret, if not the one John expected. There is a deal, and John will keep Jeff's secret."

"Although, as you said, a different deal," Betsy replied.

"Yep," Marlon said. "John and Jeff hashed it out this morning. Jeff will spend all the political capital required to get Mauricio his citizenship. Jeff could not realistically take on John's case at the same time, so John will give up his dream of a pardon. Jeff did, however, with relative ease, secure a humanitarian parole visa so John can visit his brother."

"I'm missing one piece," Betsy replied. "How would John know when to come out of the shadows? How would he know when Mauricio had divulged the truth?"

"Through me," Marlon answered. "I would have asked him for anything he had in his library about Mauricio, Jeff, and Glen. That didn't go quite as planned, either. Instead, I emailed John, Paco that is, about Jeff's testimony. Paco responded with the email, revealing himself as John."

"Oh, I see," Betsy said. "Jeff had the courage to do the right thing, risking his political career. John would do no less. John shed his disguise, not knowing for sure what would happen next."

"That's right," Marlon replied. "Or, as John said in his email: He followed Jeff down the wrong path in Vietnam. This time, he would follow Jeff down the right path."

"It seems to me," Betsy said as they rose to bus their table, "that John's plan, as you call it, had a snowball's chance in hell of working. Every card had to fall exactly his way."

"True," Marlon agreed, "but John had nothing to lose. He'd anted up everything he had a long time ago."

CHAPTER 40
BROTHERS IN ARMS

At 7:20 p.m., according to the institutional black clock hanging on the wall, Marlon walked into the waiting room. He saw Miranda sitting in a row of gray, plastic chairs. Miranda slouched, head leaning back against the chair back, eyes closed. Except for the heavily pregnant young woman sitting on the far side of the room, Miranda waited alone.

Marlon walked over to where Miranda sat, motioning to the man behind him. "Miranda," Marlon said sharply.

Miranda jumped to her feet.

"Miranda, John Evans," Marlon made the introductions. Marlon watched Miranda shake hands with the tall, slender man with faded auburn hair cropped short, freckles, and wide-set grey eyes whom Marlon had fetched from the airport.

After their murmured greetings, Marlon hustled John through the swinging doors into the corridor leading to Parker's room.

Marlon walked through the open door of Room 415, John behind him. Parker lay propped up in his hospital bed, eyes closed. His skeletal hands lay folded on the thin sheet covering his chest, which rose and fell slowly. The monitoring machines to which Parker was attached clicked and hissed.

"We're here," Marlon said, chiding himself for his falsely cheerful tone.

Parker opened his eyes, his glance instantly locking on John. At Parker's joyful smile, tears started in Marlon's eyes. He quickly backed out of the room.

An hour later, Marlon peered through the glass panel in the door to Room 415. John had apparently closed it, Marlon thought. Parker lay as he had before, unmoving, but his lips were curved in a smile.

John sat in a chair pulled close to the bed. On the tray attached to the bedside, Marlon saw two stacks of envelopes. The neatly piled, taller stack appeared to be unopened letters. As Marlon watched, John took an envelope off the top, tore open the flap, and removed a sheet of paper. Marlon could barely hear as John started to read. He listened for a minute, then left the brothers to their private communion.

Dear Parker: I forgive you for telling Dad on me. You were so young. You didn't know any better.

I am so lonely. I'm in love with a wonderful woman, but I fear the relationship can't last. Too many barriers stand in our way. I feel better when I write to you, but I am afraid of mailing these letters. I don't know how you would react. I know you volunteered and went to Vietnam. You may hate and despise your brother, the deserter. I'll just keep writing. One day, I hope, you will read them and understand.

Dear Parker: It has been four years now since I escaped from Vietnam. I have settled into this village across the Mexican border from our home.

The crippling fear I wrote to you about has lessened considerably. I still bear the burden of guilt for what I did to the dead soldier's family. As far as his parents know, their son simply disappeared. I presume he was reported as missing in action. I have found a priest who is helping me atone for that sin and my guilt lessens over time.

As for the shame of deserting, I have come to believe that my crime pales compared to others committed in that war. Fragging officers and massacring Vietnamese civilians are but some of the atrocities about which I have read.

I still feel searing regret, however. If only I had put the dog tags that I found in the grass back on the body and returned to my unit. Instead, I hid them in my pack and put my tags on the corpse. Sure, I might have been killed in battle, but John Evans is dead, all the same. This stateless man I am in Mexico is a different person. I have taken a different name.

I replay the events of that fateful day over and over, obsessing about what I don't know. How long had the dead soldier been in-country? What were the names of all the men in his unit? What led him to be in that exact place at that time? I have to find out. I am collecting every scrap of information I can find, from any source.

Dear Parker: I've discovered the dog tags I have did not belong to the downed soldier. They bear the name of a man who survived the war. I didn't know how the tags had fallen a few feet from the dead body, but it never occurred to me that the tags could belong to anyone else. So, the corpse bore no tags, and those belonging to this other man, whose name, I discovered, is Jeff, were nearby. Is it possible? Could Jeff have stolen the dead man's tags and discarded his own? But why?

I found out the man they buried as me was named Glen Hadley. I'm sending a letter to his parents. I can at least confirm to them that their son died in combat and isn't missing somewhere in the jungle.

Dear Parker: I found a photograph of four soldiers. One of them is Jeff. In this photo, Jeff is in uniform, clutching a medic's bag, wearing dog tags on a chain around his neck. From the date-stamp, the picture was taken after Glen Hadley died. I have Jeff's dog tags. So, in this picture, Jeff must be wearing dog tags not his own.

My suspicions are confirmed. I know why he did it now, too. Jeff assumed the identity of the medic to save his neck. Medics were in harm's way, but not nearly as much as regular infantrymen.

My fury at Jeff knows no bounds. He's to blame for everything that happened to me. I made that split-second decision to put my tags on Glen only because his were already missing. I would never have considered stealing the tags off a corpse.

Dear Parker: My anger has faded. I've grown up some, I guess. Jeff stole Glen's tags, but I'm the one who stole Glen's identity.

I can't exonerate myself because Jeff committed the original sin. Perhaps, though, I can use what I know to get out of this no-man's land in which I live.

I foresee this plan taking a long time to execute, unfortunately. It may be years before I see you again. In the meantime, I'll keep writing. And maybe, someday, you'll get these letters.

Marlon, having returned from his walk around the enormous hospital, opened the door to Room 415. An alarm rang. A nurse entered the room and adjusted one of the monitors.

"You've got some color in your face," the nurse, whose name tag identified him as Gerald, said. "Are you feeling better, Mr. Evans?"

"Yes," Parker and John said simultaneously. The brothers looked at each other and grinned. Marlon, eyes wet, smiled.

Hours later, just before midnight, Chad emptied the shaker. He slid the two martini glasses he had filled across the kitchen island. Miranda and Marlon nodded their thanks. Marlon grasped the stem and raised the brimming glass gingerly. Miranda followed suit.

Marlon cleared his throat. "To Parker," he said huskily.

John, whose trip from his hill town in Mexico had taken more than twenty-four hours, had accepted Chad's offer to sleep a few hours at Chad's mansion in McLean. Parker's surge of energy would not last, the doctor had cautioned, but he was sure Parker would survive until morning. Parker needed to rest, anyway, the nurse said, shooing John out of Parker's hospital room.

Marlon and Miranda whisked John across the Potomac. Chad saw him to a guest bedroom after John declined the offer of food. Chad, who slept little, agreed to wake his guest before dawn for the return to the hospital.

When Chad returned to the kitchen, Miranda informed him that she was "tired but wired," and could use a drink to calm down. Marlon said he could always use a drink.

"I know you've barely met the man," Marlon said, "but what do you think of John?"

"I think he's a good man," Chad answered, "who made mistakes, like all the rest of us have."

"He clearly loves Parker," Miranda responded, "and the feeling is mutual. You know," Miranda continued, pausing to sip her martini, "given how devoted John is to his brother, I wonder why John didn't come forward as soon as he learned how sick Parker was? Even given the risk to himself?"

"Volunteer to donate a kidney, you mean?" Marlon asked. Miranda nodded. "He couldn't," Marlon continued. "John was born with only one kidney, a trait he passed down to Roberta. He found out a decade ago when he had an MRI for gastrointestinal pain."

Marlon excused himself and left the room.

"Star-crossed, those Evans brothers," Miranda observed.

"Yes," Chad responded, sighing. "Such a pity."

He looked at Miranda closely. She knew her eyes were red, her hair was uncombed, and her cheeks were drawn.

Chad rose, walked around the island, and put his arm around Miranda's shoulders.

"You'll need a break, my dear, when this is over," Chad said.

Miranda felt her eyes welling, as they had off-and-on all day.

"After Parker's funeral, let's take our first trip together," Chad said. "Let's go see Ed. I miss him."

"And where would Ed be?" Miranda asked.

When Chad told her, Miranda paled. "I'm queasy on a plane," she said, "and that flight must take forever. What is it, a full day?"

"Don't worry, honey," Chad said, kissing the top of her head. "It won't be a bad flight because we'll be in first class. You won't even notice the time. Besides, it's worth the trip."

"Have you been there before," Miranda asked.

"Of course," Chad answered, sounding a bit offended. "I've been everywhere. Stick with me, kiddo, and you'll see the world, too."

Miranda smiled. "I'll take that offer under advisement," she said.

"Miranda, are you ready?" Marlon, who had slipped back into the kitchen, asked.

"Yeah, let's go," Miranda answered.

She hugged Chad goodbye and got into Marlon's car for the trip back to the hospital.

"It's been an interesting two weeks," Marlon said as he pulled out of Chad's driveway onto Route 123, "but I'm looking forward to plain old work. Even deposing an economist for the fifty-first time doesn't sound all that bad."

Miranda could not help but laugh.

ABOUT THE AUTHOR

Marian K. Riedy obtained her J.D. from Harvard Law School, practiced as a civil litigator for many years, and is professor emeritus, Emporia State University. She is also the author of *Fatal Accusation*.

ABOUT THE AUTHOR

NOTE FROM THE AUTHOR

Word-of-mouth is crucial for any author to succeed. If you enjoyed *Surprise Witness*, please leave a review online—anywhere you are able. Even if it's just a sentence or two. It would make all the difference and would be very much appreciated.

Thanks!
Marian K. Riedy

We hope you enjoyed reading this title from:

BLACK ROSE
writing™

www.blackrosewriting.com

Subscribe to our mailing list – *The Rosevine* – and receive **FREE** books, daily deals, and stay current with news about upcoming releases and our hottest authors.
Scan the QR code below to sign up.

Already a subscriber? Please accept a sincere thank you for being a fan of Black Rose Writing authors.

View other Black Rose Writing titles at www.blackrosewriting.com/books and use promo code **PRINT** to receive a **20% discount** when purchasing.

CPSIA information can be obtained
at www.ICGtesting.com
Printed in the USA
LVHW031044070722
722920LV00003B/131